HH
EB

continued . . .

RIVER RISING

"A fabulous relationship with a gritty glimpse inside the world of the uniform . . . No one does it better than Merline Lovelace."
—*Affaire de Coeur*

"Provides all the tension and intrigue you have come to expect from the amazing Ms. Lovelace."
—*Romantic Times*

"Perfection . . . another sure winner for this multi-talented author." —*Old Book Barn Gazette*

"Emotional . . . a guaranteed one-sitting read."
—Anne Hayes Cleary

CALL OF DUTY

"Lovelace has made a name for herself delivering tightly drawn, exciting tales of military romantic suspense." —*Romantic Times*

"Takes readers on a fast-paced, suspenseful ride that doesn't let up until the very last page."
—*The Literary Times*

DUTY AND DISHONOR

"Sizzles with excitement."   —Nora Roberts

"Exceptional . . . fresh and unique . . . powerful [and] passionate."   —*Romantic Times*

"Lovelace's command of the plot is impressive . . . intense and evocative . . . [an] unusual and well-written story."   —*Gothic Journal*

"A great yarn told by a masterful storyteller. It could have happened!"
          —Brigadier General Jerry Dalton, USAF Ret.

LINE OF DUTY

"Brilliant. . . . Fans of Tom Clancy and Scott Turow will love Merline Lovelace. . . . Exciting . . . gutsy . . . powerful."   —*Affaire de Coeur*

"The sparks flying explode off the page."
          —*Rendezvous*

"Evocative . . . high-energy . . . moves at an incredible pace . . . keeps the suspense taut and the romance hot."   —*Gothic Journal*

"Strong, action-packed stuff from Lovelace."
          —*Publishers Weekly*

"Extraordinarily powerful." —I Love a Mystery

AFTER MIDNIGHT

Merline Lovelace

AN ONYX BOOK

ONYX
Published by New American Library, a division of
Penguin Putnam Inc., 375 Hudson Street,
New York, New York 10014, U.S.A.
Penguin Books Ltd, 80 Strand,
London WC2R 0RL, England
Penguin Books Australia Ltd, 250 Camberwell Road,
Camberwell, Victoria 3124, Australia
Penguin Books Canada Ltd, 10 Alcorn Avenue,
Toronto, Ontario, Canada M4V 3B2
Penguin Books (N.Z.) Ltd, Cnr Rosedale and Airborne Roads,
Albany, Auckland 1310, New Zealand

Penguin Books Ltd, Registered Offices:
Harmondsworth, Middlesex, England

First published by Onyx, an imprint of New American Library,
a division of Penguin Putnam Inc.

First Printing, February 2003
10 9 8 7 6 5 4 3 2 1

This book is dedicated to the men and women I served with at Eglin Air Force Base. Together, we weathered hurricanes, tornadoes, plane crashes, and Desert Storm, but—thankfully!—no major catastrophes like the ones depicted in this novel.

ACKNOWLEDGMENTS

My special thanks to the personnel of the 96th Supply Squadron, particularly the panthers of 96th Fuels Flight, for their invaluable assistance.

Thanks, too, to Lieutenant Ed Ferris of the Walton County Sheriff's Department for taking time to chat with the author who wandered in off the street one afternoon and announced that she was thinking about writing a book set in his territory.

Chapter 1

Nothing good ever came out of the night.

Jessica Blackwell had accepted that grim truth long ago. As a consequence, she'd learned to function at peak performance on three or four hours of sleep snatched at random times in odd places. She'd also learned the danger of opening her door to strangers after midnight, even when they flashed a badge.

Particularly when they flashed a badge.

Eyes cold, palms suddenly damp despite the muggy June heat, Jess stared at the nickel-plated star nestled in leather and clipped to her visitor's belt.

"Lieutenant Colonel Blackwell?"

She wrenched her gaze from the shield to the man behind it. He topped her by four or five inches, which didn't happen often. At five-eight, Jess usually looked most men in the eye. Tipping her chin, she forced herself to return this one's casually assessing gaze.

"Yes."

"I'm Steve Paxton, Walton County Sheriff. I'd like to talk to you."

Common sense made her cautious. Experience made her wary. "What about?"

"An incident that happened a few hours ago. Mind if I come in?"

The glass storm door muffled his drawl, but the politely disguised demand came through with shattering clarity. Whispers of another night, another such demand, crawled along Jess's nerves. Her every instinct screamed at her to slam the inner door and shut out the darkness. Shut out the rustle of the breeze combing through the palmettos. Shut out this unfamiliar, unwanted visitor in worn jeans, white shirt, and a green ball cap emblazoned in gold with the logo of the Walton County Sheriff's Department.

The discipline gained over sixteen years as an officer in the United States Air Force stood Jess in good stead. Her hand didn't so much as tremble when she reached out and unlocked the storm door. Metal hinges that had already fallen victim to the rust caused by Florida's humidity creaked as she pushed open the door.

"Sorry to bother you so late."

The ball cap came off, revealing a pelt of tawny, sun-streaked hair. Dispassionately, Jess inventoried broad shoulders. A square chin. A nose flattened at the bridge, as though it had connected with a fist or two in the past. His skin was dark oak, weathered by sun and wind, and his eyes were a clear, startling aquamarine, as unfathomable as the vast, changeable Choctawhatchee Bay only a few dozen yards from her front door.

Jess supposed most women would consider Steve Paxton sexy as hell. She might have, too, if all that muscled masculinity hadn't come packaged with a badge.

"This could have waited until tomorrow," he said with a smile that stopped just short of apologetic, "but I saw your lights on and decided to stop. Hope I didn't disturb you?"

"No, I was just unpacking a few boxes."

His glance roamed the great room of her rented condo. Framed movie posters sat propped against various pieces of furniture, waiting for Jess to decide where to hang them. A sea of crumpled brown paper covered the parquet floors. Stacked cartons lined one whole wall.

"Looks like you still have a few boxes to go."

"Yes, I do."

Ordinarily she would've had her home in order by now. After seven moves in sixteen years, Jess had mastered the fine art of organizing her nest within a few days of reporting to a new assignment. This move was different. She'd arrived at Eglin, the sprawling air force base that ate up a good chunk of the Florida panhandle, almost a month ago and had yet to sort out her things.

A good part of that she could blame on her

new job. With only a few weeks' notice, she'd packed up, driven across country from California, and taken the helm of the largest supply squadron in the air force. The fact that her predecessor had been relieved of command and charged with attempting to cover up an illegal dump of several hundred gallons of paint solvent into an underground sewer system had certainly added a sense of urgency to the move.

The air force's three-star director of logistics had personally selected Jess for this assignment. She'd arrived at Eglin with specific orders to oversee the cleanup, get the EPA sanctions lifted, and help the JAG lawyers settle the lawsuits, all the while executing the 96th Supply Squadron's other vital missions.

The challenges of her new command thrilled Jess and consumed her daylight hours. It was the long stretches between dusk and dawn that took their toll. The tightly closed plantation shutters gracing the windows kept the night outside where it belonged, but Jess had slept even less than usual since moving into this airy, spacious condo overlooking the bay.

The stresses already surfacing in her new job were only part of it, she knew. The other part had a lot to do with a badge identical to the one her visitor had just slipped into his back pocket. Folding her arms, Jess gave him a look of polite inquiry.

"What can I do for you, Sheriff?"

"I need to know if you called or received a call from Ron Clark earlier this evening."

"The realtor who leased me this condo? No, I didn't. Why?"

"His wife found him dead a few hours ago."

Jess didn't blink, didn't twitch so much as a muscle. Her racing mind had conjured up a dozen possible reasons behind the sheriff's visit. That one came like a punch to the gut.

"How did he die?" she asked, keeping her voice carefully neutral.

"We'll have to wait for the ME to make the official determination, but initial indications are he hooked a garden hose to his Buick's exhaust pipe and sucked gas."

"And his wife found him?"

"Yes."

Jess wouldn't wish that brutal shock on anyone. Death in any form was wrenching enough. To find someone you loved with eyes rolled back and mouth agape . . .

For a moment, the condo's cool gray walls and lacquered white trim fuzzed into an institutional cream. Jess could almost see the swaying hospital curtains. Smell the pungent antiseptic. Hear the quiet click of the pump that had long since ceased to provide sufficient morphine to dull her mother's pain.

They'd had plenty of time to prepare for her death. All three of them. Jess, her stepfather, Helen herself. In the deepest, most anguished corners of their hearts, they had all prayed for it. Yet Jess would never forget the dark, still moment just before dawn when she'd gone for fresh coffee and returned to find the nurse leaning over her mother, and the heart monitor beside Helen's bed blipping out a flat, unbroken line.

The cardboard coffee cup had crumpled in Jess's fingers. Boiling liquid had spilled over her hand. To this day, the mere glimpse of the white, puckered skin webbing her right thumb and index finger reminded her of that awful moment.

Just as the sight of Steve Paxton's badge had raised instant, searing memories of another night, some twenty-five years earlier. Rubbing the puckered burn, Jess fought back the image of the older, paunchier sheriff who'd pounded on her mother's door so long ago. Paxton was a younger version of that genial redneck, but Jess didn't trust him any more than she had the original.

"I'm sorry for Mrs. Clark," she told him with utter truthfulness, "but I don't understand why you would think I talked to her husband earlier this evening. Or what difference it would make if I had."

"Well, it's like this." He toyed with the green ball cap, circling it around and around in his big hands. "Carolyn Clark said Ron developed a bad case of the jitters these past few weeks. Acted real nervous. At times seemed almost depressed. He wouldn't tell his wife what was bothering him, though. She thought it might have had something to do with the business."

Jess lifted her shoulders. "I don't know anything about his business. Or about Ron Clark, for that matter."

"Didn't you say you leased this place from him?"

"Yes, I did, but we transacted most of our business long-distance. When I found out I was coming to Eglin, I got the e-mail address of his realty office from an ad he'd placed in the *Air Force Times*."

"When was that?"

"A little over a month ago. Clark e-mailed me pictures of various properties, including this condo. He did the same with the lease, which I printed out, signed, and sent back to him."

Paxton nodded, but his glance had dropped to her hands. Only then did Jess realize she was still rubbing the old burn. Hunching her shoulders, she slid her palms in the front pockets of her ragged cutoffs.

The sheriff brought his gaze back to hers with a leisurely sweep that took in her bare legs, her braless state under the midriff-skimming UCLA T-shirt, and her total lack of anything approaching makeup. Jess couldn't decide if the glint in those unnerving, incredible eyes belonged to the man, the cop, or both.

"So you never spoke to Ron Clark personally?"

"I stopped by his office to pick up the keys when I drove into town. He had them waiting, we went over the terms of the lease, and I left. That was the one and only time I had a conversation with the man. Now suppose you answer my question, Sheriff. Why did you ask if I'd called or received a call from Clark?"

"Carolyn overheard her husband on the phone at home. Ron sounded agitated, so she went into the den to see what the problem was. According to her, Ron said your name, dropped the receiver onto the cradle, and stood looking at the wall."

Jess's skin prickled. "My name?"

"Your name, Colonel Blackwell."

He rolled the military title Southern style, slow, courteous, but Jess's heart was pounding too hard and too fast to appreciate the local flavoring.

"When Carolyn asked if he was all right, Ron turned and walked right past her. She heard the garage door open, then close. She thought he'd left for the office, thought maybe the phone call had something to do with your lease. She went upstairs to take a bath. When she came back down an hour or so later, she found her husband slumped over the steering wheel of his Buick."

Five seconds ticked by, ten. Jess's nerves were screaming when the sheriff broke the small silence.

"As far as we know, your name was the last thing Ron Clark said before he killed himself. You have any idea why, Colonel?"

"No." She looked him square in the eye. "Do you?"

If she was lying, she was damned good at it. Steve had been a cop long enough to crack the most impenetrable facades. He'd seen them all. The wide-eyed, I've-got-nothing-at-all-to-hide innocence. The belligerent, in-your-face challenge. The wounded disbelief at being questioned regarding a crime. Despite his years of separating the bravado from the bullshit, though, he couldn't get a handle on this woman. All he knew was that a blip had appeared on his internal radar screen the moment Ms. . . . correction . . . Lieutenant Colonel Blackwell had opened her front door.

Of course, the little blip might have something to do with the fact that this woman with the creamy skin, sleek spill of mink-brown hair, and killer legs didn't look like any colonel he'd ever come across during his two years as an army MP. Granted, that was back in the dark ages, before so many women had chosen to make the military a career and started hitting the top ranks. Before a ten-year stint with the Atlanta PD widened Steve's horizons considerably. Before Christy had burst into his life and widened them even more.

Burying the memory of his ex in the black pit where it belonged, he replied to the challenge in Jessica Blackwell's steady gaze. "No, ma'am, I don't know why you were on Clark's mind just before he killed himself. But I plan to find out."

"When you do, perhaps you'll tell me?"

It was a dismissal. Cool. Polite. Unmistakable. Steve's radar pinged again, but he accepted his marching orders with an easy smile.

"I expect I will."

She opened the door and waited. She was a woman used to issuing commands and having them obeyed. With a nod, Steve walked out into the night.

Hot air flavored with the sharp tang of pines seeped into his lungs. The silvery glint of moonlight on water only yards away drew him. With a rhythm older than time, the vast Choctawhatchee Bay lapped at shores fringed with short, spiky palmettos.

The bay pulled at something deep inside him. It had since the moment his Jeep had glided onto the bridge that spanned the eastern neck of the shimmering, shallow waters. He'd been on vacation, driving south at the time, intending to cut straight to the gulf and follow the ocean until something or someplace snagged his interest.

The divorce had done that to him, made him restless, rootless. After Christy had decamped with two truckloads of her fussy antiques, he'd avoided going home to an empty house and filled both his days and nights with work. He hadn't realized how close he'd come to the edge until an ex-employee had walked into a YMCA day-care center and opened fire with an Uzi.

Steve was the first officer on the scene. To this day, his stomach knotted whenever he remembered how close he'd come to emptying his own .45 into the murdering bastard's head.

The next week he'd thrown a carryall and his fishing gear into his Jeep and hit the road. He still wasn't sure why he'd decided to stop and fish the bay instead of driving on to the gulf. Maybe it was the lure of redfish and rainbow trout in the backwater bayous once paddled by prehistoric Indians. Or the clean, hot air he drew into his lungs instead of the gas fumes he'd breathed in Atlanta. Or the lack of anything approaching hustle in the sleepy village where he stopped to gas up. Whatever it was, he'd checked into the Bay View Motel and rented a bass boat the next morning.

By the following week, he'd burned, peeled, and burned again. The week after that, he'd called his boss from the marina and quit the Atlanta PD, then putt-putted out to fish the bay once more. When he'd come in that evening, the Walton County sheriff had been waiting for him. Cliff Boudreaux had heard a big-city cop was drifting around the bayous. He just wanted to say hey, and find out how long Paxton intended to stay in the area. One beer led to another, and a job offer soon followed.

That was seven years ago, and Steve still fished the bay.

Boot heels crunching on the shell walk that ribboned through the trendy condo community, he strolled past his unmarked cruiser toward the boat dock. His hip found a comfortable hitch on one of the wooden piles. With the unconscious need of a man whose mind had recognized the sense in not smoking but whose body was still waiting to be convinced, he reached in his shirt pocket. When he pulled out a pack of cinnamon-flavored Dentyne instead of the cigarettes he craved, his mouth twisted.

Unwrapping a stick, he popped it into his mouth and stuffed the paper back in his pocket. While his gaze roamed the rippling water, his mind clicked back to the scene that had greeted him when he'd arrived at the Clark home earlier this evening.

Unlike Atlanta, the Walton County Sheriff's Department didn't investigate all that many suicides. A distraught fourteen-year-old had gulped down a bottle of Tylenol after a breakup with her boyfriend last year. A lieutenant from the nearby air base had driven out to a lonely stretch of the reservation and blown out his brains some months back.

Then there was the Baptist minister down in South Walton County, whose boat had been found drifting after the storm that had whipped the usually placid bay into a frenzy last month. In all probability, the Reverend Mr. McConnell had gone overboard by accident, but until his body washed up Steve couldn't rule out anything, even suicide.

Nor would he close the books on the incident

tonight without doing some serious digging. Ron Clark's death might *look* like a suicide. It might even *smell* like a suicide. But the first axiom of police investigations was to work every unexplained death as a possible murder unless the evidence proved otherwise.

Although the Florida Department of Law Enforcement over in Pensacola held technical jurisdiction on capital crimes and had been called in to work the crime-scene analysis, the death had happened in Steve's county. He'd run his own investigation, look into the Clarks' financial assets and insurance policies. He'd also check out the woman Carolyn Clark claimed was on her husband's mind right before he died.

The gum popped, shooting red-hot cinnamon into Steve's mouth.

Lt. Col. Jessica Blackwell had triggered his interest in more ways than one. She was cool, almost too cool, but Steve had noted the flash of pity in her moss-green eyes when she'd heard how Clark's wife found him. Blackwell had also lost someone she loved, he guessed. A husband? A child?

She didn't wear a wedding ring. He'd noted that, too, right after he'd recovered from the double whammy of those mile-long legs and the trim, tight butt displayed to perfection by her cutoffs. Thinking about that rear sent another taste of cinnamon to assault his taste buds.

With a grimace of acute disgust, Steve pitched the gum into the bay and headed back to his cruiser. He'd sell everything he owned for a cigarette right now, including the thirty-six-foot trawler-style boat he'd bought at a drug auction and fitted out as his home.

Battling the acute craving, he slid behind the wheel and reached for the radio mike. "Dispatch, this is Paxton."

Wilena Shaw's husky response floated over the airwaves. "Go ahead, Sheriff."

Steve's grimace gave way to a grin. The night dispatcher was fifty-seven, carried a good two hundred and sixty pounds on her five-one frame, and kicked up the pulse of every male in the department whenever she answered or put out a call.

"I'm departing the Blackwell residence, heading home."

"Ten-four."

"Who's the duty officer?"

"Lieutenant Fairborne."

"Ask him to run a BI on Lieutenant Colonel Blackwell, will you?"

"You got it, Sheriff."

Chapter 2

Jess dug into a packing box, the muscles of her neck knotted. A good twenty minutes crawled by until she heard a car door thud and the sound of a car engine turning over. Her fists balled, crunching the paper she'd just removed from a stack of framed photos.

What the heck did Paxton do all that time out there in the dark? Had he been watching her place? Waiting to see how she reacted to his disturbing news? Thinking she might bolt?

Not this time. She and her mother had tucked tail and slunk away once when Paxton's predecessor had flashed his badge. She was damned if she was going to run again. She wasn't a scared, skinny kid anymore.

Biting her lip, she glanced down at the framed snapshot topping the stack in her hand. The black-and-white photo was one of the few salvaged from the constant moves during her gypsylike childhood. They'd moved so often, she and her mother, shedding a few more unnecessary possessions with each packing, until they could throw everything they owned in a couple of suitcases and a box or two.

Slowly Jess traced a finger over the glass protecting the photo, her heart aching at the deep grooves carved in her mother's brow. Helen couldn't have been more than twenty-eight or -nine when the picture was taken, but life had already left its mark on her face.

On her daughter's, as well. The young Jess scowled ferociously, as though she suspected whoever was taking the picture would make off with the camera. Given Helen's track record with the losers she invariably hooked up with, Jess probably had good reason to distrust him.

Sighing, she took the photo into the kitchen and set it on the white-painted shelf above the sink, where it could catch the sun.

In the days following Sheriff Paxton's late-night visit, the demands of Jess's job forced the sheriff and the unwanted memories he evoked into a separate, compartmentalized corner of her mind. There they remained during the busy daylight hours, emerging only at night to push Jess into marathon sessions of old movies and a final, frenetic flurry of unpacking.

By the time Friday morning rolled around, she'd hung all her pictures, put her closets in order, and disposed of a mound of cardboard boxes. Feeling tired but satisfied with her progress, she showered and slipped into tailored, dark blue uniform slacks and a crisply ironed light blue blouse. The embroidered silver oak leaves denoting her lieutenant colonel's rank glittered on the blouse's navy blue epaulets.

Normally she wore boots and battle fatigues to work, as did most of the military personnel on base. Today, however, she had a meeting with inspectors from the regional EPA office. They were bird-dogging cleanup of the solvents that had cost Jess's predecessor his command and weren't real happy about the slipshod procedures that had led to the dump in the first place. Neither was Jess, for that matter.

A soft breeze tugged at the hair she'd tamed into a French braid as she backed her Mustang convertible out of the garage. Giving in to impulse, Jess put the top down. The slap of the cool dawn air was worth an occasional snatch at the flight cap she tugged down squarely on her forehead.

Five minutes later she drove onto the Mid-Bay Bridge. From seven a.m. on, a steady stream of vehicles rumbled across the soaring arch of concrete. But this early, with the sun little more than a faint haze on the eastern horizon and the bay still a hazy pewter instead of its usual electric blue, she could make it from her condo to Eglin Air Force Base's back gate in just under twenty minutes.

In the weeks since she'd arrived in Florida, Jess had come to love the early-morning drive across the twelve-mile bridge. At this merging of sea and sky, of dark and light, she put the night behind her. With one hand on the wheel and the other poised to grab her hat if necessary, she relaxed and reviewed the day ahead.

It would be a hectic one. Seven-thirty, stand-up with her deputy and division chiefs. Nine, the wing commander's staff meeting. The EPA inspectors at one-thirty. At three . . .

Her mouth thinned. At three, she'd perform one of the less pleasant duties that came with command—administering punishment under Article 15 of the Uniform Code of Military Justice. She didn't look forward to busting a fourteen-year veteran who'd served with distinction in the Gulf War. Particularly since taking the man's stripe was the final punitive act before processing him for discharge under other than honorable conditions.

She hadn't met TSgt. Ed Babcock—he'd been unavailable the few times she toured or stopped by the Fuels Management Flight—but the first sergeant had briefed Jess on the man's deteriorating duty performance and off-duty conduct over the past year. It turned out his supervisor had been covering up the sergeant's repeated absences in a well-meaning if misguided effort to salvage a highly qualified fuels specialist. Only after Babcock plowed his car into a tree did Bill Petrie reveal the scope of the problem.

A serious lapse in judgment on the supervisor's part, Jess thought grimly. Instead of trying to hide the matter, he should have sent Babcock for help. After the DUI, Jess's predecessor had finally directed the NCO into a forty-day rehab program at the base hospital.

From all reports, Babcock had stayed sober after the rehab program until two nights ago, when he'd tied on the mother of all drunks and almost destroyed the casual bar at the NCO club. To add insult to injury, he'd coldcocked two of the cops who'd tried to subdue him. The first sergeant had bailed him out of jail yesterday morning and begun the inexorable paper process that would lead to his discharge.

Well, with more than three hundred active duty military and civilian personnel in her squadron, Jess figured she'd be lucky if putting a decorated war veteran out of the service was the worst personnel problem she'd face in the next few years.

The sun was spreading its humid glow as she exited the bridge and drove through the sleepy towns of Niceville and Valpariso. Traffic slowed for the approach to Eglin. Security had been extra tight since 9/11. Jess negotiated the concrete barriers slowly and flashed her photo I.D. The security force specialist squinted at her picture before whipping up a smart salute. Jess returned it and passed through the buff-and-brown-painted gate.

When she drove onto the base proper, her pulse hitched. Those massive fuel storage tanks off to the left were hers. So was the huge supply complex just beyond the tank farm. Although she'd spent her entire career in the supply business, she still found it hard to believe she now commanded the largest operation in the air force. Her people managed some 62,000 individual line items valued at $885 million, processing over a hundred thousand transactions a month for everything from pencils to laser-guided missiles. In addition to the supply items, they maintained eight hundred equipment accounts valued at another $540 million, and dispensed some 40 million gallons of aviation fuel annually.

It was an awesome responsibility, one Jess had trained for, had worked for, yet she couldn't suppress a thrill of sheer excitement at the scope of the operation. Her mind was clicking on the latest reverse post and MICAP—Mission Incapable—rates when she pulled into her reserved parking place in front of Building 500. The monstrous Harley-Davidson hogging the slot next to hers indicated her deputy was already at work.

Sniffing appreciatively at the scent of floor wax and coffee that greeted her inside the double glass doors, she nodded to the clerk on the reception desk, then hung a left. The lights in the command suite confirmed her deputy's presence. Going on forty years of civil service and Al Monroe was still the first one at work.

Tugging off her hat, she breezed through another glass door. She didn't recognize the young woman seated in one of the leather armchairs. The petite redhead clutched her hands in her lap and gave Jess a nervous smile. Jess returned it, then aimed a questioning look at the tall, scarecrow-thin civilian standing in the door to his office.

"Morning, Al."

"Good morning, Colonel." With a tip of his head, the deputy chief of supply indicated their early visitor. "This is Eileen Babcock, Sergeant Ed Babcock's wife."

"Ex-wife," the redhead corrected in a voice as thin and brittle as new ice. "Our divorce was final two days ago."

"Ex-wife," Al amended. "She'd like to talk to you."

Uh-oh. A newly divorced wife. An ex-husband about to be kicked out of the service, with accompanying loss of pay and entitlements. He'd have no job, no way to pay alimony or child support.

"I told Eileen you have to get ready for stand-up in twenty minutes," Al said, offering Jess an easy out. "With your schedule so crowded after that, I suggested she call Mrs. Burns and make an appointment."

The woman surged to her feet. Desperation darkened her brown eyes. "Please, Colonel, I just need a few minutes."

"No problem. Would you like some coffee?"

"No, thank you."

"I'll just grab a cup, then," Jess said, depositing her briefcase on the conference table in her office. "Make yourself comfortable."

"Want me to call in the first shirt?" the deputy asked quietly while Jess filled her mug. "He can handle this."

"I've got it."

Thank God the first pot of coffee Al brewed each morning before the secretary arrived was thick as sludge, with a kick like a bee-stung mule. Jess would have valued him for that alone, never mind his unfailing courtesy, steel-trap memory, and forty years of experience in the supply business.

Coffee in hand, she closed the door and took a seat at the conference table opposite the redhead. In the harsh glare of the overhead fluorescent lights, the woman looked older than Jess had first thought. Mid-thirties, maybe. And tired. Extremely tired, if the shadows bruising the skin around her eyes were any indication. Her clothes were Florida casual—a short-sleeved, loose-fitting dress in a thin black knit and low-heeled sandals. The cluster of seashells polished to shimmering iridescent beauty and looped through a black cord to form a necklace added an unexpectedly sophisticated touch.

"What can I do for you, Mrs. Babcock?"

"I heard Eddie . . . my husband—" She stopped, pulled in a breath. "I heard my ex-husband is supposed to see you this afternoon."

"Yes, he is."

"I also heard you're going to bust him. Maybe kick him out of the air force."

Jess didn't bother to ask where she'd gleaned her information. If Sergeant Babcock and this small, nervous woman had been married for any length of time, Eileen Babcock would have a good idea what a DUI, a string of failures to repair, and a recent arrest for drunk and disorderly conduct would do to a military career.

"I can't discuss your ex-husband's situation with you," Jess told her. "Even if you weren't divorced, I wouldn't discuss it until I talked to him first."

"I understand! Honestly, I do." She scuttled to the edge of her seat, gripping her hands so tightly Jess thought the bones would snap at any moment. "I just wanted you to know that what happened is my fault. *All* my fault. You've got to give Eddie another chance."

"Mrs. Babcock—"

"He never drank anything more than a couple of beers at a time until two years ago."

If the woman's eyes had looked bruised before, they were haunted now.

"He was asked to teach a course on fuel additives at the American Petroleum Institute. He was gone for almost a month. When he got home, he found out I'd slept with another man."

Jess hadn't seen that coming. Shifting in her chair, she cleared her throat.

"You don't have to say anything," Eileen Babcock put in swiftly, bitterly. "There's nothing anyone can say that would make a difference at this point. It happened, okay? I can't change that, as much as I wish I could. All I'm asking is for you to understand why Eddie went off the deep end."

She must have heard the desperation in her voice. She clamped her mouth shut and closed her eyes. When the red-tipped lashes fluttered up again, Jess felt a tug of pity for the desolation on the woman's face.

"Eddie and I started dating in high school. We were married the day after graduation. I never looked at another man until . . . until this happened. Never *wanted* another man."

Tears slid down her cheeks. Her throat working, she forced out a full confession.

"To this day, I don't know why I did it. He was younger than I was. A college kid! Down here for spring break, if you can believe that. I was flattered, I suppose. And Eddie was gone so much."

Pushing away from the table, Jess dug a box of Kleenex out of her desk drawer and offered it to the redhead. Awash in tears and self-loathing, Eileen swiped almost angrily at her cheeks.

"I'm not like you, Colonel. I didn't want a career. I've held odd jobs . . . I worked as a cashier at the BX and waited tables at the NCO club . . . but all I ever wanted was to be a wife and a mother."

"That's a career in itself," Jess said gently.

Without conscious thought, she rubbed the

puckered skin between her thumb and finger. Like Eileen Babcock, her mother had waited tables to pay the rent and put food on the table, but Helen had saved all her love, all her devotion, for her only daughter.

"Yes, well . . ." The tissue shredded, falling like snowflakes onto Eileen's black dress. "It turned out I'm sterile. Eddie and I couldn't have kids, but for all those years we had each other. Then we lost even that."

Jess couldn't help herself. Although she had no business discussing Sergeant Babcock with his former spouse, the despair in the woman's face dragged her in.

"Did you try counseling?"

"We went to the chaplain. The mental health clinic. Finally a private counselor. The more Eddie swore he forgave and forgot, the guiltier I felt. It got so I couldn't stand to have him look at me, let alone touch me. That's when . . . That's when he started drinking."

She picked at the tissue shreds, her shoulders slumping. "It's funny when you think about it. Once we separated, I qualified for a training program for displaced homemakers. Now I'm starting a career in banking I never wanted, and Eddie's losing the only one he's ever known."

Her gaze lifted to Jess, begging for understanding, for leniency, for anything that might help the man she'd hurt so badly.

"He dried out after the DUI. He really did. This latest binge . . ." She lifted a hand, let it drop. "Our divorce was final two days ago. It hit him. Really hard. Please, Colonel. Give him another chance."

The weight of her command sat heavy on Jess's shoulders. "I'll take what you've told me into consideration when I talk to Sergeant Babcock this afternoon."

It was all she would promise. All she *could* promise. Whatever had started Ed Babcock's slide into alcohol, he was the only one responsible for its impact on his duty performance.

The formalities of the official process cloaked her interview with the sergeant later that day. Offering punishment under Article 15 was a ritual, scripted out move for move, word for word. Babcock reported in, saluted, stood at attention until she returned his salute and indicated he should take the chair in front of her desk.

The first sergeant, with the diamond embroidered onto his stripes to indicate his top position in the squadron, took a seat off to Jess's right. The message was unmistakable: He was part of the command team.

Following the script, Jess read charges against Sergeant Babcock. Violation of Article 108 of the Uniform Code of Military Justice, destruction of military property. Violation of Article 134, drunk and disorderly conduct. Article 92, failure to obey a lawful order to cease and desist. Article 95, resisting arrest.

After summarizing the information on which

the charges were based, Jess stated that she intended to impose punishment for these offenses unless he requested trial by court-martial.

"I'm required to inform you that the maximum penalties I can impose upon you include forfeiture of one half of your pay for two months, sixty days' restriction to your quarters, forty-five days' extra duty, thirty days' confinement, reduction in rank of one grade, and/or a written reprimand."

The list was daunting, but all parties present knew that a military court could impose much more severe sanctions.

"If you demand trial by court-martial in lieu of punishment under Article 15, these charges could be referred for trial by either a summary, special, or general court-martial. At trial, you have the right to be represented by counsel. Do you understand your choices in this matter?"

"Yes, ma'am."

The answer was short, almost curt. Ed Babcock had been down this road before.

He wasn't quite what Jess had expected. For some reason, she'd formed a mental image that complemented his slender, almost diminutive ex-wife. Sergeant Babcock stood about five-six or -seven, but his barrel chest and wrestler's body gave the illusion of a good deal more height and muscle power. The knife-edged creases in his starched fatigues could have cut glass, and his boots were polished to a sheen that mirrored the overhead fluorescent lights.

"I'm giving you two days to decide whether you wish to request trial by court-martial," she informed him. "The first sergeant has set up an appointment for you with the Area Defense Counsel at nine tomorrow morning."

"I don't need to see the ADC. I accept whatever punishment you've decided on."

"Take the two days, Sergeant Babcock. Think about it."

His face could have been carved from granite. "With all due respect, ma'am, there's nothing to think about. I accept nonjudicial punishment."

Jess shot a look at the first sergeant. A twenty-six-year veteran who'd seen about all there was to see when it came to the vagaries of human nature, Ruiz shrugged.

"Very well," she said, turning back to the stocky sergeant. "Before we proceed, I need to advise you that you're entitled to be accompanied by a spokesperson to speak on your behalf. You may examine the police reports and statements I've considered in this matter. You may present matters in defense, extenuation, and mitigation, orally or in writing or both. You may also have witnesses present, or request these proceedings be open to the public."

"No one's going to speak on my behalf."

"Someone already has," Jess said carefully. "Your ex-wife came to see me this morning."

His stony facade cracked for a moment. Only a moment. Jess caught a flash of hope, of hurt, of fury, before the mask dropped down again.

"Whatever she said doesn't cut soap, Colonel. I'm responsible for my actions."

Jess couldn't argue with that.

"All right. Since you've declined to accept legal counsel or present matters in extenuation or mitigation, I'm hereby vacating the suspension and reducing you in rank to the grade of staff sergeant. I'm also ordering you to pay full damages to the NCO club, levying an additional fine of three hundred dollars a month for three months, and warning you that you're on notice, Sergeant Babcock."

She paused, wanting to make sure she had his attention, and leaned forward to emphasize the point.

"If you step out of line again, if you so much as spit on the sidewalk, you'll be out of the air force so fast your head will spin."

His forehead creased in a quick frown. "You mean you're not initiating the paperwork to kick me out?"

"Not this time."

His glance rifled to the first sergeant. Ruiz spoke for the first time.

"It was the colonel's decision, Babcock. I advised her to toss your sorry butt onto the street. You owe her for this one. Her and Eileen."

The stony expression that descended over the man's face again indicated a distinct lack of gratitude. Jess held his eyes, her own fierce.

"Don't make me regret this, Sergeant."

His shoulders snapped back. His chin came up. For the life of her, she couldn't tell if he was happy with this last chance or not.

"Is that all, ma'am?"

"Sign these papers; then you're dismissed."

Ruiz waited until Babcock had departed to gather the signed documents. "Well, at least Mr. Petrie won't lose his only certified fuels analyst. He was worried about that."

"He deserves to lose him. He didn't help him by covering up his repeated absences."

"Billy Jack Petrie is one of the good ol' boys," the first shirt answered with a shrug. "He takes care of his people in his own way."

She reached for the phone. "Then I'd better make sure he understands we're doing it my way from here on out."

"Yes, ma'am."

Four hours later, Jess aimed the Mustang's gleaming silver nose south over the Bay Bridge, heading toward the snow-white beaches that edged the Gulf of Mexico. A headache tugged at her temples. *Christ, what a day!*

The sessions with the EPA and Sergeant Babcock had been bad enough. A late-afternoon call from the test wing commander had upped the pucker factor even more. One of the avionics modules in a specially configured F-15 had failed and they needed a new one delivered and installed no later than noon tomorrow or they'd have to scrub a multimillion-dollar test of a new air-to-air missile.

Luckily, the major in charge of the 96th Supply Squadron's Combat Operations Support Branch knew just how to work the system. After three computer flash requests and several cajoling phone calls, she assured Jess the avionics kit had been shipped from the depot by overnight express. She also promised to track it via the computer and notify Jess immediately if it looked like it wouldn't make the promised nine a.m. delivery.

Only now, with the sun hanging low and the bay a patchwork quilt of aquamarine and emerald and deep lapis below the causeway, did Jess think about food. She'd downed a Krispy Kreme maple-glazed cruller for breakfast and skipped lunch. Hungry for chargrilled amberjack, she turned right off the bridge instead of left. A short drive past high-rise condos and snowy beaches topped with waving sea oats brought her to Pompano Joe's.

This late in the evening, the popular eatery was jammed with both locals and tourists. A smoky-voiced jazz singer crooned from the loudspeakers as Jess claimed a stool at the bar to wait for a table. The wooden shutters were raised, the windows open to the brisk evening breeze of the gulf.

Idly, Jess sipped a tall, frosted glass of iced tea and watched couples stroll hand in hand along the sugar-white sand. The tea went down strong and sweet and cold enough to make the breeze feel comfortable. The feeling that she'd failed to reach Ed Babcock didn't go down at all.

So Jess was in no mood for company when someone asked if the stool beside hers was taken. Even less when the lazy drawl registered and she looked up to find Sheriff Paxton planted squarely between her and the nearest exit.

Chapter 3

Jess's first impulse was to say yes, the stool next to hers *was* taken. Her second was to down the last of her tea and depart the premises. Still wired from her demanding day, the last thing she needed was this sudden, jagged jolt to her nerves.

With a conscious effort of will, she subdued the impulse to flee. Pride wouldn't let her run. Not this time. Not ever again. Indicating the seat next to her with a careless nod, she shrugged.

"Help yourself."

Her distinct lack of enthusiasm raised a gleam in Paxton's aquamarine eyes. "Thanks."

He slid onto the stool with an easy grace and hooked one loafer heel over a rung. From the look of them, the loafers were handcrafted and expensive. As was his suit. The charcoal-gray slacks molded trim hips. The well-cut jacket draped his broad shoulders with a touch of elegance. He'd discarded his red tie, one end of which dangled from his suit pocket, and popped the top buttons on his pale blue shirt, but the impression was still one of sophistication.

He didn't miss her quick inventory. Jess had the uneasy feeling he didn't miss much of anything.

"I was at a meeting of Florida law enforcement agencies over at Pensacola," he said in answer to the question she hadn't asked. "Thought I'd grab something to eat before leaving the bright lights of down-county."

"Down-county?"

"According to the old-timers, Walton County's developed a severe case of split personality. Up around the county seat of DeFuniak Springs, it's still old timber, Victorian homes, and Confederate flags. Since the tourist boom, down-county is now all golf resorts, high-rise condos, and Yankee snowbirds."

"With the bay keeping both cultures well separated."

"Exactly." Signaling to the bartender, he ordered a beer. "You probably got a taste of the separation when you lived here as a kid."

He let it drop so casually, anyone else might have been fooled into thinking he was just making conversation. Jess knew better.

"Did you run a background check on me, Sheriff?"

"Standard procedure, Colonel."

"Find anything interesting?"

"Several things, as a matter of fact."

She considered not taking the bait, but the need to know overcame her reluctance to continue the conversation. "Like what?"

"Like the fact that you pulled two tours in the Balkans."

"A lot of people pulled tours there."

"But not all of them led a resupply unit through heavy enemy fire. Nor were they decorated for heroism as a result."

"Did you get all that from police records?"

"No, from your official bio and the story the *Daily News* ran on you when you arrived. Our police computers contained only one entry from an old FI card—a field interview card," he expanded at her look of polite query. "Seems one of our officers responded to a report of an out-of-control juvenile. According to his report, some bratty seven-year-old had bloodied the nose of one boy and blackened the eye of another."

A bratty seven-year-old.

Jess remembered her well. All arms and legs, toting around a chip the size of Idaho on her thin shoulders. A chip that had grown with every move and every taunt from the kids at school.

They'd never accepted or understood her. She was always the newcomer, always the outsider. Always the scruffy kid whose miniskirted mother raised brows each time she marched through the halls to extricate her daughter after yet another tussle.

No wonder she and her mom had formed such a close bond. There had been only the two of them. Just her and her mother. Until Frank Blackwell. With a silent prayer of thanks for the gentle, patient garage mechanic who'd married Helen and adopted her daughter, Jess pulled her thoughts from her past to the man who kept dragging them into the present.

"The boys were too embarrassed to admit they'd been bested by a girl," he related, a smile tugging at his mouth, "so the incident was dropped with no further action taken."

The smile was potent. Too potent. Against her will, against every canon of common sense, Jess felt a stir of sexual attraction. Evidently even a badge didn't completely negate Sheriff Paxton's tawny hair, tanned skin, and lazy charm.

Cursing herself for a fool, she turned her attention to the open windows. The sun was just kissing the gulf, sandwiching a patina of gold between the darkening sky and deep emerald swells.

Paxton ignored the magnificence outside. Swiveling his stool, he planted an elbow on the bar and leaned closer. Too close. The end of his tie drifted over Jess's knee, raising a ripple along her nerves where the silk brushed the skin.

"Why didn't you mention last night that you'd lived in Choctaw Beach?"

Deliberately, she blanked the memory of a rusted trailer mounted on cinder blocks a few miles from the half dozen or so buildings that passed for the town of Choctaw Beach. Just as deliberately, she dragged her gaze back to his.

"You didn't ask, and I didn't think it was pertinent to your visit."

She might have carried off the careless reply if Paxton's glance hadn't dropped to her hands. With another silent curse, Jess saw that she was massaging the puckered flesh with her thumb. She reached for her tea to give her fingers something else to do.

"How's the investigation into Ron Clark's death coming?" she asked coolly.

"The ME confirmed the cause of death as carbon-monoxide poisoning." His long, tanned fingers stroked the frosted beer glass the bartender placed before him. "I talked to the folks at the Florida Department of Law Enforcement before I left Pensacola this afternoon. They're ready to make a preliminary determination of suicide."

Relief seeped through Jess. She was searching for a noncommittal comment when she heard Paxton's name called over the loudspeaker. He cocked his head, and Jess braced herself for the invitation she saw coming.

"Care to join me?"

Jess was already forming a refusal when she realized Steve Paxton might take that as a sign she had something to hide and dig deeper into her past. Better to go along, she decided. Besides, it wouldn't hurt to discover just how much he knew.

"That depends," she answered.

"On?"

"On whether you're still on duty."

"A cop never goes off duty." His smile remained in place. "This cop, however, is more than willing to put business aside and make small talk with a good-lookin' air force colonel for a few hours."

That line probably worked magic with most of the females he approached. Jess wasn't impressed. She flicked a look at the hand cradling his beer glass. He wasn't wearing a ring, but that didn't mean squat.

"It also depends on whether there's a Mrs. Sheriff Paxton waiting for you at home."

One sun-bleached brow cocked. "Do you always vet your dinner companions this carefully?"

"I don't like complications."

"Fair enough. There was a Mrs. *Detective* Paxton once. We were divorced a year or so before I moved down here from Atlanta."

Neither his expression nor his voice altered, but Jess sensed a definite withdrawal, as though the subject wasn't one he wanted to talk about. Apparently Paxton's divorce had left some scars. Like Sergeant Babcock's.

The loudspeaker blared the sheriff's name again. Taking her silence for assent, he slipped a hand under her elbow to help her off the bar stool. The intent might have been mere courtesy, but his touch ignited a series of small electric shocks just under Jess's skin.

Slinging her military purse over her shoulder, she broke the contact and wove through the milling crowd to the hostess stand.

When they finished their grilled amberjack and walked outside into the night, Steve had gleaned little more information about Lt. Col. Jessica Blackwell than the bare facts he'd had in his possession going into Pompano Joe's.

Through casual conversation, he'd confirmed the basic details in the background report. She was thirty-three. Single. Born Jessica Yount in Bethany, Pennsylvania, and adopted at the age of ten by a stepfather she evidently adored. Graduated from UCLA, then went on for an MBA from Stanford. Entered the air force right out of grad school. Other than that one curious incident as a child, she had no record of any brushes with the law, not even a citation for jaywalking.

Which didn't explain why Steve made her so nervous.

He'd like to believe the jumpiness she almost succeeded in concealing was physical, a reaction to his raw, animal magnetism. Unfortunately, his raw animal days were a thing of the past. Maturity and his ex-wife had taken their toll. Although . . .

Damned if all parts of him hadn't sat straight

up and taken notice when he'd cupped the colonel's arm. She'd quickly shaken him off, but not before Steve had cataloged smooth, soft flesh and a heat just under the skin that shot right from his fingertips to his groin.

The view of her backside as she crossed the parking lot wasn't bad, either. He liked the way she walked, hips rolling, long legs striking out as if she had places to go and important people to see. He also liked the way her dark blue uniform slacks shaped her rear. He slowed his pace and enjoyed the view as he followed her to a snazzy little Mustang convertible.

Tossing her purse onto the passenger seat, she reached for the door. Steve didn't fail to note how she put it between them before she turned.

"Good night, Sheriff. Maybe I'll see you around."

No thanks for the company. No polite pretensions that she'd enjoyed herself. Another man might have taken the hint. Steve wasn't finished with Colonel Blackwell yet.

"Oh, you will," he promised casually. "I still haven't pinned down why you were on Ron Clark's mind just moments before he killed himself. I'll let you know when I do."

She slid behind the wheel and keyed the ignition. "You can reach me anytime through the twenty-four-hour operations center at the Ninety-sixth Supply Squadron."

He got the message. She wasn't amenable to any more unannounced, late-night visits to her home. Wondering if she really thought he intended to play by her rules, Steve dug in his pants pockets for a package of Dentyne. As he watched the Mustang nose into the eastbound lane of U.S. 98, known locally as the Emerald Coast Highway, red-hot cinnamon set fire to his taste buds.

He claimed his unmarked cruiser a few moments later. A quick check with Dispatch revealed relative quiet for a Tuesday night. The only disturbance involved an altercation at a Little League softball game that had landed one overaggressive parent in the county jail.

"He's waiting for his wife to bail him out," Wilena reported with a deep, rich chuckle. "Just between you 'n' me, Sheriff, she plans to let him cool off for a day or two."

"Hope we don't have to respond to a ten-sixteen when she springs him," Steve drawled. As he'd learned all too well during his years on the Atlanta PD, domestic disturbances could turn deadly in the blink of an eye.

Advising the sultry-voiced dispatcher that he intended to stop at the new down-county substation on his way home, he signed off.

The Walton County Sheriff's Department substation had been constructed less than a year ago and still smelled of new paint. It was headed by one of the department's newer captains. Steve had personally selected Jay Dubois to command the ten officers assigned to the substation. Jay was experienced enough to hold their respect, yet young enough to walk the fine line between the needs of the antebellum communities of North Walton County and the booming tourist economy to the south. It didn't hurt that his wife, Pam, had a way of baking the rainbow trout Steve and her husband reeled in that could make wild dogs grovel and grown men weep.

Jay was at home, no doubt sprawled in his recliner after another of Pam's delectable suppers, but the shift officer in charge welcomed the chance to shoot the breeze with the sheriff. They traded the morbid war stories only cops could appreciate for a good twenty minutes. Steve was just getting up to leave when Wilena Shaw's voice came through the console.

"Substation, this is Central Dispatch."

"Damn!" the grizzled officer muttered, reaching for the mike. "The way that woman sounds over the radio, she could make a monk cream."

Privately, Steve agreed with him. Publicly, he refused to tolerate sexual innuendo or off-color jokes on the job. The pointed glance he sent his subordinate had the man reddening and mumbling an apology before he keyed the mike.

"This is Officer Harriman. What's up, Dispatch?"

"Is Sheriff Paxton still there?"

"He's standing right beside me."

"Be advised we have a signal-seven, Sheriff."

Steve lifted a brow. Two dead bodies in less than

a week. Business was certainly picking up. Edging the shift officer aside, he thumbed the mike.

"This is Paxton, Dispatch. What are the particulars?"

"Two kids gigging bullfrogs up around Harry's Bayou found a floater. Their mama called in the report about ten minutes ago. From what the boys told her, the body's pretty putrid."

"Who's responding?"

"Officer Martin's on the way. I've notified Captain Alexander. He's sending an investigator. Want me to call the fluff?"

Steve smiled at the local's less than flattering nickname for the Florida Department of Law Enforcement. Although he made it a point to maintain solid relations with the various state agencies his department interfaced with, the complicated jurisdictional lines could and often did blur.

Like in the matter of Ron Clark's death.

As Steve had relayed to Jessica Blackwell only a few hours ago, the state was ready to close the case. None of the probes into the realtor's business and personal financial holdings had turned up anything irregular or suspicious. But neither had investigators uncovered a clue as to what might have driven him to suicide. Or why Clark had muttered Lieutenant Colonel Blackwell's name just before he died.

The state boys could close the case if they wanted to. Steve intended to dig a little deeper.

"Go ahead and notify FDLE," he instructed

Wilena. "I'll swing by, too, and see what we have."

Steve had been fishing Choctawhatchee Bay for seven years now, but still didn't know all the inlets and coves branching off the vast body of water. There were hundreds of them, maybe thousands. After ascertaining the approximate location of Harry's Bayou from Wilena, he signed off and scrutinized the oversize map of Walton County pegged to the wall behind a thin, protective sheet of Plexiglas.

"It empties into Indian Bayou," the shift officer volunteered, peering at a section of the map. "Should be 'bout . . . here."

The inlet appeared to be little more than a shallow cove, probably clogged with weeds and inaccessible by anything other than a shallow-bottomed boat. Great for gigging bullfrogs, Steve thought. And for hiding dead bodies.

"If I remember right," the shift officer volunteered, scratching a patch of chest covered by his dark green uniform shirt, "there's a dirt road leads off Highway Twenty that runs down almost to the bayou. Kind of hard to find the road now. Used to be a dive right where it turns off. The Crab Shack, or something like that. Pretty lively place until it burned down twelve, fifteen years ago. If you look close you can still see the ruins under the kudzu."

"Let's hope Martin marks the turn," Steve replied, thinking of the stream of official vehicles that would find its way down to the bayou in the next few hours.

The drive to Harry's Bayou took Steve north across the Mid-Bay Bridge and then east along Highway 20. For some miles, signs posted on either side of the road indicated the land was part of the Eglin Air Force Base reservation, with no trespassing allowed. Another, larger sign indicated the turnoff for Site C-6, which housed the 20th Space Surveillance Squadron.

Steve had visited the isolated complex several times, originally on a familiarization tour when he'd first joined the Walton County Sheriff's Department, again some months later to pick up poachers detained by the security forces who patrolled the site. He still marveled that a phased-array radar some five stories high, which tracked over nine thousand near-Earth and deep-space objects, was tucked right here amid the tall, spindly pines of the Florida panhandle.

Once past C-6, he drove through several villages clinging to water's edge. Backed by the vast Eglin reservation and fronted by the bay, they consisted of little more than a handful of structures.

Three miles beyond the scatter of buildings with the fanciful name of Villa Tasso, the cruiser's headlights picked up a small white sign informing Steve that he was entering Choctaw

Beach, population 306. He slowed to the posted forty-five mph, squinting through the darkness at the weathered bayside cottages, the occasional trailer, the convenience store still open for customers.

Odd that Jessica Blackwell had lived in this tiny hamlet as a girl. Odder still that she hadn't mentioned that fact during Steve's visit the night of Ron Clark's death. He'd driven away from her condo with the definite impression that she was new to the area. To be fair, though, he hadn't asked about her past, only her connection to the dead realtor.

There had to be a connection, something more than a lease. Or was his cop's sixth sense working overtime? Could he be speculating about a link that might or might not exist, because the woman intrigued him?

Okay, she more than intrigued him. She turned him on in a way no woman had in a long time. *Too* long. Not that Steve had remained celibate since his marriage to Christy went bust. An all-too-willing coworker on the Atlanta PD had helped him through his anger and frustration after the divorce. Since moving to Florida, he'd enjoyed several mutually satisfying "friendships" that he was careful to keep casual.

Yet no woman since Christy had hit him with the same punch as the self-contained and completely uninterested Lt. Col. Jessica Blackwell. Shaking his head at his own contrariness, Steve checked the odometer and slowed again. The turnoff for Harry's Bayou should be around the next bend or two.

Sure enough, he spotted a glowing red light just moments later. Officer Martin had efficiently marked the turn. Steering the cruiser onto a rutted dirt track, Steve searched the dark, humped shapes on either side for the ruins the shift officer had mentioned. If a roadside dive had once existed at this location, its remains now lay buried under a thick blanket of kudzu.

Grimacing, Steve guided the cruiser down the bumpy track. The kudzu had denuded the tall cypresses on either side of the road of leaves and the feathery Spanish moss that had once draped their branches. Dark stumps now, they thrust into the night sky, making a last, painful stand against the vine that devoured them.

Steve hated the damned kudzu, felt claustrophobic every time he had to tramp or drive through stripped, silent woods like these. The stuff had been introduced into this country by some well-meaning agriculturist back at the turn of the century, supposedly to curb erosion on bare banks and fallow fields. Almost indestructible, it propagated a foot or more a day, climbing trees and telephone poles, covering fields, killing all life beneath. Long tradition had it that mothers in the South needed to keep a close watch on sleeping babies to make sure a kudzu vine didn't snake through a window and strangle them.

Finally Steve spotted lights at the end of the dark, silent tunnel. Blowing out a breath of relief, he pulled up behind Martin's black-and-white. The moment he opened the door and stepped out into the night, he caught a whiff of a putrid stench. Wilena's initial report had been right on the mark. The floater had been in the water for a while.

Gratefully, he accepted the small jar of Vicks VapoRub Martin offered him. Most of the cops carried a jar in their squad cars for situations like this. A thick smear of the powerful mentholatum under each nostril blocked even the stench of death.

"What have we got here, Martin?"

"Well, I thought at first it might be that possible drowning victim, the one whose sailboat turned over in the storm last month."

"The Reverend McConnell?"

Keeping a wary eye out for snakes, Steve approached the bayou's edge. The body—what was left of it—drifted in the weeds.

"The build's about right," Martin continued, aiming his flashlight's powerful beam at the corpse. "But . . ."

"But what?"

"If this is McConnell, I'm not sure he drowned. He's sporting a nice-size crease in his skull."

A wavelet lapped at the body, dislodging the small flap of scalp still clinging to the cranium. The bone beneath the floating hair glistened white and clean in the flashlight's beam. Even from where he stood, Steve could see the jagged edges where something or someone had smashed in the skull.

"I suppose he could've hit the rail when he went over the side of his boat," Martin observed.

"It's possible."

"Be interesting to see what the ME and the crime lab over to Tallahassee come up with."

"Yes," Steve agreed. "Very interesting."

Chapter 4

Det. Jim Hazlett arrived at Harry's Bayou some fifteen minutes after the boys from the county medical examiner's office had fished the body out of the bay.

A good thirty pounds overweight and as overworked as everyone else in the Florida Department of Law Enforcement's Investigations division, Hazlett had some twenty years of experience walking the jurisdictional tightrope between federal, state, and local agencies. He was a good man, one of only a handful of detectives in the Panama City office. He was also the FDLE officer who'd investigated Ron Clark's death.

"Evenin', Sheriff."

"Hello, Jim."

Hazlett hooked a thumb at the corpse waiting to be hauled up to the meat wagon. "Is that one of your constituents?"

"Looks like. The fish have had at him, but there's enough left to pretty well confirm that he's the man who went missing after the storm that blew in a few weeks ago."

" 'Bout time he turned up."

Dragging a handkerchief out of his pocket, Hazlett ambled over to take a closer look at the corpse. The ME's assistants obligingly unzipped the body bag and held flashlights steady while the detective took in the condition of the bloated torso.

"Well, well. Wonder how he got that dent in his skull?"

"We've been wondering about that, too," Steve put in. "And about his shoe."

Hazlett's gaze slid down. One foot had provided a feast for the fish. The other was still shod in a black leather wing-tip.

"Hmmm."

The detective waved a hand, granting permission for the ambulance crew to zip up the corpse and transport it to the ME's office.

"You took Mrs. McConnell's initial report when her husband's boat was found drifting in the bay, Sheriff. Did she happen to mention what he was wearing?"

"The last time she saw him he was dressed for work, but she indicated he kept a change of clothes aboard his boat. You'd think he'd keep some rubber-soled deck shoes, too."

"You'd think."

"I'll ask her again when I do the next-of-kin notification. Unless you want the honors," Steve asked, knowing the answer already.

"Nope, they're all yours. Until we confirm his identity and the specific cause of death, I'm only here to assist you."

"Yeah, right."

Next-of-kin notifications were never easy, even when the deceased's sailboat had been found adrift almost a month ago.

The Reverend McConnell's wife had had time to prepare herself for the worst. Still, Steve had Dispatch contact her husband's assistant pastor and request that he meet the sheriff at the McConnell residence at ten the next morning.

He wore full uniform. The gleaming Sam Brown belt, knife-creased forest-green shirt with his badge and rank insignia, and tailored gray pants with the green stripe down the sides were a mark of respect, as well as a reminder that he'd put the force of his office behind the investigation into the reverend's death.

Mabel McConnell was a small, twittery woman. Her eyes filled with tears the moment she opened her door and saw the sheriff and her husband's assistant pastor on her front porch.

"You've . . . ? You've found him?"

"We think so," Steve said gently.

Her throat worked. "Is he dead?"

"Yes."

Her hand came up to cover her mouth. Moaning, she took a step back. Steve caught one elbow, the young pastor the other. Sobbing, she allowed them to lead her into the living room.

"I knew it," she got out through her tears. "In my heart, I knew it. But I still hoped. All these weeks, I hoped and prayed. . . ."

Steve passed her a clean, folded handkerchief. Her shoulders shaking, she sank into a recliner upholstered in nubby brown-and-blue plaid. The pastor pulled in a chair from the dining room and angled it close to hers while Steve took the matching recliner.

The close placement of the plaid recliners was as telling as the homey clutter scattered around the living room. A sewing basket spilled a rainbow of embroidery threads. Books lay stacked on the maple coffee table. Framed pictures crowded the top of an upright piano. Steve caught a glimpse of a wedding shot. Clusters of school pictures. A very young, lantern-jawed Delbert McConnell in the slick-sleeved uniform of a marine recruit.

"That was before I met him," his widow said with a hitch in her voice, catching the direction of Steve's gaze. Her lips curved in a faint, trembling smile. "From what he's told me, he was pretty wild back then. I'm so thankful I met him after he found the Lord."

The faith that had formed the core of her husband's life sustained his widow now. Her fingers shaking, she reached out to grasp the young pastor's hand.

"Delbert's in the arms of his savior now. I can't grieve over that. Will you say the service for him?"

"Of course. When do you want it?"

"I don't know." Confused, she looked at Steve. "Where's my husband's body? When can we bury him?"

"The medical examiner will have to conduct an autopsy. It's required in every unexplained death."

Steve didn't go into details. He saw no need to bring up the gash in McConnell's skull until they were reasonably certain what caused it. The shoe bothered him, though. Big-time.

"When you first reported your husband missing, you said he hadn't mentioned taking his boat out that day."

"No, he didn't. But he would sneak in a sail whenever he could. It was his release, his way of communing with the Almighty. He always said he saw things clearer out there on the bay, with just the wind and the sun and the boat cutting through the water."

Steve could relate to that. He'd spent a good number of solitary hours out on the Choctawhatchee, too.

"I used to go with him when he first bought the boat, but . . ." The widow swallowed, fighting tears again. "But I didn't enjoy it as much as he did, and I always had so many things to do around the house."

She bit her lip, no doubt thinking she'd have time now for every small task she might have put aside to go sailing with her husband.

"You also indicated the reverend kept a change of clothing on the boat."

"Yes. Some shorts and an old, sleeveless sweatshirt. A windbreaker, too, I think."

"What about boat shoes?"

"Yes, of course."

"Apparently he was wearing black leather wing-tips when he went overboard, Mrs. McConnell."

She looked surprised, but could offer no explanation for why a man who sailed as much as her husband would attempt to negotiate a wet, slippery deck wearing leather-soled street shoes.

Tugging off his tie, Steve popped the top button on his uniform shirt and cranked up the air-conditioning for the drive to his office. From the McConnells' house in South Walton, he retraced his route of the night before. Across the Bay Bridge. Though Villa Tasso and Choctaw Bay. Past the intersection of Highway 20 and the dirt road that led to Harry's Bayou.

In the bright light of noon, the vine-covered clumps that had once been the roadhouse were more easily discernible. Steve gave them a once-over as he drove past, wondering idly what caused the place to burn down. Just out of curiosity, he'd pull the old reports.

Twenty minutes later he cruised under the I-10 overpass and hit the city limits of DeFuniak Springs. Steve always felt as though he had en-

tered a time warp each time he passed under
the interstate. He hadn't exaggerated when he'd
described Walton County's schizophrenic nature
to Jessica Blackwell. The beaches and touristy
bustle to the south were another universe. Here,
in the town constructed around a small, perfect,
spring-fed lake, the Victorian era still thrived in
all its gingerbread glory. Gabled and turreted
houses circled the lake. The massive Chautauqua Hall of Brotherhood, which had brought a
flourish of educational, cultural, and religious
enlightenment to the area around the turn of the
last century, still stood in all its white-columned
majesty. The hall was only one of the forty or
so structures in DeFuniak Springs listed on the
National Register of Historic Places.

The county courthouse dominated the sleepy
downtown. A jarringly modern addition to the
granite courthouse housed the county jail and
the offices of the sheriff. When Steve wheeled
into his reserved parking spot behind the jail,
a handful of prisoners in the black-and-white-
striped shirts were clipping the hedges around
the building. The rest, he knew, were chowing
down.

Which he intended to do, as well. As he let
himself in through the private entrance to his
office, he thought about taking lunch in the jail
cafeteria. He made it a point to do so at varying
times so he could answer the prisoners' inevitable complaints about the food. Today, however,

he had a reprieve. The scent of fried chicken had him making a beeline for the outer office.

Steve had inherited both his predecessor's beat-up rolltop desk and his gum-snapping, brassy-haired secretary when he let himself be talked into running for sheriff and surprised everyone, including himself, by winning. He could live without the rolltop desk. He didn't want to think about managing without Pat Sampson.

"Is that for me?" he asked hopefully, eyeing the napkin-covered plate on her desk.

"It is." Her gum popped. "The prisoners are having liver and onions today, which I know ranks right down there at the bottom of your list, so I brought you back lunch from the café."

He lifted the napkin and immediately started to salivate. Fried chicken, fried okra, *and* red beans and rice. He'd died and gone to heaven.

"Remind me to put you in for a raise come next budget cycle."

"No problem. I've already included it in the initial submissions."

Grinning, he carried the plate back to his desk, crunched into a chicken leg, and skimmed through the telephone messages stacked in a neat pile. One from the lieutenant governor's office requesting information on a recent drug bust. One from Dub Calhoun, son of former U.S. Representative John Robert Calhoun and now a candidate for his father's old office, inviting Steve for cocktails prior to the upcoming black-

tie affair that culminated the annual Fourth of
July Chautauqua Summer Arts Festival. And
one from Jim Hazlett, advising that his superiors
had signed off on a determination of suicide in
the Ron Clark case and requesting a call back if
the visit to McConnell's widow had turned up
anything new.

Steve fingered the message slip, thinking
about Ron Clark. Why the heck had he spoken
Jessica Blackwell's name? Who had he been talking to? Sprint records confirmed that the call
had come in from a phone booth.

Digging out the background check he'd had
his folks run on the colonel, he propped a foot
on the bottom desk drawer. Springs creaked as
he tilted his chair back and flipped through the
pages. There wasn't much there. Aside from that
one incident as a kid, she was clean. Squeaky-
clean.

Unlike her mother. A check on Helen Blackwell, née Yount, showed one bust for driving
under the influence of alcohol. Evidently the
woman went straight after that. Or at least
didn't get caught again.

So why couldn't he shake the feeling that
there was more to her daughter than met the
eye? Or his growing interest in the part that *did*
meet the eye?

Idly, he buzzed Mrs. Sampson. "Would you
see if you could get Lieutenant Colonel Blackwell on the line, please? She's the commander
of—"

"The Ninety-sixth Supply Squadron down at Eglin," Ms. Efficiency replied. "Hang tight, boss."

She buzzed back a few moments later. "She's on line two."

"Thanks." He hit the button, his stomach curling with a sense of pleasurable anticipation. "Colonel Blackwell?"

"Yes?"

The single syllable was cool, polite, and just a touch wary. Steve smiled into the phone.

"I thought you might like to know the Florida Department of Law Enforcement had ruled Ron Clark's death a suicide."

"Did you find out why he said my name the night he died?"

"Not yet."

The answer drew a small silence at the other end of the line. He let it spin.

"I appreciate the call," she said after a moment. "If there's nothing else, I have to get ready for a meeting."

"As a matter of fact, there is one other matter I wanted to discuss with you."

"What's that?"

"Dinner Friday night."

"I beg your pardon?"

"I've got to put in an appearance at a chamber of commerce meeting in South Walton Beach about six. How about I pick you up at seven?"

"Sorry, I'm busy Friday night."

The reply was quick, chilly, and anything but

encouraging. Steve's smile tipped into a grin. Even at her frostiest, the colonel turned him on. It was the fisherman in him, he decided, as much as the cop. He couldn't resist the challenge of getting her to rise to the bait.

"Maybe some other time, then."

"Maybe."

In other words, take a hike.

"I have to go. Good-bye, Sheriff."

Chapter 5

Disconcerted by the call and the unexpected invitation, Jess did her best to put Paxton out of her mind in the days that followed. The demands of her job helped in that regard. So did her decision to personally observe fuel-delivery operations the next time a barge docked at the off-load facility.

One was scheduled to arrive just before noon the following Wednesday. Clearing her schedule for a few hours, she grabbed her fatigue hat, told Mrs. Burns she'd be on mobile, and drove the short distance from Building 500 to Weekly Bayou.

One of Choctawhatchee Bay's innumerable inlets, the finger of water poked right into Eglin base proper. At its mouth, the base maintained a sandy beach, a Fam-Camp with RV hookups, and boat slips with rentals for base personnel. The pristine beach had taken a severe hit in the tropical storm that had swept the area just days after Jess's arrival, but most of the debris had been cleared and the recreational facilities were again open for business.

Luckily, the storm hadn't damaged the fuel dock. It floated at the tip of the bayou, little more than a stone's throw from the massive storage tanks. Jess parked at the entrance to the dock and sat for a moment in the air-conditioning blasting through the Mustang's vents. Iridescent waves of noon heat shimmered outside the windows as she surveyed the scene.

There wasn't much to see. A long, white-painted wooden pier. A hookup to the underwater pipeline that ran to the storage tanks. Scattered pieces of emergency fire-suppressant equipment. A small building that served as control center and office for the dock NCO.

Shutting off her car's engine, Jess braced herself and climbed out. Although her baggy camouflage fatigue pants and loose-fitting shirt were supposedly designed to allow air to circulate, she knew she'd be swimming in perspiration within minutes. As the natives were fond of saying, that was Florida in mid-June for you.

Her black boots clumped on the boards as she walked out onto the floating platform. The familiar tang of aviation fuel flavored the air. Although she'd spent her entire career in the supply business, she'd never become directly involved in the fuels operation. She was learning more about the complex task of keeping aircraft refueled, cocked, and ready with each passing day.

When he saw her coming, the NCO in charge of the docks threw her a surprised look and a hasty salute. "Good morning, Colonel."

"Good morning, Sergeant Weathers."

"What can I do for you?"

"I understand you've got a barge on the way in."

"Yes, ma'am. The tug captain just radioed that he's ten minutes out. We're getting to deploy the booms."

"Mind if I watch?"

"No, ma'am," he replied warily.

He was even newer to the base than Jess was, having reported in just two weeks ago. The prospect of having his commander look over his shoulder obviously made him nervous. He started down the dock, but the sound of a vehicle pulling up brought a sweep of relief to his face.

"There's Sergeant Babcock. He had this job for years before he took over the lab. He can answer any questions I can't."

Jess turned, narrowing her eyes against the glare as a government vehicle parked behind her silver Mustang. When the short, stocky NCO made his way out to the dock, her glance went to the stripes on his sleeve. If Ed Babcock resented the fact that he now wore one less than he had the last time he saw her, he didn't show it.

Shifting a wooden case containing a rack of glass vials to his left hand, he saluted with his right. "Colonel."

Jess returned the courtesy, waiting until Weathers had scurried off to take another radio call from the tug captain to inquire how Babcock was doing.

"I haven't touched a drink since that night at the club, if that's what you're asking."

She didn't pretend otherwise. "It is, and I'm glad."

The forthright reply surprised him. The glass jars rattled as he shifted his kit again.

"I didn't thank you the other day for not handing me my walking papers. I wasn't expecting another chance."

Jess hadn't expected to give him one, either, but knew better than to mention how persuasively his ex-wife had pleaded his case.

"Sergeant Weathers mentioned that you used to be in charge of the docks," she said instead. "Why don't you talk me through the off-load procedures?"

Off-loading a million or more gallons of jet fuel, she discovered, required patience, vigilance, and a good deal of muscle power. The Defense Supply Center purchased Eglin's aviation fuel in bulk from refineries in Houston and New Orleans. The military package contained a variety of additives that included everything from the ice inhibitors to the conductivity eliminators necessary for aircraft that might deploy to bases strung from the Arctic to the Sahara. Exxon in turn subcontracted with various tug companies to supply Eglin, Hurlburt Field, and Tyndall Air Force Base, farther east on the coast. The tug captains hired their own crews and made the fourteen-day round trip at scheduled intervals.

"Most of their crews are foreign nationals," Babcock told her. "Too many of them either ignore or aren't able to read safety warnings. Once, I caught a man dragging a pack of cigarettes out of his shirt pocket during an off-load operation. He was just about to light up when I tossed him and his cigarettes into the bayou."

Suddenly the merciless noon heat blazing down on Jess's head and shoulders didn't seem quite so unbearable. She could only imagine the inferno that would erupt if several million gallons of jet fuel ignited.

As a consequence, she took a somewhat personal interest when a long, flat barge appeared a few minutes later. A second followed, nosed along by the squat black-and-white tug that churned up a steady wake as it approached the dock.

When Sergeant Weathers's people climbed into a motorboat and putt-putted out to deploy the floating booms behind the tug, Jess relaxed a bit. Only a bit. The booms would contain minor spills, but a spill of forty gallons or more would have to be reported. After her last session with the EPA, she wasn't anxious for another.

She didn't breathe easy until the barges were tied to the dock.

"We're off-loading a million-point-two gallons this shipment," Babcock informed her. "It should take about eighteen hours. I'll draw samples from all eight compartments in each barge before they begin off-loading, halfway through the discharge, and again when they finish."

"Looking for?"

"Sediment. Water contamination. Prohibitive levels of conductivity. I also have to make sure the refinery put in the required additives."

He hesitated a moment before extending a grudging invitation.

"You're welcome to come back to the lab and watch while I run the tests."

"I'll do that."

By the time Sergeant Babcock finished taking his initial samples, sweat plastered Jess's fatigue shirt to her back and her breasts. With a heart-felt prayer of thanks for the Mustang's air-conditioning, she followed Babcock's truck up Eighth Street past sprawling, brown-and-tan-painted airmen's dormitories to Building 89.

Refuelers were lined up outside the building, ready to fill up and dispense JP-8 to the test aircraft parked along the aprons stretching to the east. The planes were only a fraction of those supported by the 96th Fuels Management Flight. The fighter wing on the other side of the base flew sleek F-15s. In addition, the transient aircraft that stopped at Eglin gulped down millions of gallons of fuel each year.

Babcock parked at the rear entrance to the Fuels Management building and hauled out his samples. When Jess's Mustang pulled up behind his truck, he punched in a cipher code.

"The lab has its own entrance. We can go in here."

"I'd better let your lieutenant know I'm here," Jess told him, mindful of protocol. "I'll join you in the lab in a few minutes."

"Yes, ma'am."

She walked around to the front of the small building. Jess had toured Building 89 during her initial orientation and visited several times since. Even so, the trophy case crammed with awards and citations from the American Petroleum Institute impressed her all over again. The 96th fuels operation had won the API award for best in command seven of the last eight years.

Passing under a shield depicting a snarling panther, she saw that the fuels officer wasn't in and moved to the adjoining office. A glimpse of the occupant through the glass partition stopped her in her tracks.

The fuels superintendent was bent over his desk, his legs braced wide and his fists balled on the littered desktop. His mouth was a thin, tight slash, his face as white as the newspaper spread across his blotter. From where she stood, Jess couldn't make out the details of the picture that held his intense concentration.

"Mr. Petrie?"

Billy Jack Petrie jerked around. When he spotted Jess, his skin seemed to blanch even more.

"Are you all right?" she asked, taking a step into the office.

"I'm fine." His fist closed over the newspaper. Wadding it into a tight ball, he tossed it into the dented metal wastebasket beside his desk. "What can I do for you, Colonel?"

"I was down at the docks observing the offload. I wanted to let the lieutenant know I was in the building. I'm going to watch Sergeant Babcock perform the initial analysis."

"Why?" the supervisor asked swiftly. "Don't you trust him?"

Don't you trust me? was the question that hovered in the air. Jess hadn't minced words when she'd reminded Petrie of his responsibilities as Ed Babcock's supervisor.

"Obviously I trust his skills," she replied, "or I wouldn't have allowed him to remain in his present position."

"You don't think he's been drinking, do you? I've been on him like ticks on a coon dog, and haven't seen any—"

"No, I don't think he's been drinking. I just want to observe the tests."

Straightening, Petrie seemed to collect himself. He was a tall man, lean and rangy, with a shock of coal-black hair that belied his age and years of service. He took in her heated face and her sweat-drenched fatigues and extended a grudging offer.

"You'd better cool down some before you go into the lab or the fumes will get to you. There's a pop machine in the break room. Can I get you something to drink?"

"A cold Coke would be great."

She reached in the pocket of her fatigue pants for her wallet, but Petrie waved aside her money.

"I've got it."

When he disappeared down the hall, Jess's glance snagged on the wastepaper basket. With a quick look over her shoulder, she retrieved the wadded newspaper. The grainy, black-and-white photo on the front page of the *Daily News* caught her notice instantly. Centered in the picture, a T-shirted man smiled benignly at a crew of what looked like volunteer construction workers.

Local minister, shown here directing a Habitat for Humanity project, will be missed.

Jess read the caption twice before moving to the article that followed.

Forensics experts at the Florida Department of Law Enforcement have tentatively identified the body recovered from Harry's Bayou last Friday as Rev. Delbert McConnell, pastor of the Dunes Baptist Ministry in South Walton County.

Reverend McConnell's wife reported him missing after he failed to return from a fishing expedition. He disappeared almost a month ago, the same day Tropical Storm Carl lashed the coast.

Carl had done its share of damage, Jess thought. The same storm that had torn limbs off trees on base, deposited mounds of debris on the Fam-Camp beach, and whipped the bay into a frenzy was now presumed to have claimed Reverend McConnell's life.

Coast guard and local marine patrols conducted an exhaustive search and located his overturned boat, but found no trace of the popular minister until his badly decomposed body was discovered submerged in the weeds in Harry's Bayou.

The sound of footsteps brought her head up. Petrie stopped short in the doorway, a Coke can clutched in one fist. His glance whipped from her face to the newspaper and back again. When he didn't speak, Jess gestured to the photo.

"Did you know him?"

Her question hung on the air. His throat working, Petrie opened his mouth, shut it again.

"Yes," he finally got out. "I knew him. Everyone 'round these parts knew Delbert McConnell. He . . . he was a good man."

Whatever she might have said in answer was lost when Sergeant Babcock appeared just behind Petrie.

"I'm all set up, Colonel."

"Right."

She moved to the door. Petrie backed away, giving her room to pass through. Stopping before him, she held out her hand.

"Thanks for the Coke."

"What? Oh, yeah." He practically shoved it at her. "You're welcome."

Despite the air-conditioning that dewed the windows with condensation, sweat runneled down Billy Jack Petrie's cheeks as he snatched up the telephone receiver. His finger shaking, he stabbed at the keypad and waited in a swelter of impatience until a voice roughened by decades of cigarettes growled out an answer.

"Yeah?"

"She was just here," Petrie hissed. "In my office."

A long, hacking cough came through the receiver. Deep and swimming with phlegm, it ripped all the way up from the bottom of his listener's chest.

Grimacing, Petrie held the phone away from his ear. "Did you hear me?" he demanded when the vicious rattle finally died. "She was just here."

"So?" There was another hack, and the splat of spittle hitting something tinny. "She's your boss, ain't she? She's come to your office before."

"Not without calling first. She just showed up, I tell you, right when I was reading about Delbert."

"Reading what about Delbert?"

"Didn't you see today's paper? Jesus Christ, it's right on the front page."

"I ain't got around to going into town for a paper yet," his listener said in a snarl. "You want to tell me what the fuck you're talking about?"

"The police made a positive ID. They know it's him."

"They say how he died?"

"No, only that he disappeared the day the storm hit. Jesus, what if they do an autopsy and don't find water in his lungs?"

"Why wouldn't they find water in his lungs? He drowned, didn't he?"

"Yes, but what if—"

"Shut up, for crissakes! You're starting to sound as bad as Clark!"

His stomach roiling, Petrie swiped an arm across his forehead. First Delbert, then Ron Clark. Where would it end? Where *could* it end?

If he didn't know the finish, he knew when it had started. Twenty-five years ago, on a night he'd wiped clear out of his head until Lt. Col.

Jessica Blackwell arrived at Eglin and stirred beasts best left slumbering.

"She keeps ragging me about one of my men," he said hoarsely. "She wants to lay the blame for his troubles on me; I know she does. Between that and—"

"Shut up, I said! You're making my head hurt worse than that bottle of Jim Beam I killed last night."

"That's another thing, dammit. You keep swilling a fifth or more every night and you're going to say the wrong thing to the wrong person. I don't know about you, but I sure as hell don't want—"

With another snarl, his listener crashed down the phone. Billy Jack winced and hung up. His head pounded. The grits and sausage patties he'd downed for breakfast threatened to rise up and choke him. Swallowing, he forced the bile back down his throat and dragged his gaze to the crumpled newspaper.

Delbert McConnell smiled up at him from the front page of the *Daily News*.

Hunching over his desk, Billy Jack Petrie buried his face in his crossed arms and fought the urge to bawl like a baby.

Bill Petrie wasn't the only one feeling the weight of Lieutenant Colonel Blackwell's presence in Building 89. Sweat soaked Ed Babcock's armpits and slicked his hands as he showed the colonel how to ground herself and reduce the static electricity in her clothing. Once inside the small, windowless lab, he pointed out the safety features.

"The exhaust vents will prevent the fumes from reaching noxious levels, but if you start to feel sick, either slip on an oxygen mask or go outside."

Nodding, he indicated the oversize shower-head suspended over the center of the room like a giant Kansas sunflower. "If something should spark and ignite the fumes, the shower will drench the entire lab in a half second."

"You've actually timed it?"

"As a matter of fact, I have."

With the tender care a mother might give her newborn, Babcock aligned the samples he'd drawn from the barges on a stainless-steel work-table. The pale gold liquid looked so innocuous, yet Ed accorded the highly flammable fuel the respect it deserved.

"For safety purposes, the maximum amount of fuel we bring into the lab at any one time is ten gallons."

Jess stood a few feet away, her green eyes curious while he measured various agents into five of the glass jars.

"What are those?"

"Chemicals to verify the presence of required additives. This one tests specifically for Biobor JF. It combats fungus and other microtive life in hydrocarbons. This"—he measured another agent—

"checks for diethylene glycol monomethyl ether, which is an anti-icing additive."

The fuel fumes thickened, tainting the air. Ed could feel them seeping into his pores. Nervous as a cat in a yard full of stray dogs, he poured the samples through a series of filters to assess the sediment levels.

Was she watching his hands to see if he had the shakes? Did she think he couldn't do his job? Resentment at being on probation like this percolated through his head. He was good at what he did, damned good, but his nerves were strung wire-tight when he readied for the final test. Centering a beaker of fuel in a special oven protected by a giant metal hood, he closed the glass door and set the temperature gauge.

"The military fuel package contains a special additive to increase its flash point to a hundred degrees. This allows high performance jet aircraft to burn off most of the residue that builds up in the engines and, theoretically at least, prolongs engine life."

The colonel nodded, her eyes riveted on the oven's temperature gauge. The seconds ticked by, sliding slowly into minutes, while the needle inched from green, through white, toward red.

Ed had taken pride in his job, had loved knowing what he did contributed directly to the air force mission. So much he'd sweated through college courses at night to complete first a bachelor's, then a master's degree in chemistry. Over the years, he'd turned down lucrative offers from Exxon, from Texaco, from the American Petroleum Institute.

Until his marriage fell apart at the seams, he'd never seriously considered the offers. Until he started burying his ache for Eileen in a bottle, he wouldn't have imagined that he'd trade a stripe, maybe even his right to wear an air force uniform, for a drink. But now, with the woman who had the power to destroy him standing just a foot or so away, he craved a slug of tequila so badly his entire body screamed with need.

He knew it was irrational, knew he was transferring his frustration and pain over his failed marriage and rapidly disintegrating career. But at that moment he hated Colonel Blackwell for stringing him out like this with passion as hot as the flames that suddenly erupted inside the oven.

Chapter 6

Once a year the commanders on base threw a huge, formal bash for the local dignitaries and their wives. Eglin's Christmas ball, the Logistics Group commander informed Jess the last steamy Monday morning in June, was the social event of the year and Eglin's way of saying thank-you for the surrounding communities' support.

The locals reciprocated, Colonel Hamilton advised, with a number of must-attend events. One was the City of Fort Walton Beach's answer to Mardi Gras, the Billy Bowlegs Parade and Pirate Ball. Another was the Niceville Mullet Festival. The Okaloosa County Chamber of Commerce's by-invitation-only dove hunt and poker night at a private hunting lodge had traditionally been an all-male gathering until a previous female commander had broken through the barriers. Jess could expect an invitation to that event come dove season.

The black-tie affair that culminated the Chautauqua Summer Arts Festival, traditionally held over the Fourth of July weekend, constituted another mandatory function. The party took place up in DeFuniak Springs and gave the Eglin folks a chance to mix and mingle with the Walton County bigwigs on their own turf.

Ignoring his key staff's groans at the prospect of getting all gussied up in formal dress uniforms on one of the hottest nights of the year, Hamilton informed them they *would* all show, and they *would* all have a good time.

Somewhat to her surprise, Jess did have a good time, at least at first. The only military woman present, she stood out among the bejeweled and gowned flock. Luckily, the severe lines of her midnight-blue formal mess dress uniform flattered her. The straight, floor-length skirt was slit to the knee on one side to allow movement. The tuxedo-style jacket in the same dark blue was paired with a snow-white blouse and satin cummerbund. Embroidered silver epaulets announced her rank, while the two rows of miniature medals decorating her jacket gave her instant status. In a concession to the occasion, she'd piled her honey-brown hair on top of her head and attacked the rambunctious strands with a curling iron. The feathery crown of curls added an unexpectedly feminine touch to the otherwise starkly military ensemble.

Reserved at first, Jess soon relaxed. The eclectic mix of military, local businessmen, and artists made for lively conversation. What was more, the setting for the lavish soiree proved magical. The turn-of-the-century Victorian home of the party's host was a gem, with fanciful mansards, a three-story turret, and encircling verandas overlooking the small lake fed by the springs that gave the town its name.

After an hour or so of the required mingling, Jess slipped through the tall French doors to the veranda. Old-fashioned wooden paddle fans churned the evening air, while very modern humidifiers discreetly hidden behind banks of ferns sprayed just enough chilled moisture into the night to make it bearable. Clutching a dew-streaked glass of perfectly chilled Riesling from the local Chautauqua Winery, Jess leaned a hip against the railing and gazed at the stately mansions and elaborate cottages encircling the lake. They were all illuminated in honor of the occasion, with additional white lights strung through the trees to add to the festive atmosphere.

The sight stirred a long-forgotten memory. Vaguely, Jess remembered taking quick swipes at a melting chocolate ice-cream cone while she and her mother completed a walking tour of Circle Drive one Sunday afternoon. Helen had read about each house from a printed brochure. A little later a band had set up in the gingerbread bandstand beside the lake, and mother and daughter had stretched out on a grassy bank to listen to the songs of a bygone era. The concert had ended with a rousing rendition of "Dixie" enthusiastically chorused by all listeners.

That was the last Sunday Helen and her daughter had spent in Florida, or in the South. Blanking the humiliating events that followed from her mind, Jess lifted her glass and sipped the fruity white wine.

"Enjoyin' the view, Cuh-nul?"

The curvaceous blonde who joined her wore a cheerful smile and a name tag that identified her as Maggie Calhoun, wife of State Senator Dub Calhoun.

"Yes, I am."

Jess remembered her from their long ago school days. Vaguely. When they'd met in the receiving line earlier it was obvious the bubbly blonde didn't have a clue that they'd once attended the same school. That was fine with Jess. She couldn't quite decide whether the woman's effervescence was a factor of her own personality or her husband's political ambitions. She'd already heard the rumors that smooth, handsome Dub Calhoun intended to follow in the footsteps of his father, once one of Florida's most colorful and powerful U.S. representatives. Jess didn't doubt for a moment that this stunning blonde draped in a sheath of flame-colored silk would prove a decided asset to Dubba's career.

"I've lived here most all my life," the politician's wife confided, "and never do get tired of seein' the circle lit up like this. It's something, isn't it? Oh, my stars," she murmured, her glance snagging on something just over Jess's shoulder. "So is that."

Jess angled around to follow the woman's admiring gaze. The sight of a tall, tanned figure in a full-dress uniform had her breath hissing out.

It was the first time she'd seen Paxton wearing the full accoutrements of his trade. He didn't wear them often, she guessed. Probably only on formal occasions—weddings, funerals, command performances like this one. The forest-green jacket and gray trousers with their green stripe down the sides were tailored with military precision. A black leather Sam Brown belt polished to a glassy sheen crossed one shoulder and circled his waist. But it was the silver eagles on the collar points of his white shirt that grabbed her attention.

She was well aware that most civilian law-enforcement agencies employed the same rank structure as the military. Lieutenants headed flights, captains ran branches, majors managed departments. County sheriffs and chiefs of police in large cities were the equivalent of full colonels and wore the silver eagles denoting their exalted status.

Although she was forced to respect the responsibility that went with those eagles, the visual reminder that Paxton outranked her set Jess's teeth on edge.

Maggie Calhoun's admiring gaze lingered on the sheriff for some moments before drifting back to Jess. "I swear, sometimes there are distinct disadvantages to being a married woman."

Jess made no comment as the politician's wife took a delicate, catlike sip of her wine.

"I gather from what I read in your bio that you're not similarly afflicted."

"No, I'm not married."

"Have you met our handsome sheriff yet? I'd be happy to introduce you."

"Yes, I have."

Something in her reply must have alerted Mrs. Calhoun to the fact that Jess harbored no desire to join the ranks of Steve Paxton's admirers. The blonde indulged in a few more moments of small talk before gliding over to join the sheriff. Tilting her head back, she laughed at whatever he said in greeting and tucked a casual hand into the crook of his elbow.

They made a striking pair, Jess decided objectively. Both tanned and tawny gold. They could have been carved from the same gleaming marble. More to the point, the senator's wife obviously enjoyed Paxton's company. So Jess wasn't the only one he surprised when he disengaged a few moments later and headed across the porch. For a second or two, Maggie Calhoun looked almost waspish.

"I've been working my way through the crowd to you," he said when he reached Jess's side.

"Have you?" she replied with a credible show of nonchalance. "Why?"

"I reeled in a twelve-pound redfish this afternoon. It's all filleted and ready to grill. I thought you might want to come over to my place tomorrow and compare my culinary skills to Pompano Joe's."

"To your place?"

"Yes, ma'am." His mouth curving at her obvious surprise, he conducted a leisurely inspection of her curls. "I like your hair like that, by the way."

"Thank you." Jess pasted on a smile. "I appreciate the invitation, Sheriff, but—"

"Steve. The name's Steve."

"I appreciate the invitation, *Sheriff*, but I'm still learning my job. Aside from official functions like this, I don't have time for socializing."

"Don't think of it as socializing," he said, his eyes glinting. "Think of it as Sunday dinner."

So much for polite pretenses.

"Let me put it another way, then. I'm not interested. In you or in Sunday dinner."

"Sure you are. You just aren't ready to admit it yet."

She didn't bother to dignify that with a reply. With a small nod, Jess walked away.

Shoving one hand in his pocket, Steve held his drink with the other and treated himself to the pleasure of watching her walk. The swish of her long blue skirt and accompanying flash of leg put a kink in his groin that stopped just short of painful.

Correction. It hurt like hell. He might as well be honest. He'd had a hard-on for the colonel since the first night she'd opened her door to him wearing those skimpy cutoffs and half a T-shirt. The woman fascinated him almost as much as the mystery of her link to the dead realtor. He was chewing over that link again when a ripple of throaty laughter brought his head around.

"My stars, darling." Maggie Calhoun sauntered over, her eyes bright and brittle. "I couldn't help overhearing. The colonel certainly put you in your place."

"It happens every once in a while," Steve admitted with a careless shrug.

"Oh, well, that's how it is with these Yankees. They just don't appreciate our native charm."

"This one should. She lived down in Choctaw Beach for a few years in the late eighties."

"Really? That wasn't in her bio." Maggie tapped her lower lip with a pointed, pink-tinted nail. "We're the same age, give or take a year or two. We must have gone to school together, but I sure don't remember any Jessica Blackwell."

"Her mother's name was Yount. Helen Yount."

"Yount! That's Jessie Yount?"

His companion swung around to shoot an incredulous glance at the woman in uniform, slop-

ping her champagne over the sides of the flute
in the process. With a muttered, un-Maggie-like
curse, she dabbed her napkin at the spot on her
silk sheath.

"You knew her?" Steve asked when she
tossed the crumpled napkin onto a nearby tray.

"Not really. She was a couple years behind
me in school, and everyone pretty much steered
clear of her. Not just because she was an outsider. Truth is, she was the skinniest, scrappiest
kid you ever saw. Seemed like she was always
getting into fights."

"Why?"

"Probably because of her mother." Maggie's
nose wrinkled delicately. "Much as I loathe to
put people in boxes, Helen Yount really fit the
definition of poor white trash. There were all
kinds of rumors about what she did with the
customers out at the Blue Crab."

"The Blue Crab?"

"Oh, that's right. You wouldn't know it. The
place burned down years ago, long before you
moved here from Atlanta."

Steve didn't correct her. He knew the place,
all right. He'd tramped past its vine-covered remains just last week.

His gaze slid past Maggie and found a tumble
of warm brown curls. No doubt it was only a
coincidence that Reverend McConnell's body
had tangled in the weeds of Harry's Bayou, just
a few dozen yards from the ruins of the roadhouse dive where Jess Blackwell's mother once

worked. And it might have been mere coincidence that Jess's name was the last thing Ron Clark said before he killed himself.

The problem was, Steve had been a cop for too long to believe in coincidence. More intrigued than ever, he pulled on a lazy smile and pumped Maggie Calhoun for more information.

Jess wasn't sure when she first noticed the sidelong glances. Right after the fireworks display that lit up the night sky and poured showers of green and red and blue stars into the pond, she thought afterward. Certainly well before the lavish cocktail party began to break up.

She didn't have any doubt as to the source of the murmured rumors that whispered through the crowd like a hot, dry wind through a wheatfield. She'd turned her back on the sheriff's tête-à-tête with Maggie Calhoun, but hadn't missed the glances the blonde sent her way shortly when she drifted back inside and sidled up to her husband. After a brief exchange, Dub Calhoun's smile had slipped and he'd pinned Jess with a long, hard stare.

She'd expected the stares, Jess reminded herself grimly during the long drive home. Sooner or later, she'd expected the rumors to begin. What she hadn't expected was the little sting that accompanied each intercepted glance and murmured aside. Or the familiar anger that ignited little fires just under her skin.

Her bunched fist hit the Mustang's steering wheel. She was so sure she'd put the anger behind her, dammit. She hadn't allowed herself to get all tight and raw like this in decades. Not since the night Steve Paxton's paunchy predecessor had pounded on the door to Helen Yount's trailer, suggested she pack herself, her belongings, and her kid into their rattletrap of a car, and escorted them out of town.

As Jess pulled into the garage attached to her condo, the memories of that humiliation rushed at her like demons of the night. Letting herself in through the kitchen door, she bypassed the living room and went straight down the hall. Her clutch purse hit the seafoam-green chair tucked in the alcove off her bedroom. Her high heels thudded into the gray carpet, one after another, as she kicked them away.

With each uniform item she yanked off and tossed on the bed, the images grew sharper. She could almost see the sheriff's jowls, hanging loose and flabby like a bloodhound's dewlaps. Hear again his genial warning that Helen had best put a long stretch of miles between herself and the Blue Crab.

She could hear, too, the taunts she'd endured from the older kids at the regional elementary school she'd attended. They'd called Helen trailer trash, had jeered and quoted their daddies as saying the waitress served up sex along with the Blue Crab's watered-down whiskey.

Jess had never heard the term *whore* until the day she took two boys down in the schoolyard's dirt playground.

The sheriff had come to their trailer that night, too, she remembered, and suggested Helen put a check-rein on her kid before she got into a fight she couldn't get out of. Jess had never told her mother what sparked that particular brawl, just as she'd never asked why Helen often dragged home only short hours before dawn some nights.

Seven-year-old Jessie Yount might not have heard the term *whore* before, but she'd learned to recognize the particular stench men left on her mother's body.

Nothing good ever came of the night, she thought savagely, yanking on her favorite T-shirt. *Nothing!*

With the T-shirt skimming her high-thigh bikini briefs, she retreated to the kitchen and yanked open the fridge. Armed with a giant-size bag of Lay's potato chips, and a diet Coke, she settled in front of the TV for a serious bout of late-night movies.

Inevitably, the rumors that made the rounds at the party began to circulate the squadron.

Jess had expected that, too, since most of the civilians she commanded had lived in the local area all their lives. It took less than a week after the gala in DeFuniak Springs for the ugliness to get back to her.

She heard them first from her deputy. As usual, the tall, cadaverous Al Monroe beat her and everyone else in to work. Tossing her briefcase onto her desk, Jess accepted a mug of throat-closing Valvoline he brewed before Mrs. Burns could dilute it to less toxic levels.

"What do you do, Al? Sleep here?"

"Not much to interest me at home since Luanne died."

During her brief association with the man, Jess had discovered that he rarely talked about the wife he'd lost a few years ago. And it was rarer still for him to plop down in one of the chairs beside Jess's desk and shoot the breeze. Al was usually all business, ready to brief her on the night's activities before their seven-thirty stand-up with the division chiefs.

This morning, however, he slouched in the leather armchair and rested his mug on his ornate silver belt buckle. Jess still found it remarkable that this quiet, gray-haired civil servant had purchased his first motorcycle a few months after his wife's death, then pushed the Hog through wind and rain and stinging Death Valley sands to win a three-thousand-mile cross-country race sponsored by Harley-Davidson.

"What's this I hear you lived around these parts as a kid?" he asked after Jess had skimmed the MICAP report from the previous night.

Carefully she laid the report on her desk. "Yes, I did."

"You never mentioned it."

"I lived a lot of places as a kid."

Bethany, Pennsylvania. Dothan, Alabama. Choctaw Beach, Florida. Odessa, Texas. Apache Junction, Arizona. Those were the stops Jess could remember. There were others, made less than memorable by a whole string of roach-infested apartments and musty trailers as Helen drifted from job to job and man to man.

Al's long, bony fingers played with the handle of his mug. "Rumor has it your mama once waitressed at the Blue Crab."

"Rumor has it right. She did."

"Can't say I ever stopped in there myself, but I heard tell Wayne Whittier had a lively business going until the place burned down."

"My impression is you didn't miss much," Jess replied coolly. "I seem to remember my mother telling me that ol' Wayne watered his drinks and mixed lump whitefish into his so-called blue crab special."

They were dancing, each waiting for the other to flirt close to the real issue. Jess folded her hands around her coffee mug and left the next move to Al.

"Eglin's the largest employer in this neck of the woods," he said after a moment. "The only employer, really. At least half of the civilians on base have lived around here all their lives. Some of the people who work for you probably remember your mama."

Some might even have had sex with her. He didn't say it. He didn't have to. He was just trying in his own quiet way to warn Jess that the gossip mill had started churning out its inevitable grist.

"I *hope* they remember her."

She wasn't aware she'd set her mug aside until her left thumb went to work on the scarred tissue of her right hand.

"She was a good mother, Al. I loved her very much."

The soft, fierce reply seemed to answer the rail-thin deputy's inner questions. With a nod, he turned the conversation to the status of the special wing struts urgently needed by one of the fighter squadrons.

The blasted wing struts still occupied Jess's mind when she cruised onto the Bay Bridge just past nine that night. After a whole day spent fielding increasingly frantic calls from the fighter squadron commander and hourly updates from her combat operations chief, Jess had secured a promise from the depot manager to expedite the struts.

She'd call the ops center later to verify that the expedite had been placed in-system, she thought as the wind whipped her hair and the Mustang's headlamps stabbed the slowly darkening bay. Traffic was slow tonight, thank goodness, with only the occasional car whizzing by. One nosed up behind Jess, its lights glaring in her rearview mirror.

She'd just reached up to flip the mirror to

night driving when the vehicle behind her
pulled out to pass. The next instant it swerved
back, slamming into the Mustang's left rear
fender. Like lovebugs locked in a grotesque mat-
ing dance, the bigger, heavier vehicle shoved the
convertible sideways.

"Shit!"

Jess fought the wheel for two or three terrifying seconds before the Mustang crashed through
the bridge's side wall and sailed into the
darkness.

As long as she lived, Jess would remember
the few terrifying moments while the Mustang's
twin headlights sliced an insane arc through the
night and the black, silent bay rushed up at her.
They seemed to last ten lifetimes, those few seconds. If she screamed, she didn't hear it. If she
swore a vicious stream of oaths while her hands
clamped like a vise around the wheel, she had
no awareness of it. All she saw, all she knew,
was that she was going to hit and hit hard.

Arms braced, legs stiff, boots shoved hard
against the floor, she still wasn't prepared for
the impact. Metal shrieked. Glass shattered. She
flung an arm up to protect her face and died a
thousand deaths while the Mustang seemed to
hang suspended, nose-down in the water, rear
wheels high in the air, then slowly, so slowly,
sank into the inky blackness.

Chapter 7

Wilena Shaw contacted Steve aboard the thirty-six-foot Albin trawler-style boat he called home a little before ten o'clock to advise that a vehicle had gone off the Mid-Bay Bridge.

He'd just popped the top on an ice-cold brew and propped his crossed ankles on the rear deck rail. The air around the rickety dock where he kept the *Gone Fishin'* moored was alive with night sounds. Lulled by the rhythm of waves lapping against the hull, of frogs croaking in the reeds and the occasional splash of a night-feeding predator, Steve was mulling over the report he'd received this afternoon from the Florida Department of Law Enforcement on the McConnell case. The gruesome finality of the remains the ME's office had released for burial pretty well closed the case. Just to be sure, though, Jim Hazlett had conducted another interview with the widow.

No, Mabel had reiterated, she didn't know her

husband had decided to take out his trim little sailboat the day Tropical Storm Carl had whipped up so unexpectedly.

No, she couldn't imagine why he was wearing dress slacks and his favorite wing-tips when he went overboard instead of shorts or jeans and rubber-soled boat shoes.

Yes, she understood that the blunt trauma to his skull was consistent in shape and size with the cleat on the gunwale, and that the small volume of water in his lungs indicated he'd in all likelihood hit his head and lost consciousness before he drowned. She was grateful, she *must* be grateful, that he hadn't thrashed about in the angry bay, terrified and increasingly weak, until he slipped beneath the gray waters a final time.

Steve might be grateful, too, if not for those damned wing-tips.

The shrilling phone jerked his thoughts from Reverend McConnell's footwear, and Wilena's report of the incident on the Mid-Bay Bridge claimed his instant attention.

Although the bridge was in Okaloosa County and thus technically not Steve's responsibility, the rescue operation had closed down three of its four lanes and was starting to back up traffic along the major arteries feeding onto the bridge.

"Captain Dubois said to tell you he's got a squad car working traffic control down-county along Ninety-eight," Wilena advised in her smoky, come-hither contralto. "He says traffic is still moving along Highway Twenty, but thinks we should put out an advisory."

"Tell him to go ahead. Has Okaloosa requested any other assistance?"

"Negative, Sheriff. They're getting all the help they need from the coast guard and from Eglin. More than they need, probably, since it was a military officer who went in."

"Have they fished him out?"

"Her." The dry response was an unspoken comment on his sexism. "Yes, they have. Funny thing, you running a background check on the colonel just last week, and tonight she ends up in the bay."

"Christ!" Steve's heels hit the deck. "Are you saying it was Lieutenant Colonel Blackwell who went off the bridge?"

"Ten-four, Sheriff."

"What's her condition?"

"I don't know, but I'll find out. Hold on."

He sat clutching his beer, his jaw tight, until Wilena came back on the line.

"Word is she's pretty shaken up, but all in one piece."

"What hospital did they take her to?"

"Apparently she doesn't require medical attention. She's still at the scene."

Emergency-response vehicles lined the bridge when Steve arrived. Squad cars flashed strobe lights. Portable spots illuminated the gaping wound in the side wall where repair crews sweated to rig a temporary fix. A coast guard patrol boat from the nearby Destin station idled below, its powerful searchlights stabbing the black water around a flashing buoy that presumably marked the location of the submerged vehicle.

Steve wasn't interested in the vehicle, only its driver. She was huddled in the back of a squad car, a lightweight blanket around her shoulders. Her wet fatigues clung to her like a second skin. Her hair straggled down in limp tendrils, and the angry bruise on her right cheek tied Steve's gut in knots. The flash of recognition, of welcome, in her eyes when she spotted him loosened the knots a little. A very little.

Wondering how Jessica Blackwell had gotten to him so hard and so fast, Steve hunkered down beside the squad car's open door. "You okay?"

"More or less." The welcome disappeared, replaced by the careful distance she always maintained with him. "What are you doing here? Isn't this outside your jurisdiction?"

"I heard you decided to go parasailing without a chute. Thought I'd come view the results."

A shaky hand reached up to finger the swelling on her cheek. "From the feel of this, I'm guessing they're pretty ugly."

"Think so?"

Curling a knuckle under her chin, he tipped her face to the light. Her pupils dilated instantly, and the tight cinch around Steve's chest eased another couple of notches. She didn't appear to be in shock. Or doped up. Or suicidal, all of which were distinct possibilities when someone drove off a bridge.

"I've seen worse," he said with considerable understatement. "Still, you should let the EMS folks transport you to a hospital."

She drew back, breaking the contact. "It's just a bruise."

"What happened?"

"I was sideswiped." Fury surged into her voice, set her shoulders to shaking under the blanket. "Some idiot pulled out into the passing lane, then evidently changed his mind. When he swerved back in, he rammed my car's fender and shoved me right through the side wall. I don't know if the bastard was drunk or blind or both, but he should have stopped. Dammit, at least he could have stopped."

Christ, a bump and run. It took a real slime to send another driver sailing off a bridge and flee the scene.

"Sit tight. I'm going to go talk to the officer in charge."

The Okaloosa County deputy sheriff controlling the scene was more than willing to share the data he'd collected so far with Steve.

"We've got two good sets of skid marks. The colonel's, where she jammed on the brakes just before butting through the wall, and the second driver's."

With Steve pacing beside him, he walked about twenty yards past the sparks showering from the acetylene torch welding the temporary guardrail into place. The pencil-thin beam from his flashlight picked up the black scars on the concrete.

"The son of a bitch fishtailed to a stop right about here."

"Think he was DUI?"

"Hard to tell. You can see how he laid a good three feet of rubber when he took off again."

"Did Colonel Blackwell note the make or type of the vehicle that hit her?"

"All she could see in the rearview mirror were its headlights. But chances are it left a shitload of paint scrapings on her car. Soon's they haul the wreck out of the bay, we'll send the fragments off to the lab in Tallahassee, see if they can find a match in the National Automotive Paint File."

Fortunately, the NAP File allowed labs across the country to establish the color, year, and make of an automobile from microscopic chips of paint. Unfortunately, the case backlog in Tallahassee meant it might be weeks or even months before their specialists got to these particular paint chips.

Like every other state agency, the forensics lab was understaffed, underfunded, and unable to keep pace with the recent boom in DNA analyses, ballistics tests, and drug IDs. In the heirarchy of demands, an incident that didn't involve death or serious injury got shoved to the bottom of the pile.

"I'm guessing a turnaround time of eight to twelve weeks on the paint samples," the deputy warned, confirming Steve's guess. "I've got a drug case from last December I'm still waiting for labs on. Meantime, we'll send out an alert for any damaged vehicle matching the color of the scrapings."

"Would you keep my office posted on the responses to the alert?"

"No problem."

Steve's glance went to the woman in the backseat of the patrol car. "Are you finished with Colonel Blackwell?"

"Yes, sir. We were just waiting on the coast guard to verify the name of the salvage vessel that's going to retrieve her vehicle before we drove her home."

"I'll take her. You can radio our Dispatch when you get the information and I'll relay it or call her at home."

"Okay by me."

When Steve hunkered down beside the patrol car a second time, Jess's brief flash of fury at the driver who'd sideswiped her had obviously faded. Even the cool, collected Colonel Blackwell wouldn't have the strength to sustain a raw emotion after what she'd just gone through. He'd bet she'd used every ounce of reserve she possessed to claw her way out of her car after it nose-dived into the bay.

As if to prove him right, a sudden bout of shudders racked her. She wrapped her arms around her waist and made a valiant attempt to subdue them, but Steve knew she'd relive those seconds when the black, silent water shrouded her a thousand times, ten thousand times, before the terrifying memory dimmed to merely frightening.

"Come on; I'm going to take you home."

Impaled on a spear of quiet panic, she stared at him with wide, blank eyes. Steve cursed under his breath and drew her out of the patrol car, handling her as carefully as a first-time father would a new baby. The blanket slipped from her shoulders. She took one step, or tried to. Her knees buckling, she went down. Steve caught her before she hit the pavement.

"I can walk," she protested as he scooped her into his arms. "I . . . I just need a moment to get my land legs back."

"My car's right here, Jessica."

She mumbled something inarticulate.

Steve bent, drawing in the scent of wet, starched canvas from her clammy fatigue uniform. "What?"

"Jess. I prefer Jess."

"Right," he replied, shifting her higher against his chest. "Jess it is."

Despite those long, slender legs and trim rear, the colonel was no lightweight. He liked the feel of her, the firm, solid flesh, the curve of shoulder and hip and thigh.

Shielding her body with his, he carried her past the sparks still geysering from the acetylene torch to his vehicle. He felt her small, almost imperceptible flinch when she saw the bristling antennae and gold star painted on the side panel, but she made no comment as he reached for the door handle.

The drive home helped Jess regain a small measure of her shattered equilibrium. She stared straight ahead, hands gripped tight in her lap. She ached to huddle next to Paxton, to siphon off more of his strength and warmth.

She fought the urge, remembering all too vividly her spear of sheer, mindless relief when she'd first spotted him. Tall, solid, his jeans riding low on his hips and his shoulders taut under a faded red T-shirt, he'd cut a straight path through the swarm of emergency vehicles. She'd come within a breath of sobbing out his name, and that disturbed Jess almost as much as her dive into the bay.

When she climbed out of Paxton's patrol car, her legs were shaky and the acrid taste of fear still thickened her throat, but she managed what she considered a very credible poise given the circumstances.

"Thank you, Sheriff."

She held out her hand, intending to send him on his way and retreat into her sanctuary.

"It's Steve, Jess. Remember?"

She remembered. She also remembered how

she'd deliberately refused to use his first name when he'd offered it at the cocktail party up in DeFuniak Springs.

He remembered, too, which was no doubt why he ignored her outstretched hand.

"Let's get you inside."

Snagging her elbow in a sure grip, he escorted her to her front stoop. Only then did it dawn on Jess that she'd lost her keys, her purse, and all her ID along with the Mustang.

"My keys," she got out on a ragged note. "They're at the bottom of the bay."

"Don't you hide a spare key?"

"No."

"Hang loose while I check the windows."

"They're all locked."

He gave her a pitying look and disappeared around the side of the condo. Hugging her arms, Jess leaned against the porch railing and waited. Against her will, the shimmer of moonlight on the water drew her gaze. She could just see the bay through the scattering of live oaks draped with Spanish moss, just hear the faint rattle of rigging from the boats tied to the dock.

She paid an extra thirty dollars a month for the view from the condo's front windows. She didn't think she'd ever look out on it again without feeling her stomach clench. She squeezed her eyes shut, blocking out the moon and the bay and the dark, feathery beards of moss, only to jerk them open at the rattle of the glass storm door.

"You should install a security bar on the sliding patio door in your living room," Paxton commented as she brushed by him. "Your bedroom, too, if you've got another set of patio doors in there."

"I do. I will."

Shoving back her damp hair, she tried to send him on his way once more. He wasn't ready to be sent. Taking her chin in one hand again, he tipped her cheek to the light. She didn't like the concern that darkened his eyes from turquoise to sea green. She liked even less the way her nerves snapped whenever he touched her.

"It's just a bruise," she told him for the second time that night. "I hit the side window when I went into the water."

"You should have let them take you to the ER for X rays."

"I'll call a cab and go in if it starts to hurt worse."

"Worse?"

Releasing her chin, he dropped his hand to her shoulder and propelled her in the direction of the hall.

"I'll fix an ice pack while you pop some Tylenol and change."

"Look, I appreciate the ride home, but I'm—"

"Go change, Colonel. You're beginning to smell like dead fish."

She wasn't about to take orders in her own home. If he hadn't already turned away and made for the kitchen, she would have informed him of that fact. But she was left facing his back, and the effort of continuing the battle between them suddenly seemed too huge, too heavy. She'd take a quick shower, she thought, dragging herself down the hall. Change into something that didn't stink of bay water and terror. Then tackle the sheriff.

When she emerged from the bedroom some fifteen minutes later, he was still in the kitchen. He held an ice cube–filled Baggie in one hand and the framed three-by-five photograph he'd lifted from the white-painted shelf above the sink in the other.

Like an animal sensing a new and unexpected danger, Jess went still. The various aches that had just begun to make themselves felt all over her body got lost in a sudden, icy rush.

He swung around then, his handsome face registering only casual curiosity. "Is this your mother?"

"Yes."

"You look like her."

Afterward, Jess could only blame her terrifying ride into the bay for the emotion that spewed out raw and hot. Marching forward, she snatched the photo out of his hand and thrust it back on the shelf.

"Why don't you just ask me if I'm like her in other ways, too?" she demanded, whirling on him. "I'd rather you do that than stir up old rumors, the way you did at the cocktail party the other night."

He didn't deny it. Damn him, he didn't even try to deny it.

"Maggie told you that I pumped her for information about you?"

"No, she didn't. She didn't have to. She told everyone else at the party, though. They aimed enough sidelong glances and speculative looks at me to pierce even my thick hide."

"I'm sorry, Jess. It wasn't my intent to—"

"Save the bullshit, Sheriff. You intended to do exactly what you did. String out questions. Stir the waters." Her head went back. Fire flashed in her eyes. "Go ahead. Ask me. Am I like my mother?"

"All right. Are you?"

"Yes." The reply cracked through the air, as swift and lethal as a rifle shot. "In every way that counts. The only difference between us is that I don't have to sleep with anyone to cover my rent. The air force pays better than hustling drinks at the Blue Crab."

"I should hope so," he said mildly. Too mildly.

The evenness of his temper sent Jess's soaring. She never lost control. Couldn't remember the last time she'd vented her feelings. The violence that ripped at her now shocked her, yet she couldn't seem to harness it. Her fingers curled into claws, and she let loose with both barrels.

"What are you thinking? That Helen Yount's daughter is as easy as she was? That you might get lucky? Is that why you're conducting this one-man inquiry into my past? Why you keep trying to hit on me?"

Disregarding her furious hiss, he laid the ice pack gently against her cheek.

"I've definitely got a case of the hots," he admitted, sliding his other hand around her nape to hold her in place when she would have jerked away. "But my feelings for the daughter don't have squat to do with the mother. And one of these days, Blackwell, you just might unbend enough to admit you've got the hots for me, too."

"In your dreams, Paxton."

Jess could have kicked herself when a glint sprang into his eyes. Her gut told her he wasn't the kind of man to resist a challenge, whether issued by a woman or a striped bass. She expected him to swoop, wasn't prepared when his mouth brushed hers with a touch so light, so gentle she might almost have imagined it.

"What?" he asked when he drew back and caught a glimpse of her expression. "Did you think I was going to wrestle a woman who just got fished out of the bay to the floor?"

"It wouldn't have surprised me."

The reply was churlish and not worthy of either of them. Jess recognized that, but was damned if she'd take it back. His thumb traced her lower lip. Once. Twice. She tolerated it, refusing to look away.

"Someone did a real number on you," he said softly. "Or on your mother."

"I think you'd better leave. Now. *Please!*"

He must have recognized how close she was to the edge. His hands dropped, but not before his mouth made another gentle pass.

"I'm going, Jess. I'll be back. You know that, don't you?"

Her breath left on a shuddering sigh. "Yes," she murmured. "I know."

Night surrounded Steve as he sat in the cruiser, one wrist draped over the wheel, his gaze on the bay glistening in the moonlight just yards away. He didn't like leaving Jess alone and still shaken.

He had no evidence that the accident on the bridge wasn't just that, an accident. It was probably just his cop's sixth sense was working overtime that had him reaching for his radio mike.

"Dispatch, this is Paxton."

"Go ahead, Sheriff."

"Advise the South Walton substation that I want a periodic drive-by of Colonel Blackwell's residence."

"For the rest of tonight?"

"Until further notice."

"Ten-four."

Chapter 8

It was Wilena Shaw who fit together the first pieces of the puzzle. She was on duty when Steve stopped into Central Dispatch around two a.m. the following morning. He'd been out riding patrol with one of the rookies, keeping his hand in and himself visible to his people, and stopped to cadge a cup of coffee before heading home.

The dispatcher's chair squeaked under her two hundred–plus pounds as she wheeled around. Flipping up the mike on her headset, she ripped the top sheet off her notepad.

"One of the Okaloosa County deputies called to tell you the paint scrapings are on their way to Tallahassee. Said they were yellow. Bright yellow."

"Did they run a check of local repair shops?"

"They're in the process of calling them."

Nodding, Steve took a cautious swig of the scalding-hot brew that kept the dispatchers alive and alert during the small hours of the morning.

"Heard a rumor that your Colonel Blackwell's momma once worked at the Blue Crab," Wilena continued in her velvety drawl.

It was a small town, Steve reminded himself, and an even smaller department. He wasn't surprised the rumors Jess had accused him of stirring had percolated through the ranks to Central Dispatch.

"She's not my colonel."

"Huh!"

Wilena declined to point out that the whole department was buzzing over the fact that the sheriff had carried Colonel Blackwell off in his arms, but her sly grin spoke volumes.

"What do you know about the Blue Crab?" Steve asked to divert her attention.

"Not much. It wasn't the kind of place a woman would feel comfortable in. Sheriff Boudreaux kept his eye on it." Her forehead crinkled in thought. "Seems I recall an incident years ago where some customers roughed up a waitress. It happened right after I came to work as a dispatcher. I took the call, and the sheriff checked it out. It would have been about the time your colonel lived in Choctaw Beach. Wonder if the waitress was her mother?"

"I wonder, too," Steve said slowly.

Morning dew glistened like tears on the bearded moss when Steve radioed in the next morning and advised Dispatch he was heading up to Liberty to get in a little fishing.

That was one of the nice things about being the boss, he mused as he drove north out of DeFuniak Springs on Highway 83. He put in long days and late nights, but could pretty well choose when and how to compensate for them.

In anticipation of his expedition, he'd opted for comfortable jeans and a cool white shirt with the sleeves rolled up this morning. With his mirrored sunglasses and green ball cap to protect his eyes and an extra supply of Dentyne tucked in his shirt pocket, he was ready for the bright summer sun.

Elbow propped on the open window, he steered his cruiser through the patchwork quilt of farms that rolled from DeFuniak Springs clear to the Alabama border. This stretch of Walton County was rich land. Good land. Originally inhabited by friendly Euchee Indians who were more than willing to share their fertile valley, the area had attracted settlers since the early 1800s. Its sandy loam, underlaid by clay subsoil, produced abundant crops of wild satsuma, grapes, pears, and figs, along with the staples of corn, soybeans, peanuts, and forage crops.

Local peanut farmers had taken a hit last year, Steve knew. With such a large portion of his constituency dependent on the land for their livelihood, he'd developed a personal dislike for the Spotted Wilt Virus that had attacked the peanut runners and forced so many farmers to destroy their diseased crop. The new crop looked healthy enough. Tender green and low to the ground, it covered the rolling hills in neat rows.

He reached the turnoff to his destination long before the sun got hot and the fish got lazy. The dirt road stretched straight as a scar through the new-green fields. Thick red dust plumed behind the cruiser, announcing Steve's arrival as effectively as any security system. Sure enough, when he pulled up his host was waiting in the shade of the porch that wrapped around the house at the end of the dirt track.

The house was relatively new, put up a few years before the present occupant bought it, when peanut prices had rocketed and the communities in North Walton County had enjoyed a building boom. But it was the string of catfish ponds behind the columned, redbrick residence that gave the property its real value in Steve's mind. Climbing out of the cruiser, he greeted the heavyset figure in the shade of the porch.

"Hey, Sheriff."

"Hey, yourself, Sheriff."

"Sure wish I could retire and become one of the idle rich."

Cliff Boudreaux's heavy jowls folded into a grin. "Your day will come. Or it would if you weren't such a lazy son of a bitch. You've been camping out on a houseboat for near on seven years now. When the hell you going to move into something a little bigger and a little dryer?"

"One of these days."

"Don't know 'bout you, boy." Shaking his

head, Steve's predecessor gathered the rods propped beside the porch in a meaty fist. "I figured once you took over the county, you'd put down a few roots."

"I have. They're just anchored in silt instead of clay."

"Next good-size storm's going to blow that boat of yours halfway to Alabama."

"The last one did enough damage," Steve commented as he hefted a bait bucket and a glass jug. Ice chinked in the jug, sloshing the sun-brewed tea Boudreaux swilled by the gallon. "Not just to my boat," he added. "We lost that two-hundred-year-old oak in the courthouse square . . . not to mention the Reverend McConnell."

Nodding, the older man led the way around the house to the path that cut through a stand of spindly pines to a flat, green pond.

"Too bad 'bout Delbert. Once he grew out of his wild ways and found the Lord, he did some real good for folks 'round here."

Steve stowed the bait bucket and jug and waited while the man who had served as sheriff of Walton County for thirty-six years settled his bulk on the rowboat's transom seat. Untying the line that anchored the skiff to the small wooden dock, Steve pushed off with one foot and manned the oars. The sun warmed his shoulders as he dropped the blades into the still water. The pond looked more brown than green now that they were on it. Gnats and dog flies

swarmed just above its surface, dodging respect-
fully around the occasional iridescent dragonfly.

"Funny thing about McConnell," Steve said
casually. "You'd think a man who sailed as
much as he did would wear rubber-soled deck
shoes when he took out his boat."

"You'd think so," Boudreaux agreed,
scratching the belly that threatened the buttons
on his green plaid shirt. He'd always been a big
man and had carried his bulk with complete indifference for as long as Steve had known him.
"Heard the hole in Delbert's skull matched up
exactly with the metal cleat on the aft port
gunwale."

Steve didn't even bother to ask how he'd
learned the specific details of the ME's report.
Boudreaux was still a force to be reckoned with
in the local communities.

"Looks like his feet might have gone out from
under him and he took a dive."

"Looks like," Steve agreed.

"Is that what you came up here to talk
about?" Boudreaux asked, slanting him a curious look.

"I came up here to fish."

"Uh-huh."

"And to ask about an incident that occurred
at the Blue Crab years back," Steve admitted,
grinning.

"There was always something going on in
that shithole. You'll have to be more specific."

"Wilena mentioned a waitress who got

roughed up. We think her name might have been Helen Yount. Is that specific enough?"

"Maybe, maybe not. Pull over there, under the shade of that tupelo."

For all his paunch and fleshy, hound-dog face, Cliff Boudreaux was nobody's fool. In his thirty-six years as sheriff, he'd taken the art of making a subordinate sweat to the level of a master. His deputies—Steve among them—had found themselves swallowing curses and changing shirts on a regular basis, as well.

He swallowed a few oaths now as he waited for Cliff to bait his hook. With a flick of his wrist, the former sheriff sent the squirming minnow in a smooth arc. It hit with a plop and disappeared beneath the surface. Steve cast to the opposite side of the boat.

"You going to tell me," he asked after a few moments, "or make me drag it out word by word?"

"Not much to tell. I didn't even remember the incident until I heard Helen Yount's daughter was back in the area." He tested the line, squinting into the sun. "Happened a good twenty-four, twenty-five years back."

Along about the time Jess bloodied the noses of two classmates. Giving his own line a gentle tug, Steve waited.

"Helen was flying high that night. Rum and coke—the kind you snort, not drink. Jiggled those big tits of hers up against every man in the Blue Crab. That's what they claimed, anyway."

"They?"

"The five men who stretched her out on a table in the back room and had at her."

"Oh, hell!"

"One of the other customers thought he heard muffled screams and called in a nine-one-one."

"Was it rape?"

"If it was, she wouldn't file charges. Probably figured she couldn't make them stick if she did. Helen had taken a few men into the back room before. More than a few."

Which probably explained that incident in the schoolyard. Jess would have heard the rumors about her mother. Hell, she probably had them thrown at her every day. Kids could be real pissers.

"Wasn't pretty what they did to her, though."

Wrenching his thoughts from a dusty schoolyard, Steve caught the flash of disgust on Cliff's face. Boudreaux didn't spell out the details. He didn't have to. They were both cops.

"She was in bad shape when I got to the Blue Crab, but she wouldn't let me take her to the hospital. That woman was some stubborn."

So that was where her daughter got it from. Well, Jess had warned Steve that she was just like her mother in every way that counted.

"I had a talk with the boys who roughed her up," Cliff ruminated, "then stopped by Helen's trailer later that night and suggested it might be better if she moved on."

"Better for her?" Steve drawled. "Or the men who assaulted her?"

"Both, to my way of thinking. The talk was sure to turn ugly, and that scrappy little kid of hers had already 'bout got herself kicked out of school." He angled a look at Steve, his brown eyes sleepy beneath their drooping lids. "That young'un was so skinny she couldn't make a shadow if there was three of her bundled together."

"She's filled out some."

"Must have, if you're sniffing after her."

"Jesus, is there anything that goes on in this county that everyone else doesn't hear about before I do?"

"Not much."

Reeling in, Steve checked his bait and recast. The ripples had spread halfway across the dappled surface of the pond before he asked the question Boudreaux obviously expected.

"So who were these fine, upstanding citizens?"

"The recently deceased Delbert McConnell was one," the sheriff drawled. "He was just getting ready to go into the marines and feeling his juice. I figure that nasty little incident was one of the reasons he eventually turned to Jesus."

Steve had seen too many righteous fall and sinners redeem themselves to comment on what led a rapist to God.

"Who were the others?"

"Old man Calhoun was there."

"Congressman Calhoun?"

"He wasn't a congressman at the time. Just a

pissant used-car dealer and state senator like his boy is now."

Steve gave a soundless whistle. "I'd heard he catted around some up in Washington, but—"

"Some?" Boudreax snorted. "Rumor is it was a particularly nasty strain of herpes that ate into the ol' boy's brain and landed him in that nursing home. Dub and Maggie like to put out that he's gone senile, but my bet is his loose dick finally did him in."

"A loose dick's one thing. Rape is something else."

"He didn't see it as rape. None of them did."

"Yeah, well, a jury might see it differently. Not to mention public opinion."

Was that why Dub Calhoun had walked around looking like he'd bitten into a hot pepper the night of the big Fourth of July shindig? Had he heard the rumors about his father and a coked-up waitress? Had he recognized Jess Blackwell as that waitress's daughter and worried what effect an alleged rape might have on his campaign to claim the old man's seat in the U.S. Congress?

"Who else was at the Blue Crab that night?"

"Wayne Whittier. He owned the place. Son of a bitch has always had a reputation for screwing his hired help."

"That's three."

"Billy Jack Petrie makes four." Boudreax spit over the side of the boat before adding a casual kicker. "Petrie works at the base. In the supply squadron."

The vicious irony sucked the air from Steve's lungs. One of the men under Jess's command had assaulted her mother. Petrie must be sweating blood these days . . . assuming he'd recognized Helen Yount's daughter. Steve would bet he had.

The coils around his gut squeezed tighter. There were too many coincidences, too many threads slowly coming together to weave a picture he didn't particularly like.

"Who was the fifth?"

"Just between you, me, and that snapping turtle sunning himself on the branch over there, it was Ron Clark."

Steve had already figured that out, but hearing the realtor's name said aloud hit him harder than he wanted to admit.

Boudreaux took an absent swipe at the dog fly buzzing his ear, but his gaze was narrow and hard as it rested on Steve.

"Looks like you got yourself an interesting set of circumstances here, Sheriff. Five men sexually assault a woman twenty-five years ago. Her daughter returns to the area, and two of the five turn up dead. Next thing you know, someone rams said daughter's car and sends her into the bay. You have to ask yourself why."

Slowly, deliberately, Steve reeled in and laid his rod in the bottom of the boat. He had little interest in catfish at the moment, and no desire to pretend otherwise. Leaning forward, he draped his wrists over his knees.

"All right, Cliff. You've obviously asked why. What's the answer?"

Boudreaux took another swipe at the persistent fly. "The statute of limitations on Helen Yount's rape would have run out years ago, even if she was still alive to bring charges. So none of the men involved needed to fear anything except public humiliation if Helen's daughter exposed them."

"Which she hasn't."

"No, but the fear of it might have sent Delbert McConnell out on the bay to pray and decide whether to cleanse his soul of past sins."

"And Ron Clark out into the garage, to suck up carbon monoxide?"

"It's a stretch," Boudreaux admitted. "A real stretch."

So was the idea that Jess Blackwell might be seeking a very personal, very private revenge and had somehow engineered the two deaths. Yet the ugly doubt wormed into Steven's mind, and the cop in him couldn't get it out. As a homicide detective, he'd investigated too many clever murders disguised as accidents and suicides. Locking his gaze on the turtle sunning, he forced himself to assess the matter dispassionately.

She could have done it. She could have gone

out for a sail with McConnell, shoved him hard enough to knock him into the gunwale. She was strong enough to bring him down, then heave him overboard. Smart enough, too, not to leave any incriminating prints when she brought the boat close in before swimming ashore and abandoning it to the oncoming storm.

Likewise, she could have made the call Ron Clark received the night he died, maybe arranged to meet him somewhere. Pat Clark said she thought her husband had gone out for a while, was sure she'd heard the garage door open and close. Whoever he'd met could have slipped him something. God knew there were plenty of drugs available for the right price, drugs that acted fast, were totally absorbed into the blood system, didn't show up in an autopsy. Maybe the killer drove Clark back to his garage in his own vehicle. Left the car running. Walked away.

And maybe, just maybe, one of the remaining rapists had worried that he was next on the killer's list and decided to make a pre-emptive strike.

"What are you thinking, boy?"

Steve dragged his gaze back to Cliff Boudreaux. "I'm thinking I'd better have a talk with this Billy Jack Petrie and Wayne Whittier. Congressman Calhoun, too, although I doubt it will do any good."

"Last I heard, the old reprobate dribbles his dinner down his chin."

"His son, then."

Laughter rumbled up from Boudreaux's belly, deep and rich. The startled turtle scudded off his branch and dropped into the water with a plop, disappearing instantly beneath its brown-green surface.

"Wish I could listen in when you ask our future congressman about his daddy," Walton County's former sheriff wheezed. "He's got twice the old man's ambition, but half his balls. Dub can't even keep that little wife of his in line. She sunk her claws into you yet?"

Steve was too much the gentleman to admit Maggie had tried and settled for a noncommittal grunt.

"Never mind." Boudreaux chuckled. "There's some things an old retired fart like me is better off not knowing. Now throw your hook back in the water and let's catch us a mess of cat."

Steve tackled Wayne Whittier first. That very afternoon, in fact.

The former owner of the Blue Crab lived a few miles outside Ebro, close to the river that fed into the bay and gave the vast body of water its name. As Steve learned from various sources in the small, unincorporated town before driving out to Whittier's place, the one-time bar owner had developed a reputation as a mean drunk with no visible means of support except Social Security. Somehow he managed to stretch the meager pension enough to keep himself in cigarettes, booze, and bait.

The hovel Whittier called home substantiated both his limited income and his meanness. With a cautious eye to the mangy, furiously barking Rottweiler staked out at the end of a long chain, Steve picked his way through the rusted cans and refuse littering the hardscrabble yard. With each step, the animal's frenzy escalated until his entire body was one earsplitting, slathering snarl after another.

Whittier's wooden-frame shack looked as if it were about to lose its last battle with termites at any second. Steve stepped onto a front porch missing as many boards as a picket fence when the glint of red plastic taillight covers caught his eye.

Flattening himself against the wall to avoid the Rottweiler's frantic lunges, he edged to the end of the porch and squinted through his sunglasses at the '76 Cadillac parked beside the shack. The fin-tailed behemoth was more rust than metal. It also sported an interesting collection of creases and dents, Steve noted, some old, some not so old. The hot Florida sun had faded most of its paint, but there was enough left to see it was once a bright canary yellow.

"Shut up!"

The hoarse bellow came from right behind Steve. So did the empty whiskey bottle that sailed over his shoulder and caught the Rottweiler in midlunge. The animal's throat-ripping snarl ended on a yelp. Tail down, ears flattened, it slunk away to crouch beside its overturned water dish.

"Stupid fucking bitch. Doesn't know when the hell to shut her yap."

Peeling off his sunglasses, Steve gave the animal's owner a careful once-over. Gray whiskers bristled on his unshaven cheeks. His eyes were rimmed in red, their pale blue irises turned almost opaque by cataracts. Rank body odor rolled in almost palpable waves from the sweaty armpits revealed by his stained, sleeveless T-shirt.

Steve was tempted to run the bastard in, if for no other reason than his stink and his cruelty in keeping an animal chained in the hot sun with no water.

"Are you Wayne Whittier?"

The blurred eyes squinted at the gold star on Steve's ball cap before dropping to the badge clipped to his belt.

"Yeah."

His voice was low, washboard rough, and as grating on the nerves as an engine cranked too long and too hard.

"I'm Steve Paxton, sheriff of Walton County. I'd like to ask you a few questions."

"About what?"

"About where you were about nine, nine-thirty the night before last, for one thing."

"Right here. Why?"

"There was a hit-and-run on the Mid-Bay Bridge. We're waiting for paint analysis to pinpoint the type of vehicle involved."

"Yeah, well, you kin wait till hell freezes over. I was right here, asleep on the couch."

Passed out on the couch, more likely.

"If that's all," Whittier got out in his hoarse croak, "I got things to do."

"No, it's not all. I also want to ask you about an incident at the Blue Crab involving you, four other men, and Helen Yount."

He half expected a blank stare. Maybe a pretense of surprise. Instead, the man's narrow chest heaved in a rattling, lung-deep hack that brought up a thick glob of mucus. Steve barely restrained a quick jerk back as Whittier spewed the grayish yellow mass over the porch railing.

"So ask," he growled, dragging the back of his hand across his mouth.

The onetime bar owner sang the same song to Steve that he'd evidently sung to Boudreaux all those years ago. It wasn't rape. Helen Yount had begged for just what she got.

Steve hadn't expected anything different, so he was more disgusted than disappointed when he climbed back into his cruiser fifteen minutes later. His glance on the rusted Cadillac, he keyed his mike and requested everything the department could pull up on Whittier. He also asked Dispatch to give Eglin's security desk a heads-up.

"Advise them that I'm coming on base to interview a civilian regarding an off-base incident."

"Roger, Sheriff."

"And verify the duty location of one Billy Jack Petrie, would you?"

"Will do."

Petrie had left work when Steve arrived at the 96th Fuels Management Flight.

"He got a call about a half hour ago," the round-faced lieutenant who introduced himself as the fuels officer explained. "He had an emergency at home. Asked for a couple of hours of annual leave and rushed right out. Can I help you with something?"

"No." Extracting a card from his wallet, Steve handed it to the officer. "Just tell Mr. Petrie I'd like to speak with him."

"Sure will."

Steve took the time to share a cold Pepsi and shoot the breeze with the commander of the security forces before climbing back into his car to depart the base. As he approached Eglin's back gate, he passed the massive building with *96th Supply Squadron* lettered prominently over its double glass doors. Steve was tempted, really tempted, to make another stop.

Not yet, he decided with a twinge of genuine

regret. Despite the kink Jessica Blackwell put in his gut whenever he was in her immediate vicinity, he wasn't ready to confront her just yet. Not until he'd talked to each of the men who'd allegedly assaulted her mother.

Chapter 9

Jess supposed a new car was the least she deserved after sacrificing her Mustang to the water gods. Since it would have cost more to restore the salvaged convertible than pay it off and sell the thing at auction, her insurance company agreed to arrange for its disposal.

Consequently, Jess got pre-approved for a loan and spent most of the weekend hitting the local car dealerships. On Monday afternoon she stopped by the Eglin Credit Union to finalize the paperwork on a new, midnight-blue Expedition. Compared to the sporty little Mustang, the oversize SUV handled like a tank. On the other hand, it would take another tank to shove this monster off a bridge. The solid thud of steel on steel when she pulled up at the credit union and slammed the driver's-side door gave her immense satisfaction.

Squaring her fatigue hat with its subdued silver oak leaf on the crown, she crossed the park-

ing lot and pushed through the credit union's
front door. Even that short walk in the broiling
sun stuck her fatigue shirt to her back. Pro-
foundly grateful for the air-conditioning that
streaked the interior windows with condensation, she signed in with the receptionist, stated
the purpose of her visit, and was shown to a
loan officer's cubicle.

"Hello, Colonel Blackwell." Rising, the petite
redhead held out her hand. "It's good to see
you again."

It took Jess a few seconds to place her.

"You, too, Mrs. Babcock."

"Please, have a seat."

In a reversal of roles from their last meeting,
Jess took the chair in front of Eileen Babcock's
desk. As before, the woman was simply but ele-
gantly dressed, this time in a lightweight, short-
sleeved blouse and knee-length walking shorts
in pale pink. She'd pinned her flame-colored
hair atop her head and applied her makeup with
a skillful hand, but nothing could disguise the
dark shadows bruising the skin under her eyes.

"I understand you want to finalize a loan for
a new car."

"Yes. A Ford Expedition. My Mustang took
an unexpected early retirement."

Sympathy poured from the other woman. "I
read about the accident in the paper. You must
have been terrified when your car went off the
bridge."

"It wasn't an experience I particularly want to repeat," Jess admitted, glancing around the neat cubicle. "I remember you mentioned that you'd begun a new career in banking, but I didn't know you worked here at the credit union."

"Actually, I just completed my training program. You're one of my first customers."

Uh-oh. Bracing herself for a long and possibly painful session, Jess handed over the paperwork from the car dealer. To her surprise, Eileen Babcock produced the necessary documents for her signature with a few clicks of her computer keyboard.

"There's not much to finalizing a car loan these days," she admitted when Jess praised her efficiency. "You didn't even need to come in. We could have done this by phone. I'm glad you did stop by, though," she said, sliding the papers across the desk for Jess to sign. "So I could thank you for giving Eddie another chance."

"You don't have to thank me. It's to the air force's advantage to keep someone with Sergeant Babcock's expertise in uniform . . . if he'll straighten up and fly right."

"He will! I know he will. He hasn't had a drink since . . . since the day our divorce was final."

"How do you know?" Jess asked gently.

"He stops by my apartment sometimes. We

have coffee. Talk about work." Flushing, she looked away for a moment. "About everything, really, except what went wrong between us."

Pity for two people snared in the web of human frailty tugged at Jess, followed almost instantly by an unexpected pang of envy. She'd never loved a man with such wrenching despair, had never experienced the dizzying highs and plummeting lows of that fragile institution called marriage.

She'd come close once, but her brief engagement to an air force lawyer had unraveled shortly after she took him home to meet her mother and stepfather. Helen had hit the jackpot when she met and married Frank Blackwell. Unfortunately, neither the garage mechanic with half-moons of axle grease under his nails nor the former cocktail waitress who frizzed her hair and troweled on eye shadow thought much of the too-handsome, too-tanned JAG. The feeling, Jess discovered during the short, disastrous visit, was mutual.

"The first time Eddie stopped by my place was right after a fuel barge docked," Eileen Babcock said. "You had spent the afternoon looking over his shoulder." The beginnings of a smile tugged at her lips. "You made him nervous."

"He didn't let it show."

"No, he wouldn't." Playing with a ballpoint pen, Eileen gave a small, sputtering laugh. "I'll admit my stomach dropped clear to my knees, though, when Eddie mentioned that a sheriff showed up at the fuels building Friday afternoon."

"A sheriff stopped by Building Eighty-nine?"

"Yes. When Eddie first told me, I thought maybe he had . . . I was afraid he was . . . Well, you know. In trouble again."

"Yes, I know." Carefully, Jess tucked the folded papers in her black leather clutch purse. "Did he happen to say which sheriff? Or what he wanted?"

"I think it was Sheriff Paxton from Walton County. He was looking for Mr. Petrie."

"Did he find him?"

The edge to the question earned her an odd look.

"I don't know. Eddie didn't say."

"I see. Well, thanks for your help with the loan." Forcing a smile, Jess rose. "You may not have wanted a career in banking, but you've obviously got a knack for it. This was the easiest thirty-thousand-dollar debt I've ever racked up."

Once she was outside, her smile curled up and died like a leaf on a hot sidewalk. Why had Paxton stopped by *her* fuels section, to talk to *her* people, without clearing the visit with her first? Had he heard more rumors about her mother? Decided to check them out personally?

What did he know?

The questions tumbled furiously through her mind as she grabbed the handhold and swung up into the dark blue Expedition. She still couldn't quite believe she'd curled into his arms like a weak, helpless kitten that night on the bridge. Or that she'd let him kiss her there in her condo. Not once, but twice.

The fact that she was having trouble distinguishing the man from the badge bothered her. The fact that her pulse skipped when she remembered how she'd wanted to lose herself in his strength bothered her even more. Frowning, Jess shoved the Expedition into gear. It took her less than five minutes to reach her office, another five for Mrs. Burns to put a call through to the Walton County Sheriff's Department.

"The sheriff's in a meeting," she reported to Jess via the intercom. "Do you want to leave a message?"

"Yes, please. Tell him I'd like to talk to him. ASAP."

She and Paxton played telephone tag for the rest of the afternoon. When he returned her call, it was Jess's turn to be in a meeting. She tried again, only to be informed the sheriff was conducting a shakedown of the county jail. After a long and particularly boring briefing at wing headquarters, Jess found a stack of yellow message slips on her blotter. The one from Paxton was short and to the point.

Tonight. Seven-thirty. Fried catfish.

Below the succinct message Mrs. Burns had scribbled the directions to his place.

*   *   *

She was waiting when Steve navigated the narrow, red-clay road leading to the dock where he moored the *Gone Fishin'*.

He'd cleared enough of the tupelos and palmettos at the bayou's edge to allow for a good-size turnaround. The dark blue Expedition with the dealer's tag was parked a few yards from the dock. With a nod of silent approval for the SUV's solid bulk, he pulled up alongside and waited for Jess to kill the idling engine, shoulder open her door, and abandon the vehicle's air-conditioned comfort for the swampy heat of the bayou.

She'd taken the time to go home and change out of her uniform, Steve saw in a quick glance. The long length of thigh showing beneath her gauzy, red-plaid shorts made his pulse jump a couple of erratic beats. When paired with a red tank top that hugged her breasts and a ball cap that allowed her honey-brown hair to swing in a loose ponytail, the overall effect was enough to send a man straight into cardiac arrest.

Steve managed to keep his heart pumping. He even managed to ignore the now familiar ache Jess Blackwell started just below his belt as he reached for the bag of groceries stashed on the cruiser's backseat.

"You're early," he said by way of greeting, noting the tight set to her mouth. "Not to worry. It won't take long to get the grease hot and the catfish sizzling and spitting."

"I can't stay for dinner."

"Too bad. The fish is fresh. I caught and filleted it myself."

"I just want to talk to you."

"Well, come aboard and grab something cold
to drink. You can talk while I mix the cornmeal
batter. You may not be hungry," he added
mildly when she started to protest, "but I am."

Leading the way down the rickety pier, he
made the transition from dock to deck with
surefooted agility and deposited the grocery
sacks before turning around to help Jess aboard.

"Watch your step."

Reaching out a hand, he steadied her while
she negotiated the two-foot gap between the
pier and the boat rail. Even with the warning
and his assistance, she wasn't prepared for the
way the deck tilted under her weight.

His feet spread, Steve caught her as she
pitched forward. The fusion of chest and hip
jolted through him, shocking his entire system.
Hers, too, judging by the way her head snapped
back and her green eyes widened.

A wise man would have set her on her feet
and retreated to high ground at that moment.
Particularly if that man was a cop who hadn't
yet found the answers to the questions stacking
up in his mind.

He'd only take a taste, he decided. Not much
more than the brief brush of lips he'd allowed
himself at her condo. Dipping his head, he covered her mouth with his.

Too late, Steve realized his mistake. A kiss wasn't enough. Not from Jess Blackwell. He wanted more, and he wanted it badly. Taking advantage of her temporary immobility, he widened his stance.

Stunned surprise held Jess rigid. This kiss bore no resemblance to the gentle brush of Paxton's lips after the accident. Nor did he cradle her against his chest with anything approaching the incredible tenderness he'd shown that night.

She could break the hold. She'd learned some particularly incapacitating moves in her various self-defense courses, although she suspected the sheriff might be able to employ a few countermoves.

She could break the kiss, too, if she wanted to. All she had to do was jerk her head back. Puncture his arrogant masculinity with an ice-coated barb. Walk away. She might have done just that if he hadn't dragged his head up at that moment.

Red singed his cheeks. The muscles in his arms were corded and quivering. Regret rippled across his face. Or was it wariness? Jess couldn't decide which.

"In case you're wondering," he said gruffly, "I didn't plan that."

She shifted, one brow arching when her hip pressed against the bulge of his crotch.

"Or that," he added.

Maybe it was the tight line to his jaw. Or the undisguised hunger in his eyes. Or the realiza-

tion that she'd kept her cool while his hung by
a thread. Whatever it was sent a heady sense of
power sweeping through Jess. The hot, sweet
rush was more intoxicating than wine, and far
more urgent.

She wasn't a tease. Nor was she promiscuous.
If nothing else, those long nights waiting for her
mother to come home, wondering where Helen
was, who she was with, had generated a bone-
deep aversion to sexual games and one-night
stands. Jess had never denied her needs, however. She was a woman, with a woman's wants
and cravings.

Like her mother.

And she wanted Steve Paxton. Despite his
badge. Despite every dictate of caution and common sense.

"I didn't plan on staying for dinner, either,"
she admitted slowly, "but I seem to have developed an appetite."

He didn't pounce. She'd give him that. His
body was rock hard everywhere it touched hers,
yet he didn't swoop in with a grunt of male
triumph to take advantage of her hesitant
admission.

"You've been sending mixed signals, Jess.
You'll have to tell me what you want."

She thought about it, gave a sigh of real regret,
and stepped back. "I want to talk. Just talk."

A muscle ticked in the side of his cheek. His
face hardened. In anger? Frustration?

"Fine. We'll eat. Then we'll talk."

Chapter 10

Wound tighter than a new reel and all too aware that it showed, Steve snagged the bag of groceries, shoved the hatch back, and went below deck.

Suffocating waves of heat erupted from the interior, heavy with the scent of varnish and the ever-present mildew that was every sailor's bane. Depositing the groceries in the galley, he flicked the switch to the small air-conditioning unit built into the rear bulkhead. He'd had to call in a few favors to get the county to string a power line down to the dock. The same with the phone company. Electrical and telephone lines were necessities in his line of work, as was the sleek little computer sitting atop the drop-down mahogany shelf that did double duty as desk and dining table.

His old cast-iron frying pan gave an angry rattle when he drew it from the cupboard above the stove. Forcing his hands to slow, he assembled the ingredients for corn-bread batter and hush puppies and tried to decide which he wanted more at the moment—to have Jess flat on her back in his bunk or off the boat before he made a fool of himself trying to get her there.

He hadn't yet made up his mind when her foot appeared on the top step. Stooping, she descended halfway down the steps and peered into the cabin.

"Close the hatch," he instructed. "You're letting in the mosquitoes."

The prospect of sharing a meal with Steve scraped at Jess's nerves, already strung tight after the steamy interlude on the deck. Ultrasensitive to every move he made in the cabin's minuscule galley, she watched him put together a simple feast of store-bought coleslaw, fried catfish, and hush puppies.

Steve's nerves evidently hadn't defused, either. He didn't need her help, he informed her curtly when she volunteered her services. Her main task—her only task at the moment—consisted of keeping out of the way.

That proved a challenge in a living and work area not much larger than her condo's walk-in closet. Jess took one of the captain's chairs bolted to one side of the eating area, but had to duck each time Steve reached for something in the cabinet above her. After the third or fourth duck, she abandoned the chair and squeezed onto the cushioned bench behind the drop-down table.

She couldn't help but contrast the sleek little high-tech computer on the table with the scarred, if lovingly polished slab of mahogany it rested on. The wood showed its age in every nick and scratch. Like the rest of the creaking, rocking boat, it had weathered a few storms, Jess guessed.

As had the boat's owner. Her glance went to the man handling both spatula and cast-iron frying pan with consummate skill. He stood with his legs spread against the gentle roll of the boat, his jeans snug against his thighs.

Smothering an oath at the sudden spear of heat in her belly, she wrenched her gaze back to his face, only to discover he'd been looking her over while she did the same to him.

"Don't you get claustrophobic living on a boat?" she asked, more to divert the sardonic comment she saw forming on his face than to make conversation.

"No."

Her fingers drummed on the closed computer. Evidently he wasn't ready for polite chit-chat yet. Well, she supposed she couldn't really blame him. She was still strung wire-tight herself. Blowing out a breath, she refrained from further comment while he transferred the catfish to a plate, heaping the browned fillets alongside hush puppies glistening with a sheen of grease.

"Move the computer, would you?"

She edged the notebook to the seat beside her. Jess had never considered herself a real catfish aficionado, but the aroma that steamed from the cracked blue platter Steve put in front of her had her mouth watering. Wedged in place behind the table, she could only sit and wait with mounting impatience while he retrieved a plastic container of coleslaw from the fridge, along with a sweating glass jug of iced tea. Finally, he set out plates, glasses, and utensils and seated himself in the captain's chair on the other side of the table.

"Help yourself."

Taking him at his word, Jess forked several hush puppies and a large fillet onto her plate. The catfish flaked white and succulent under its crisp coating. The hush puppies, she discovered when she bit into one, bit back. Her eyes watering, she grabbed her glass of tea and downed half of it in several large gulps.

"Sorry," Steve offered, the harsh planes of his face softening for the first time since they'd come below deck. "I should have warned you that I include a touch of Tabasco when I mix up the batter."

"A touch?" Jess gasped, her tongue still on fire. It took another few swallows to douse the flames. Cautiously, she poked at the fish. "Did you use the same batter on this?"

"That's just plain cornmeal, egg, and milk. Tabasco would overwhelm the delicate flavor."

"No kidding."

She nibbled cautiously on a small piece. It tasted every bit as moist and delicious as it looked. Relieved, she followed Steve's lead and settled in to satisfy the hunger now emitting low warning growls from the vicinity of her stomach.

With the boat rocking under them and the air conditioner humming busily just above their heads, they emptied the platter of all the catfish and most of the hush puppies. Jess reached her limit before Steve, who polished off the last of the coleslaw.

Digging a package of gum out of his shirt pocket, he offered her a piece. Jess declined, but now knew the source of the cinnamon that had flavored his kiss. The memory of how her tongue had danced with his had her shifting on the bench, edgy and annoyed, until he hooked his hands over his stomach and stretched his legs under the table.

"All right. Let's talk."

Jess blew out a short breath. Evidently filling his belly hadn't mellowed his mood. Okay, so maybe she owed him more than the grudging apology she'd offered earlier. Might as well get that out of the way first.

"Look, let's try to get past what happened up on deck. It . . . it surprised me as much as it did you."

He looked as though he had a few words to say on the matter, but clamped his mouth shut and gathered the dirty dishes instead.

Jess slumped back against the cushion, drumming her fingers on the laptop's lid. It was an Apple G-4, she saw, billed as the fastest computer on the planet. Wondering if its fifteen-inch screen lived up to the hype, she raised the lid. At her touch, the darkened screen blinked to life. She was reaching for the lid, intending to close it and put the computer to sleep again, when the name at the top of the screen leaped out at her.

Helen Yount Blackwell

Frowning, she skimmed the lines of print below her mother's name. With each word, Jess's throat closed a little more, until she couldn't breathe, couldn't drag so much as a gasp into her lungs.

"Jess?"

She lifted her stunned gaze to find Steve with the rest of the dishes in his hand and his narrowed gaze locked on her face. She swallowed, trying desperately to work the paralyzed muscles, and lifted the laptop onto the table.

"What *is* this?"

He flicked a glance at the screen. His jaw went tight. "Those are my notes."

"About my mother?"

"About an incident that reportedly occurred at the Blue Crab twenty-five years ago."

She flattened her palms on the table, whether to steady them or absorb strength from the smooth, thick wood, she didn't know. Carefully, so very carefully, she measured her words.

"Is this part of a police report?"

"No." His eyes held hers. "There was no official report. I got the information from Sheriff Boudreaux."

"Sheriff Boudreaux." The little air she'd managed to pull into her lungs hissed out. "I remember him."

"He remembers you, too."

"And he said . . . ?" She cleared her throat again. "He said my mother was raped?"

Was it an act? Was she feigning that bruised look around the eyes? For all his years of interrogating suspects, Steve was damned if he could tell.

The cop in him took over. Shoving the remaining dishes into the sink, he hooked his chair around and sank down to her level. He wanted to gauge every flicker of facial muscle, needed to read every emotion.

"According to Boudreaux, five men assaulted your mother. It happened the same night you and she left town."

"The same night Boudreaux ran us out of town," she countered swiftly, bitterly. "Did the sheriff name the five men? Are they here, in your computer?"

She hit the page-up key an instant before he reached over and snapped down the laptop's lid. She glimpsed the list, or enough of it to whisper the first name.

"Delbert McConnell."

"He was a local minister," Steve said into the silence that followed. "He drowned some weeks back. You might have read the story in the newspaper."

Something flickered in her eyes. Shock? Surprise? Guilt? It was gone before he could put a label to it.

"Ron Clark was there, too."

She didn't make a sound. Not a damned sound. But she clamped her mouth shut as tight as a safe to keep something back. In anyone else, the white lines cutting into her cheeks might have given Steve a primal satisfaction. Now he experienced only the twisted hope that she'd keep her lips sealed. At least until he figured out just what the hell she might say.

"Boudreaux said Wayne Whittier was also one of the five. Along with Congressman Calhoun and—"

Her dry, harsh laughed stopped him in midsentence. "He didn't even recognize me."

"Congressman Calhoun?" The skin on the back of Steve's neck tightened. "You went to see him at Silver Acres?"

"I saw his son. At the reception up in De-

Funiak Springs." Her mouth twisted. "Until Dub's wife whispered in his ear, he didn't even recognize the girl who once rubbed his nose in the dirt."

Like a boat plowing through angry waves into the calm eye of a hurricane, she seemed to steady. Only her hands moved, slipping into her lap, white at the knuckles, one thumb kneading a pocket of puckered flesh.

"Who was the fifth?"

"Billy Jack Petrie."

Her mouth opened. Snapped shut. Opened again.

"Is that . . . ?" With a quick shake of her head, she started over. "Is that why you went to see Petrie today?"

"Yes."

The tiny pop of Steve's gum was the only sound in the cabin for long, heavy moments.

"Bill Petrie thinks I got on his case about how he handled one of his men," she said at last. "Now . . ."

"Now?"

Her mouth curved into a slow, feral smile. "He's going to sweat blood by the time I finish with him."

Before he could stop himself, before he could decide whether he even wanted to stop, the cop in Steve moved in for the kill.

"Is that all he's going to do, Jess? Sweat? Or will he turn up dead, like Delbert McConnell and Ron Clark?"

The smile froze on her face. The thumb kneading her scarred flesh ceased its slow circles.

"Is that what you think, Paxton? That I arranged Clark's suicide and McConnell's drowning?"

He considered every possible reply before giving the only one he could. "I'm beginning to wonder if someone did."

"Someone who couldn't trust the local law-enforcement officials to bring her mother's rapists to justice, you mean?"

For the first time, Jess allowed emotion to whip into her face and voice.

"Someone who already had a taste of Walton County justice when Sheriff Boudreaux hustled her out of town in the middle of the night?"

"Cliff Boudreaux had his reasons for suggesting you and your mother leave town. They run a little different from the ones you remember."

"Oh, yeah? Why don't you try a couple on me to see how they fit?"

"Your mother refused to bring charges against the men. She wouldn't go to the hospital to have a rape kit done, so there was no evidence to support charges in any case. According to Boudreaux, she didn't want the public ordeal of a trial."

"According to Boudreaux," Jess echoed with a twist of her lips.

"Could be he sympathized with her and with a knob-kneed kid who'd already started down the road to trouble," Steve said evenly. "Could be he figured it would be better for both of you to get out of town, given the circumstances."

Jess weighed the arguments and came up short on one side of the scale. "And it could be your predecessor just didn't want a cocktail waitress making trouble for some of his buddies. Did that occur to you?"

"Of course it did. It also occurred to me that those same buddies could get real nervous if the waitress's daughter showed up after all these years and decided to make a little trouble herself. So nervous one of them might just force her Mustang off a bridge."

"What!"

The shock looked real. Too real to be feigned. Yet Steve had heard too many suspects proclaim their innocence in the same stunned tones to trust anything but his own instincts. The problem was, he wasn't completely sure he could rely on those instincts where this woman was concerned.

"Why don't we just cut through the bullshit here, Jess? Tell me exactly how much you knew about what happened at the Blue Crab."

As shaken as she appeared at that moment, she knew better than to fire off an answer to that one. Steve felt a stab of satisfaction, though, when her thumb went to work on that right hand again. He'd gotten through to her. Thank God, he'd gotten through to her.

"What if I tell you I didn't know *anything* about it?"

"I'll believe you."

"Why?"

"Mostly because I want to," he replied with brutal honesty. "And I don't have any evidence to prove otherwise."

Yet.

The unspoken caveat hung between them, as thick and heavy as the odor of congealing grease.

"All right," Jess said slowly. "I didn't know anything about it. My mother never told me she'd been raped at the Blue Crab. She never explained why Sheriff Boudreaux showed up at our door that night, or why we left Choctaw Beach so suddenly. If she had . . ."

"If she had?"

Her clear green eyes didn't waver.

"I probably would have sneaked out, snitched the rusted old double-barrel shotgun Mom kept in the car trunk, and tried to blow off those bastards' balls."

Chapter 11

Jess spent the rest of the night huddled on the couch in her living room. A blaze of lights and the condo's white plantation shutters held the darkness outside at bay, but nothing could keep the past from haunting her thoughts.

She stared blindly at the black-and-white Busby Berkeley musical flickering on the TV. The three Ziegfeld chorus girls played by Judy Garland, Hedy Lamar, and Lana Turner sang and hoofed their way across the screen in a succession of exotic costumes. Yet all Jess could see was the hazy image of a dishwater blonde in a miniskirt that barely covered her rear and a blouse unbuttoned low enough to display the generous breasts spilling out of her black lace bra.

Was that why those five animals had thought they had the right to sexually assault her? Jess speculated angrily. Because Helen was proud of her body? Because she liked to show off her breasts?

To this day, Jess's stomach cramped whenever she remembered the stricken look on her mother's face when the oncologist had urged her to consider a radical mastectomy. In the end, even that brutal disfigurement hadn't saved Helen. Just as the local authorities hadn't saved her from the pain and humiliation she'd endured at the Blue Crab.

God! She was raped! Held down and assaulted right there at the bar, according to Paxton. And Sheriff Boudreaux hadn't even tried to build a case against the scum who attacked her.

Jess's long-buried resentment at the paunchy police officer flared into fury. Fed by the coals Steve had shoveled on tonight, it burned as fierce as a phosphorous flare. Yet the white-hot heat didn't begin to compare to the searing anticipation of facing Billy Jack Petrie at work tomorrow. Only this time she'd make sure he was aware that she knew about the Blue Crab. This time there wouldn't be any doubt.

"Sorry, Colonel."

Lieutenant Ourek's round cheeks glowed brick red from the heat. JP-8 fumes rose in waves from his fatigues. When he whipped off his ball cap to wipe the sweat from his forehead, the band left a damp ring in his carroty hair. Jess had caught him on the ramp outside Building 89, where refueling trucks were lined up, awaiting their turn at the pumping station.

"Mr. Petrie's not here," he told her. "He took off Friday around noon to handle some kind of minor emergency at home, then called in yesterday morning and asked for administrative leave for the rest of the week. Anything I can do for you?"

Shrugging off her sharp stab of disappointment, Jess smiled. "No. Thanks."

"Mr. Petrie's not, uh, in any kind of trouble, is he?"

"Why would you think so?"

"Well, the Walton County sheriff came looking for him Friday. Now you want to see him." He hesitated. "If one of my people has a problem, I should know about it."

Billy Jack Petrie had a problem, all right, but it wasn't one the lieutenant needed to know about. Not just yet, anyway.

Still, Jess owed Ourek an answer. He was years younger than most of the men and women he supervised, but he obviously took his responsibilities as chief of the fuels flight seriously.

"I'll let you know if there's a problem," she promised, then turned the subject. "I see you've got a string of refuelers loading up."

"Yes, ma'am. We just got word a C-5 is inbound and has requested a full load."

"How about I ride along and observe?"

"No problem."

Eager to show off his operation, the lieutenant escorted Jess to the refuelers. The R-11s were the military equivalents of the tanker trucks that hauled commercial fuel to gas stations all over the country. Painted a uniform mud brown, each R-11 could carry approximately six thousand gallons of fuel.

Topped off, the trucks drove to transient operations and parked on the apron to wait for the monstrous C-5 cargo plane's arrival. The gray-painted Galaxy swooped down some ten minutes later, impossibly huge, incredibly graceful, and taxied to its designated spot. Jess had a bird's-eye view while the rear ramp lowered and two companies of army rangers with full gear poured out and scrambled into trucks, en route to refresher training at the ranger camp located on Eglin's vast reservation.

The Galaxy required more than an hour to refuel. One of the largest aircraft in the world, the fantailed C-5 carried twelve internal wing tanks that gobbled up more than fifty thousand gallons of jet fuel. Jess's admiration for the personnel of the fuels flight escalated each time they dragged another heavy hose from the R-11s to the aircraft.

The brutal heat reflecting from the ramp spread a shimmering haze over the entire operation. Fuel fumes added rainbows of iridescent color to the thick, almost unbreathable air. Sweat poured from the T-shirted men and women who wrestled the hose nozzles into place. It was hard, backbreaking labor that technology had yet to make easier.

Jess spoke personally to each of the fuel operators before she and the lieutenant departed transient ops. Back at Building 89, she thanked Ourek for his time and started for the Expedition she'd parked out front. Her path intercepted that of a familiar, stocky figure cutting his way through the parked vehicles.

The salute Ed Babcock snapped off was respectful, his greeting less so. "Ma'am."

"Good morning, Sergeant Babcock. Did another barge dock?" she asked, eyeing the samples in his kit. "I didn't see it on the schedule."

"No, ma'am. These samples are from the Thirty-third. One of the maintainers reported higher than usual coke residue in a couple of aircraft. I just wanted to recheck the batch of fuel they're burning."

The busy Air Combat Command fighter wing on the other side of the base was one of Jess's biggest customers. If there was a problem with their fuel, she needed to know about it.

"I'd like to see the results of your analysis."

"Yes, ma'am."

With a nod, she reached for her car door. Babcock turned away, hesitated, then swung back.

"Eileen told me she saw you at the credit union yesterday," he dragged out with obvious reluctance.

"Did she?"

"She said you complimented her on the way she processed your loan application."

"She deserved the compliment. She shuffled those papers like a pro."

"Yeah, well, she also said I should get down and kiss your feet for giving me another chance."

"No feet kissing is either required or desired," Jess assured him. "I'm just glad to hear you're maintaining the lines of communication with your wife."

"Ex-wife," he corrected, but the grim lines in his face relaxed. The blunt features softened, and Jess caught an unexpected glimpse of the man Eileen Babcock still cared about.

"We're keeping something open," he admitted with a shrug. "I'm damned if I know what."

Jess wouldn't presume to offer advice that wasn't asked for, but she drove off hoping Ed continued to drop by his ex-wife's apartment.

Frowning, Ed carried his samples into the lab. The brief conversation with the colonel weighed on his mind. Almost as much as last night's visit to his ex-wife.

He'd tried to stay away. What little was left of his pride shredded a bit more each time he knocked on Eileen's door. She didn't want him; she'd made that clear. She'd flinched every time he got too close. Yet still he couldn't stay away.

She was his lodestone. His center. He'd loved her since high school, had never wanted anyone else, couldn't imagine wanting anyone else. When he lost Eileen, his whole world had tilted off its axis.

Cursing, Ed grounded himself and entered the lab. When he placed the sample kit on the stainless-steel counter, his hand shook so badly the glass jars danced and rattled in their slots.

He wanted a drink. Christ, he had to have a drink! Just one. To steady his hands and tame the wild beast clawing at him from the inside out.

Yanking open one of the drawers under the counter, he shoved aside the jumble of funnels and calipers. His fingers searched with frantic urgency until they found the bottle stashed at the back of the drawer and slammed it onto the counter. The tequila sloshed, settled, whispered to him.

Legs spread, arms outstretched, fingers gripping the edge of the counter, Ed stared at the red-and-green label and imagined the sharp bite. The liquid incandescence sliding down his throat. The gradual relief from care. The blessed, soothing relief.

But right there, next to the square-shaped bottle, was his sample kit, the pickle jars half-full with fuel that should have gleamed a clear, pale gold. Unlike the tequila, the fuel was hazy. Too hazy.

With an ache in his bones like that of an arthritic old man, Ed uncurled his fingers and released his death grip on the counter. His hands still shook when he reached for the tequila and shoved it back in the drawer, but the sediment clouding the fuel now had his full attention.

He could see it with the naked eye, for God's sake, which meant the contamination level exceeded tolerance. How the hell had this much sediment slipped through the filters? Why hadn't the initial off-load analysis picked up the impurities? Frowning, he donned his protective gloves and apron and assembled the tools of his trade.

Two hours later, he was still frowning. He went looking for his boss, only to learn from a coworker that Mr. Petrie was on administrative leave.

"When's he coming back to work?"

"End of the week, I think."

Chewing on the inside of his lower lip, Ed went back to the lab.

Steve didn't have any better luck locating Billy Jack Petrie. Petrie didn't answer either his telephone call or his knock when he stopped by the neat frame house occupied by the civilian and his wife.

Eyeing the rolled newspapers lying in the front yard, Steve walked back to his cruiser. Evidently Petrie had decided to take off in a hurry. So much of a hurry he hadn't bothered to cancel the newspaper or ask a neighbor to pick it up.

The scattered papers were still on Steve's mind when he pulled into the parking lot of the

Silver Acres Retirement Center on the outskirts of DeFuniak Springs. Discreet lettering at the bottom of the elaborate, leaf-shaped sign advised that the facility offered assisted-living services and memory-impaired suites.

Opened just a few years ago and privately funded, it was one of a chain that stretched across the South and catered to those with the means to afford the steep fees and luxurious surroundings. Yet even the breezy ferns decorating the white-railed porch and huge sprays of bloodred gladioli in the foyer couldn't quite disguise the scent of antiseptic and urine.

His entry triggered a silent alarm and brought a receptionist with a pixie cap of brown hair bouncing around the corner.

"Hello, Sheriff."

Steve didn't need the name tag clipped to her collar to identify the teenage daughter of De-Funiak Springs' High School principal.

"Hi, Trish. I didn't know you worked here."

"I started after school let out for the summer."

"How do you like it?"

"It's okay. Kind of sad at times, but I'm learning a lot. I may specialize in geriatric medicine when I do my residency."

Since she had at least four years of college and three of med school ahead of her before she'd decide on a residency program, Steve refrained from comment.

"Did you need to see the director?" she asked. "He's in his office."

"No, I'm just here to visit Congressman Calhoun."

"He's in the solarium." Trish's pert, freckled nose wrinkled. "Trying to lift the skirt of every female resident who passes."

Senility hadn't slowed the old coot down, Steve mused as he followed the teen's directions to a sun-washed parlor occupied by several octogenarians in wheelchairs. Two were hunched over a game table. The third had assumed a strategic position by the door and didn't try to hide his disappointment when Steve strolled in.

"Hello, Congressman."

Craning to one side, the skeletal figure crowned with a lion's mane of white hair searched the hallway.

"Where's that snippity little piece I heard you talking to?"

"She's keeping out of range."

Calhoun's age-spotted face screwed up into a scowl. Thoroughly disgruntled, he sank back into his chair.

"How about we take a little walk?" Steve suggested.

Releasing the brakes, he wheeled the congressman out of the sunlit game room to an alcove halfway down the hall. He took a striped satin chair and angled it around to face the frail, hunch-shouldered politician.

"Do you remember a dive down on Highway Twenty called the Blue Crab? It burned down eight, ten years ago."

"Can't say as I do."

"A waitress named Helen Yount used to work there. Remember her?"

"Hell, boy, why would I remember a waitress if I can't recall the dive she worked in?" His watery eyes narrowed to a squint. "Can't say as I recall you, either. Who are you?"

"Steve Paxton. I'm sheriff around these parts."

"What happened to . . . ?" He lifted a hand, sketched a circle in the air. "Big man. Gut hanging clear to his knees. Face like a bloodhound."

"Sheriff Boudreaux. He retired a few years back. About this waitress . . ."

"Did she have big tits and red hair?"

Before Steve could answer, the bony hand made another circle.

"No, no, that was the pharmaceutical lobbyist who came sashaying into my office just before the vote on Medicare reform. Or . . ." His bushy brows snapped together. "Or maybe that was my legislative assistant. Seems I recall bending her over my desk and going at it a time or two. Was her name Helen?"

Steve didn't know and didn't care. "You bent this particular Helen over a table at the Blue Crab and went at her. You and four other men. Roughed her up pretty bad."

"I told you, I don't remember any Blue Crab! And I sure as fire don't remember roughing up any woman." His querulous expression gave way to a cagey grin. "Didn't need to. Never got

an itch for a female who wouldn't drop her
drawers for a member of Congress. Get it, boy?
A *member* of Congress?"

Patiently, Steve waited for Calhoun's gleeful,
wheezing whoops to subside. "The incident I'm
referring to happened before you were elected
to the U.S. House of Representatives. You were
still in the state senate. This would have been
around September, October of 1977."

"How the hell do I know where I was in September, October of seventy-seven? You'll have
to ask Maggie."

"Your daughter-in-law?"

"You know who I mean! The one with the
yellow hair and nice, tight ass."

The realization of how close the congressman's description fit his daughter-in-law came
home to Steve the following evening, when he
found Maggie Calhoun slouched in one of the
chairs on the rear deck of his boat. She qualified
as a sunshine blonde, and her ass was definitely
round and tight.

" 'Bout time you got home, Sheriff."

With the sinuous grace of a well-fed cat, she
tipped the deck chair back and stretched her arms
above her head. Hibiscus red and cropped short at
the waist, her knit top inched upward and bared the
skin above her matching drawstring slacks.

"Hope you don't mind me comin' for a private little visit?"

"I don't mind," Steve replied, propping a hip against the rail, "but I'm thinking Dub might."

"Only if he finds out about it." Her generous mouth tipped. "I won't tell if you won't."

"Trusting a man to keep quiet about a 'private little visit' is a pretty risky proposition for someone whose husband has his sights set on a seat in the U.S. House of Representatives."

"You have to take a few calculated risks, even in politics. *Especially* in politics. You know that as well as I do. You're an elected official. You run for office every four years. You can only kiss so many butts."

"True."

"Dub and I both learned how to play the game a long time ago. From a real master at it, I might add."

"Your father-in-law?"

"My father-in-law." Letting the deck chair legs drop back down, she raked a leisurely hand through her hair. "I heard you paid the old fart a call yesterday afternoon."

"You heard right."

"Was there any particular reason for your visit, or were you just feeling neighborly?"

"I could ask you the same thing."

Her smile widened. "Come on, Steve. We both know I've felt more than neighborly toward you for some time now. You've just been too cautious to follow up on the invitations I keep sending your way."

"Guess I'm still too cautious. Invitations like that scare the crap out of me."

Her smile turned sly. "Not when they're issued by Jessie Blackwell, evidently. Well, you know what they say. Like mother, like daughter."

"What do you want, Maggie?"

Slipping her feet into a pair of thonged sandals, she abandoned the kitten act. "I want to know why you went to see the congressman. He gave me some garbled story about you asking if he balled his legislative assistant. He balled a number of them, actually, but for some reason he seemed to think this one was named Helen. I assume it was Helen Yount you asked him about."

Steve wasn't surprised she'd made the connection. Everyone, Dub included, acknowledged that she supplied the brains and drive behind what they both intended as the next generation of a political dynasty.

"What's going on, Steve? Is Jessie Blackwell out to pay back a few snubs and, oh, by the way, scuttle Dub's campaign by claiming her mama did it with his father? If so, the scheme will backfire. The way I heard it, her mama did it with just about everyone."

"As far as I know, Colonel Blackwell's not out to scuttle anything."

Which was true. At this point, Steve couldn't state with any degree of certainty just what Jess Blackwell was out to do.

"I hope you're right," Maggie said softly. "I surely to goodness hope you're right. We've sunk too much time and money into this campaign to let it go sour on us now."

Swaying over to where he stood, she trailed a finger along his jaw. Her touch was light, almost playful. The edge to her voice was neither.

"You can tell the colonel that next time you two get together."

"I will."

Her fingers made another graze, then tapped him lightly on the cheek. "See you, Sheriff."

He waited until she'd gathered her purse and started for the step to the dock. "Where were you a week ago tonight?"

"Last Tuesday?" She threw him a considering look. "I was with Dub, in Tallahassee. The governor called in the legislature for a special session to sort through the avalanche of recommended fixes after the presidential election mess. Why?"

"No particular reason."

Except one. On Tuesday night, an as-yet-unidentified driver had forced Jess Blackwell's car off the Mid-Bay Bridge. Unless and until the crime lab in Tallahassee confirmed the paint scrapings came from a rusted yellow Cadillac, there were still too many unanswered questions in Steve's mind.

The state capital was only a little more than a hundred miles from DeFuniak Springs. Added to that was the fact that Maggie Calhoun had collected a bucketful of speeding tickets in her regular commutes to and from Tallahassee.

Steve was pretty sure neither Maggie nor Dub drove a canary-yellow vehicle, but it wouldn't hurt to run a check on the rental agencies in and around the state capital. Maybe get a complete list of the folks who worked in Dub's campaign office and run a check on their vehicles, too.

Chapter 12

By Thursday morning, Jess was already feeling the effects of a long week. Grimacing at the image in the bathroom mirror, she smoothed on an extra layer of pancake makeup in a futile attempt to hide the shadows under her eyes. The grayish circles looked ghoulish enough on their own. When combined with the mottled black and drab brown of her fatigue uniform, she showed all the color of a corpse.

She couldn't remember the last time she'd slept more than four or five hours at a stretch. Not since returning to Florida, she thought. Certainly not since her visit to Sheriff Paxton's boat three nights ago. Every time she relaxed enough to lower her guard, her skin would start to prickle with the remembered feel of his hands and his mouth.

And every time she closed her eyes, her restless mind would carry her to the back room of a smoke-filled roadside dive.

Bill Petrie's administrative leave ran through the end of the week. Tomorrow was Friday. He had four more days to hide from her. A whole weekend to sweat. Even if he called in to request additional leave, sooner or later he'd have to return to work. Sooner or later he'd have to face Jess.

The past few days had given her time to think about that meeting. The officer in her, the military executive who took pride in both her uniform and her leadership skills, shied away from crossing the line between personal and professional.

Yet the daughter who'd watched her mother die an agonizing death couldn't help but wish some of that same pain on the men who'd hurt her. On all the men who'd used and abused Helen until she'd found Frank Blackwell.

Dropping the bottle of makeup on the bathroom shelf with a clatter, Jess flattened her palms on the edge of the shell-shaped porcelain sink. *Thank God for Frank!* Every day of her life she would say a silent prayer of gratitude for the gruff, unpretentious garage mechanic who'd won Helen's love, blundered his way past Jess's bristling hostility, and offered them both the precious gifts of security and happiness.

She needed to give him a call, Jess thought, bringing her head up again. Needed to hear him grouse about the house she'd bought for him a few years ago, after Helen's medical and funeral bills had devoured every penny of Frank's meager retirement fund. He hadn't wanted his adopted daughter to go into debt, had insisted he didn't need two bedrooms. Luckily, Jess had just come out on the list for promotion to major and countered his protests with assurance that she could make the payments on the small two-bedroom house and still live comfortably.

Thank God for Frank, she thought again, a smile softening her face. Steady as a rock and just about as talkative, he'd acted as her anchor all through Jess's teen years, never pushing but always ready with a strong shoulder to lean on when she needed it.

Like Steve Paxton.

Jess's smile faded. How could she trust him? Much less the need that swept through her whenever she was with him? He'd compiled a file on her mother, for pity's sake. Had practically accused Jess of having somehow arranged the death of two of the men who'd assaulted Helen.

No, that wasn't right. He hadn't accused her. He'd warned her. With a wrench, Jess killed the insidious wish that she could talk to him, just talk, and sort through the conflicting emotions that had kept her sleepless the past few nights. He was a cop, she reminded herself. She needed to tread warily with him.

And with Billy Jack Petrie, she thought grimly. Her mouth tight, she finished applying her makeup.

*   *   *

As it turned out, she wasn't the only one worrying about the deputy chief of the fuels branch.

Lieutenant Ourek reported to her office that afternoon, a troubled look on his young face. "I'm concerned about Mr. Petrie. I haven't been able to reach him at home or at the emergency number he left."

Jess's chest squeezed. She could almost hear Steve speculating in that soft, dangerous tone whether Petrie would turn up dead next.

"Why are you trying to reach him?"

The lieutenant eyed the paper he clutched in his hand. "It's this analysis Sergeant Babcock did on the fuel over at the Thirty-third. I understand you told him you wanted to see it."

"Yes, I did. I expected to have it on my desk yesterday, as a matter of fact."

"Sergeant Babcock indicated as much, but . . . Well, I wanted to run the interim report by Mr. Petrie first, since he authorized the deviation."

"Deviation?"

"It wasn't significant," Ourek assured her. "Only seven parts per billion above the acceptable norms."

"You've lost me. Seven parts per billion above what norms?"

"Naturally occurring sedimentation levels."

"Let me make sure I understand this," Jess said carefully. "You're saying we received a shipment of fuel that contained higher than normal levels of pollution? And Mr. Petrie authorized acceptance of the shipment?"

"Yes, ma'am."

Her first thought was that she had him. If Petrie had screwed up here, as he had when he'd covered up Sergeant Babcock's drinking problem, Jess would nail his hide to the wall and enjoy hammering in every spike.

Some of her grim anticipation must have shown on her face. Gulping, the lieutenant rushed to clarify matters.

"We have local authority to approve up to ten parts per billion. Anything over that, we notify the Defense Fuels Center and they make the determination whether to accept the load or not. Mr. Petrie didn't consult them in this instance, as the sediment levels were within our approval parameters."

Frustration bit into Jess with sharp, jagged teeth. "So what's the problem here?"

"That's just it. We're not exactly sure." Ourek's nose twitched like a nervous rabbit's. "After the Thirty-third maintenance personnel reported gummed-up engine nozzles, Sergeant Babcock reanalyzed the fuel. We're pretty sure it came from the last shipment. The one you observed during the initial off-load."

"I thought the samples from that shipment tested clean."

"They did, on all but the last compartment. It showed elevated sediment levels, but seeing as that particular sample came from the bottom of the compartment, where the trash would have settled during the trip from the refinery, Mr. Petrie okayed the deviation. Still, that level of sediment shouldn't have resulted in the amount of residue now showing up in the Thirty-third's engines. Sergeant Babcock thinks . . . Well, he wants to run some special tests."

"Special how?"

"There's a new additive floating around out there. SF445. It's supposed to make fuel flow through pipelines more smoothly, reducing friction that could result in an explosion. It's kind of like liquid Teflon. It coats everything it touches, including the filters."

"So the fuel . . . as well as the trash . . . passes through more easily."

"Yes, ma'am. SF445 is designed mostly for oil-field operations, where the product is transported long distances via pipelines. The refinery isn't supposed to include SF445 in the military fuel package. We don't even have the proper chemicals to test for it."

Jess had only a hazy concept of refinery operations. She knew they produced massive quantities of both heating and engine oil, each with its own particular characteristics and specifications. How they kept the various specs straight during production and distribution went well beyond her level of expertise.

"The SF445 could have been added at the refinery by mistake," Ourek explained. "Or it could have been present in a previous load the barge delivered, and the barge wasn't fully purged after delivery. In any case, Sergeant Bab-

cock has asked a buddy at the American Petroleum Institute to pull up the latest data on the
stuff and advise what chemicals we need to test
for it."

A dozen questions rifled through Jess's mind.
How long before Sergeant Babcock's buddy got
back to him? Where could they obtain the necessary chemicals? If tests showed that Eglin's last
load contained SF445, could the contamination
that slipped through the filters cause a jet engine
to fail in midflight? Should she alert her boss?
Advise the flying wing commanders? What
about the other bases supplied by the same
barge? Were they finding the same unexplained
levels of residue?

Suddenly the ghosts that had haunted her for
the past few weeks took a backseat to reality.
This involved more than memories. This situation was immediate, with the potential for disaster written all over it.

"Tell Sergeant Babcock to let me know if he
doesn't hear from his friend at the API within
the next hour. If necessary, I'll make some calls,
too. In the meantime, leave the interim report
with me and let me digest it."

"Yes, ma'am."

Just under an hour later, Ed Babcock showed
up at her office. By then, Jess had read his interim report twice and passed it to her deputy.

She trusted Al Monroe's judgment, had used
him as a sounding board on almost a daily basis

since her arrival at Eglin. The gray-haired, part-time biker confirmed her initial worries, but cautioned Jess to take it one step at a time before issuing a contaminated fuel warning.

Ed Babcock, on the other hand, urged her to err on the side of caution.

"No one really knows much about SF445. OPEC glommed onto it as soon as it went on the market, but it hasn't been out long enough for any definitive studies of the long-term effect on high-performance engines. The Defense Fuels Supply Center has nothing on it in their database. Nothing useful, anyway."

"How do you know so much about this stuff?"

His wrestler's shoulders lifted under his fatigue shirt. "That's what the air force pays me such big bucks for."

"Yeah, right."

"I'm just doing my job."

Which, Jess decided, he performed exceedingly well. More thankful by the moment that she hadn't booted him out of the service, she leaned forward.

"Okay, give it to me straight. If you do find traces of SF445 in our fuel, what course of action do you recommend?"

He didn't hesitate. "Shut down flying operations, purge the fuel tanks on all assigned aircraft, and clean every engine nozzle. At the same time, we'll need to resample the contents of the entire tank farm and drain any contaminated fuel."

"How long would that take?"

"Well, Dulles Airport closed down for three days after a contractor pumped contaminated fuel into its tank farm a couple years ago. In that case, the contaminant was the red dye the IRS requires to differentiate motor oil from heating oil. As I recall, the amount was infinitesimal. The equivalent of less than a quart of dye. But it polluted about a million and a half gallons of jet fuel, all of which had to be trucked out before the storage tanks could be cleaned."

"Good Lord!"

"Similar incidents have happened at least twice at LaGuardia that I know of. Once each at Honolulu and Miami International. When a contaminant like SF445 gets into the hydrant system, everything fed by that system bites the dust."

"Let's hope you're speaking figuratively," Jess said with some feeling. "When will you know for sure whether we're dealing with SF445 here at Eglin?"

"By this afternoon, I hope. The Advanced Concepts Technology Branch at the research lab here on base keeps a stash of the chemicals I need, but they're telling me I have to get their commander's okay before they'll let me mess with their stuff."

Jess reached for the phone. "I'll take care of that."

Three minutes later she'd obtained the necessary authorization for Sergeant Babcock to invade the white-coated sanctity of the Air Force Research Lab.

"Thanks, ma'am." A reluctant respect glimmered in his eyes. "You just saved me a half dozen phone calls."

Despite the tension crawling up her neck, Jess managed a quick grin. "Just doing my job, Ed."

She didn't find much to grin about during her subsequent meeting with her boss. Colonel Hamilton listened intently enough, but wasn't ready to raise the red flag until Babcock concluded his tests and the colonel obtained more definitive information about residue levels in the 33rd's aircraft.

"Even if this SF445 is present in our fuel, we don't have proof that it's causing these increased coke deposits." Frowning, the director of logistics tapped his pen on his blotter. "We could be talking internal engine corrosion. Improper nozzle spray angle. Any one of a dozen possible problems."

"That's true."

"We also don't know if the soot has made any discernible impact on engine performance. I'll ask maintenance to conduct some run-ups, collect more data."

"Yes, sir. While we're waiting for that data, I'll have my people start collecting samples from the storage tanks. Just in case."

"Incidentally, what did Petrie have to say about this business?"

She fought to keep the edge from her voice. "Mr. Petrie didn't have anything to say about it. He took leave this week. Lieutenant Ourek's on top of the situation."

"Is he?" Clearly skeptical, the colonel nevertheless gave the brown bar the benefit of the doubt. "I hope so."

Actually, Jess put more faith in Ed Babcock than in either Ourek or Petrie, but didn't say so. Hamilton had voiced doubts about her decision to give the sergeant one last chance.

Ed Babcock called Jess at six-forty-five. In a more animated tone than she'd yet heard him use, he confirmed minute traces of SF445 in the samples he'd pulled earlier that day.

"We need to notify the Defense Fuels Center," he said. "The lieutenant's standing by, waiting your okay."

"Tell him to go ahead."

"When will the flying wings stand down?"

"They're not going to stand down. Not right away, at least. Colonel Hamilton wants maintenance to conduct some run-ups and collect more data on the residue."

The silence at the other end of the phone was thunderous.

"Tell Lieutenant Ourek to press with sampling the storage tanks," Jess ordered. She didn't want to sit on her hands any more than Ed did. "Keep me posted on the results."

"We can pull the samples, but I can't get more

chemicals from the research lab until tomorrow. They're running a test of some superclassified propellant tonight. Said I'd need a clearance from God himself to get past the front door."

"All right. Do what you can."

It was after eight when Jess walked out into the summer night. Clouds trailed across a smoky blue sky, playing hide-and-seek with a moon already glowing white-gold and full.

Still wired, Jess clicked the remote to unlock the vehicle she'd privately dubbed Big Blue and swung up into the bucket seat. The new-car smell wrapped around her. It was a man smell. Rich. Leathery. Stirring the senses when it should have soothed.

She sat for a moment, wrists draped over the wheel. The events of the day swirled through her mind. She needed an outlet for this nervous energy. Even more, she needed someone to talk to. As they had this morning, her thoughts zinged to Steve.

Caution warred with a sudden, intense craving to hear his voice. Maybe he'd received the results of the paint analysis of the vehicle that crowded her Mustang off the bridge. Maybe he had a handle on Bill Petrie's whereabouts.

And maybe she didn't need an excuse to call him except the obvious one. Quickly, before common sense stayed her hand, she fished her cell phone and the number of the Walton

County Sheriff's Department out of her black leather clutch.

A dispatcher who must have been a sultry torch singer in an earlier life put Jess's call through. She could hardly hear over the rattle of plates and cutlery when Steve answered and regretfully declined her invitation to share a pizza.

"I'm in Freeport, at a Lion's Club banquet," he telegraphed over the din. "Soggy broccoli, tire treads disguised as roast beef, and a roomful of teenagers waiting to be recognized for their participation in the Just Say No program."

The intensity of her disappointment should have warned Jess.

"Too bad," she tossed off with a credible show of nonchalance. "I was going for broke tonight. Anchovies, Italian sausage, and pineapple."

"What? Hang on a second."

Drumming her fingers on the leather-wrapped steering wheel, she hung on.

"Look, I've got to get up and make a speech," he informed her when he came back on the line. "Call in your order. I'll be at your place in an hour."

"Do you really want pizza after soggy broccoli and tire treads?"

"No, Jess. I want you."

Chapter 13

Jess's unexpected phone call destroyed any faint hope Steve might have harbored of enjoying the rest of the banquet.

He managed to make his speech. Even managed to hold his ummarked cruiser to just a few miles over the speed limit for most of the drive from Freeport to South Walton, although the demons hopping up and down with anticipation inside his head shouted at him to hit the siren and strobe lights.

He'd laid it on the line during his brief phone conversation with Jess, had told her the absolute truth. He wanted her. Despite the unanswered questions, despite his growing conviction that the dark incident from her past somehow still shadowed the present, he wanted her. The fact that she hadn't slammed down the phone or told him to piss off when he'd admitted as much had put Steve into an instant sweat.

He stayed in a sweat until halfway across the Mid-Bay Bridge, where the cruiser's headlights picked up the temporary repairs to the side wall. The shiny new metal patches speared right into his gut.

Like a leaping tiger, the cruiser jumped forward. Cursing, Steve wrestled it and himself back under control, but the effort ate a considerable bite out of what was left of his willpower. As a consequence, he wasn't as diplomatic as he might have been when Jess answered her doorbell.

Light spilled from inside the condo, painting her tumble of hair a warm, honey brown. The same glow rendered her white linen camp shirt damned near transparent. Her obviously braless state hitched Steve's breath. Her frown when she took in his uniform produced another, less pleasurable effect.

His job required him to wear civilian clothes more often than Walton County's green-and-gray, but every time Jess saw him in uniform, she froze. Swearing under his breath, he yanked open the glass storm door.

"I'm not Boudreaux. I'm not here to hustle you out of town."

Taken aback by his curt tone, she returned fire. "So I gathered from our phone conversation. You intend to hustle me into bed instead."

"Do you have a problem with that, Blackwell?"

"Maybe."

"Then this time we'd better deal with it *before* we get all hot and bothered."

He walked past her into the living room. The door behind him closed with a thud.

"You're pretty sure of yourself, Sheriff."

"You called me, remember?"

"I don't suppose it occurred to you that I just want to talk?"

His summer-weight Smokey the Bear hat with its shining leather chin strap went sailing toward the sofa. The brim skimmed mere inches above the coffee table littered with the remains of her pizza. Hooking his thumbs on his Sam Brown belt, Steve called her bluff.

"We haven't conducted a single discussion yet where I didn't have to drag every word out of you. You want to converse, we'll converse. As long as you're prepared to go wherever the conversation leads us."

She backpedaled instantly. He saw the shutters come down, had fully expected them. Although the cop in him acknowledged that she was smart not to lay herself bare, the swift withdrawal rubbed a raw spot.

"Decide, Jess. Which will it be? Do we talk, or do we pick up where we left off on the boat?"

"There *are* other options."

"I don't think so. Not tonight."

Her arms folded over her chest. A bare foot tapped the plush gray carpet. She didn't like being pushed. After driving across half the county in a sweat, Steve was definitely in the mood to push.

"Need some help making up your mind?"

Sliding a hand under her hair, he drew her forward. Her rigid shoulders gave him a perverse satisfaction, as did the tight set to her lips when he covered them with his own.

He took his time, tasting her, taunting her, stroking his thumb against the side of her neck. She remained stiff, her mouth softening a mere fraction to accommodate his, but he knew her decision before he lifted his head.

Whatever else might lie between them, the heat was there, just under the surface of the skin, needing only a touch, a breath, to spark it. The flames crept into her cheeks, darkened her eyes to smoky jade.

"You laid down the ground rules last time, Jess. Want to try it my way tonight?"

A shudder went through her. For a moment he thought she might bolt, but she surprised him by standing her ground.

"That depends on what your way entails."

"It's slow," he warned, feathering his thumb along the tendon in the side of her neck. "Real slow. Might take all night. I don't promise you'll get much sleep."

"Then I guess it's fortunate I don't need much."

The shadows under her eyes made a liar out of her, but this wasn't the time to debate the matter. Steve's concentration narrowed down to a single focus. It would probably kill him, but he intended to make good on his promise to savor every minute of the next few hours. Without another word, he scooped her up and headed down the hall.

"If I remember from the night I broke in, your bedroom is right about"—he nudged a door with his left knee—"here."

Like the living room, her bedroom was awash in light. Steve formed a swift impression of cool gray walls, arched windows shuttered in white, and a needle-nosed palm sprouting from a white wicker basket in one corner. Artfully framed movie posters made bright splashes of color against the walls, but it was the queen-size bed smothered in pillows that held his attention. When he lowered her to her feet beside the bed, the slide of her hips against his fly had his throat going tight and his hands reaching for the buckle of his Sam Brown belt.

Jess stood silent, mere inches away, while he shrugged out of the belt and holster. After all these weeks of dancing around each other, she hadn't expected him to be so confrontational tonight. Or so damned direct.

Her nerves had been screaming for the past hour. Steve's blunt response to her phone call had shattered her illusions that she could control the hunger that drove them both. She could have said no, of course. Or turned aside his declaration that he wanted her with a mocking laugh.

Instead she'd let her startled silence speak for itself, then spent the next hour alternating between feverish anticipation and a resolve to talk matters through with him when he got here.

So much for her resolve! Steve had put her on the defensive the moment she'd answered her door. In a few terse sentences, he'd somehow managed to fire both her anger and her desire.

Now she could only curl her fingers into tight, sweaty fists as he shed his gray shirt with its knife-sharp creases and silver eagles on the collar. The broad expanse of chest and shoulders covered only by his crew-necked T-shirt made her mouth go bone-dry.

Her nails dug into her palms. She kept her fists at her sides, fighting the need to reach out and stroke those hard ridges and smooth, rippling curves. She'd just about crawled all over the man before bringing matters to a screeching halt the last time they got this close. She wasn't going to initiate anything this time.

Or end it, she swore silently.

When he started on the buttons of her linen shirt, the raw hunger she'd tried to keep harnessed broke free. Sudden, selfish greed punched through her. She wanted this. She needed it. No talking. No thinking. Just the brush of his knuckles against her breasts when he peeled off her shirt. The slide of his palms along her ribs. The warm wash of his breath as he nuzzled her throat.

Her lids drifted down. Her head went back.

His teeth nipped the cords in her neck, sharp enough for pain, careful enough for pleasure. She shuddered again, as much from the tiny shock as from the air-conditioned chill on her nipples.

"Did I hurt you?"

She lifted her lids and sank into the treacherous turquoise of his eyes. "No."

He took another bite, lower this time, in that vulnerable jointure of neck and shoulder. Pleasure darted up and down her spine. A single step brought him closer, so close her bare breasts brushed his chest. Needles of sensation shot from her nipples to her belly. When he eased back and broke the contact, she almost groaned aloud.

"No," he ordered softly, "don't move."

His hands went to the waistband of her cut-offs. With maddening deliberation he popped the snap and found the zipper. Jess sucked in a breath, her stomach hollowing at the glide of his knuckles against her belly.

She had to touch him. The need was all-consuming, impossible to resist any longer. Her palms flattened against his chest, winged up and across his shoulders. The downy cotton T-shirt was cloud-soft under her fingertips and still smelled faintly of bleach. It fused with the woodsy tang of his aftershave, but the faint wash of cinnamon on his breath was all Steve. Wondering if she'd ever taste the spice again without thinking of this man and this moment,

Jess locked her arms around his neck and drew his mouth down to hers.

One kiss and she wanted more. Two and she was hot with need. He took her down to the bed, where they rid themselves of the rest of their clothes, but he refused to hurry his pleasure or hers. Within moments her body had slicked and her hunger had taken on a feral urgency.

Still, he played with her. "Slow, Jess. We're taking this slow, remember?"

Demonstrating his intent, he cupped her mound and initiated a lazy, unhurried friction. He knew just where to rub, just when to ease the pressure. Ripples of pleasure built into waves. With each stroke, each press, the waves came closer and closer to cresting.

Jess stood it as long as she could. Panting, she jerked away from his touch and rolled onto her side. When she wrapped her fingers around his rigid flesh, her smile was lethal.

"Let's see just how slow you can take it."

His shoulder, she decided two cataclysmic orgasms later, made for a hot, lumpy pillow, but she couldn't summon the energy to separate their bodies. She found enough to protest, though, when he stretched a hand to the bedside lamp and flicked the switch, plunging the room into darkness.

"What are you doing?"

He mumbled something unintelligible against

her hair. Struggling up on one elbow, Jess blinked to adjust to the gloom. The digital clock on the bedside table glowed a bright green warning.

"Steve, it's almost three. You'd better not go to sleep now or you'll—"

"I'm not sleeping. Just recharging my batteries."

"If you charge them any more," she drawled, "we'll both be dead by morning."

Smirking, he opened one eye. "I can think of worse ways to go."

"So can I, but not here and not now."

His other eye opened. His smirk faded.

Without saying a word, they both acknowledged that there were, in fact, worse ways to go. Drowning, for example. Or sucking in carbon monoxide while your unsuspecting spouse puttered around upstairs in your bedroom.

The lethargy seeped out of her bones. Leaning across Steve's chest, she snapped on the bedside lamp and forced the shadows to retreat to the far corners of the room. An awkward twist dislodged the tangled sheets from under her hips. She pushed upright, taking a corner of the sheet with her, and shoved her hair out of her eyes.

"The lieutenant in charge of my fuels branch came to see me today. Yesterday."

Tucking his arms under his head, Steve gave her a sidelong glance. "I met him," he said after a moment. "A moonfaced kid. Seemed sharp enough, though."

"He is. He's also worried about one of the men who works for him."

"Billy Jack Petrie."

It wasn't a question, but a flat statement of fact. Jess shifted, wanting to see his face more clearly. Needing to see his face more clearly.

"The lieutenant tried to call Petrie's house. There wasn't any answer."

"He and his wife aren't there. I drove by the house a couple days ago and saw the newspapers littering his yard. I've had one of my men keeping an eye on the place since."

Her heart began a slow thump against her sternum. "Did you also drive by Wayne Whittier's house?"

"The hovel he lives in hardly qualifies as a house."

"Was he there? Did you speak with him?"

"I did. I also spoke to Congressman Calhoun."

"Are you going to tell me what they had to say about my mother . . . or about me?"

"Calhoun didn't remember your mother," he said slowly. "I doubt if he remembers his own, for that matter."

"And Whittier?"

"Whittier claims Sheriff Boudreaux read matters wrong, that the waitresses who worked at the Blue Crab all understood the rules. If they took a customer into the back room to earn an extra tip, they split it with the owner."

Her lip curled. "Nice guy."

"No, he's not."

Lowering his arms, Steve pushed upright. The sheet rode up his flanks and bared his hip. The rigid flesh that had driven into Jess such a short time ago lay flaccid amid its nest of wiry gold curls.

"He's slime," Steve said flatly, wrenching her gaze to his face. "The kind who deserves to be blown away. If the bastard doesn't drink himself to death first, chances are someone will do just that. But not you, Jess. You won't be the one to pull the trigger."

The yeasty scent of sex still hung in the air. Her skin tingled from a rash of whisker burns, and her lips seemed swollen to twice their size. Yet all she could feel, all she could hear, was the implacable, unshakable certainty in Steve's voice.

"How do you know it won't be me? I told you before, I would have snitched my mother's rusty old shotgun out of the trunk and gone after every one of those bastards if I'd known what they did to her."

"But you didn't know, did you?"

Her knuckles whitened on the sheet. "I do now."

She'd dodged the question. Again.

Anger flushed through Steve's veins, all the more dangerous because it was so rigidly restrained. Even now, after moaning and straining against him, she wouldn't give him a straight answer. With a vicious curse, he swung to the side of the bed and yanked his pants from the heap of pillows and garments on the floor.

"Steve, listen to me—"

"No, you listen!" He swung back, his anger beating against the chains that held it. "I'm a cop. I've seen about every atrocity a sick, twisted mind can devise. I've had to watch lab techs scrape evidence samples from under the fingernails of an eighty-seven-year-old who was sodomized and beaten to death with his own cane. I know what it feels like to tell a parent their runaway son was cut up and sold for body parts."

"Good Lord!"

He bent over, slapping his palms on the headboard, caging her against the wood.

"I also know what it feels like to stand amid the carnage of a day-care center and hold your forty-five to the head of the man who gunned down a half dozen three- and four-year-olds. I wanted to squeeze the trigger so badly my whole body shook with it, Jess. I wanted to paint his brains against the wall. You know why I didn't? Because I wouldn't profane those children by splattering them with that murderer's blood."

Christ! Where the hell had that come from? He hadn't talked about that day to anyone. Not the departmental shrink. Not even his partner, who had cuffed the YMCA shooter and quietly, urgently talked Steve back from the edge.

Shaken, he shoved away from the bed and

grabbed his shirt. By the time he'd thrust his arms through the sleeves and forced the buttons into the closest holes, he'd blanked the image of those small, desecrated bodies from his mind. His voice was calm, his hand steady when he turned back to the woman who watched him, wide-eyed and mute.

"I didn't do it, Jess, and you won't profane your mother's memory by putting a bullet between Wayne Whittier's eyes or hounding Billy Jack Petrie out of his job."

That was what he believed. What he wanted desperately to believe.

Gathering the rest of his belongings, Steve left her still naked, still silent.

Jess heard the front door slam, listened for the revving of the cruiser's powerful engine. Only after it had faded did she relax her grip on the sheet.

Shame coursed through her as she padded to the bathroom and reached into the shower stall to twist the knobs. She'd never asked Paxton about his past, had never even wondered about it. Since her return to the Florida panhandle, her own had consumed her.

It still consumed her. It would until she'd confronted Bill Petrie and Wayne Wittier. As for Congressman Calhoun . . .

Her heart pounding, Jess stepped into the tiled shower stall, lathered a washrag, and soaped all traces of Steve Paxton from her body.

Chapter 14

Summer weekends on Florida's Emerald Coast were made for sun and sand and splashing through waves of impossibly green water topped by lacy curls of white.

On any other Saturday afternoon, Jess might have considered stretching out on the beach and soaking up the sun's rays. She might even have returned Steve's call when he left a message inviting her to take the *Gone Fishin'* out with him later in the day.

Not this Saturday.

The SF445 problem consumed most of her day. Sergeant Babcock and the crew he'd pressed into service had worked around the clock to finish sampling the fuel in the storage tanks and underground distribution system. To Jess's relief, tests confirmed traces of SF445 in only one of the six massive tanks.

"Looks like we'll only have to empty one storage tank," a weary, oil-stained Ed Babcock reported. "Since the Defense Fuels Center manages the contract for delivery of all fuels, it'll work the contract for its removal."

"Have the folks at DFC been notified?"

"They will be, as soon as I leave here." He swiped the back of his hand across his forehead, smearing dirt and oil from temple to temple. "With the polluted fuel isolated, our biggest problem is going to be underground pipeline. We have to shut the entire system down and purge the lines."

"Which means we'll have to truck fuel to the flying wings," Jess said, chewing on her lower lip. Not only to the test wing and fighter wing on Eglin proper, but also to the reserve wing based at one of the auxiliary airfields some twenty-five miles away. With the pipeline down, there was no way the 96th's fleet of refuelers could sustain the current level of flying operations and service transient aircraft.

"We can request the loan of additional R-11s from other bases," Babcock said, anticipating the problem. "We loaned two of our trucks to Fort Rucker after they got hit by a tornado last year. Sent a couple to Keesler, too, to help support their open house and air show. I figure we can draw from bases throughout the South if Headquarters gives our request priority."

"If they don't, I'll call the LG."

The three-star director of logistics at air force headquarters had handpicked Jess for this job.

She'd packed up and moved with only a few weeks' notice. She figured it was payback time.

"Get the request ready and I'll sign it. I want it to go out this afternoon."

Babcock flashed her a grin. "Yes, ma'am."

He was halfway to the door before she stopped him. "That was good work, Ed. I'm glad we're on the same team."

"Yeah," he replied. "Me, too."

Jess left the squadron just after two. Her satisfaction with the morning's progress stayed with her when she stopped to grab a burger, which she ate during the drive across the bridge. By the time she reached her condo and exchanged her uniform for jeans and a cool, sleeveless shirt, the demands of her job had taken a backseat to the need that had been festering in her for days.

She thought about calling Steve, but she had a good idea what he'd say about the obsession that took her east along Highway 98. A few miles from Panama City, she cut north on State Road 19, heading for the small town of Ebro, where the former owner of the Blue Crab now lived. Jess had retrieved Wayne Whittier's address from the phone book and directions to his residence from a door-to-door Internet map service.

North of the dazzling white-sand coast, the landscape took on a different character. Short, stubby pond pines skirted by palmetto and tough wiregrass dug their roots into the clay. Where rivers and streams combined to form a swamp, cypress domes humped above the otherwise flat terrain.

Some miles north of the turnoff, Jess passed a sign carved from native blackgum announcing *Pine Log State Forest*. A few more miles took her to the intersection with the two-lane county road that led to Whittier's place.

Swerving several times to avoid roadkill, she checked the odometer carefully to clock the distance specified in the Internet directions. Aside from a few hand-painted signs nailed to tree trunks, there were no markers to identify the red-clay side roads. Most of the rusted, tiptilted mailboxes planted at the juncture of these dirt roads lacked numbers of any sort. Jess drove well past one bullet-riddled box before deciding it must belong to Whittier.

Backing up, she rested her arms on the Expedition's steering wheel and stared at the holes in the rusted tin mailbox. Buckshot, she guessed from the random spray pattern, although she certainly didn't consider herself an arms expert. Under Frank Blackwell's close supervision, she'd fired her mother's shotgun maybe three, four times as a teenager, badly bruising her shoulder each time. As part of her officer-training program, she'd qualified on both the M-16 and 9mm service Baretta.

She'd also made a special visit to an off-base firing range to qualify with the Smith & Wesson

.38 Special she'd purchased during an assignment to the Space Systems Division in L.A. The dealer had categorized it as a ladies' piece—airweight, uncomplicated, just point and shoot. Perfect for a woman living alone in a city noted for its high crime rate. Perfect, too, for a woman about to stand face-to-face with someone like Wayne Whittier.

The snub-nosed revolver rested in the overhead compartment of the Expedition, along with Jess's updated permit to carry a concealed weapon. Reaching up, she slid open the compartment door and extracted the revolver. The hard rubber grip fit her hand perfectly. The matte-gray nickel finish gleamed dully in the afternoon sunlight. She cradled it in her hand for long moments, testing its weight, considering everything she'd heard about the man she'd come to confront. Her mouth set, she slipped the .38 into the pocket of her straw shoulder tote.

The Expedition took the dirt side road like the tough utility vehicle it was. Pine branches scraped at its sides and rooftop as the high carriage jounced over ruts. Clamping her jaw tight to keep her teeth from rattling, Jess navigated the narrow track until she reached a clearing that backed onto a swamp.

Her lip curled in disgust as she surveyed the flat, treeless stretch. If this *was* Whittier's residence, the man's idea of landscaping evidently consisted of tossing his trash out the window and waiting for it to sprout. And if that was

Whittier's Rottweiler snapping and leaping at the end of its chain, the owner deserved to be staked out beside the animal in the broiling sun. Or worse.

Keeping a cautious eye on the snarling animal, Jess hitched her straw tote over her shoulder and climbed out of the SUV. Thank God she'd chosen jeans and sneakers instead of shorts and sandals for this excursion. The thick rubber soles and tough denim protected her from the broken glass and insects that swarmed around her ankles as she crossed the yard.

When she approached the sagging front porch, the Rottweiler's frenzied howls escalated to a deafening crescendo. Cautiously, she mounted the rickety steps and had just raised a fist to pound on the door when it was yanked open from the inside.

The stench of sweat, old bacon grease, and whiskey rolled out, sending Jess back an involuntary step. A shirtless, bleary-eyed male who slapped a palm against the door frame to support himself. His other hand, Jess noted, was wrapped around the neck of a half-empty Jim Beam bottle.

Squinting at her with red, irritated eyes, he pitched a hoarse shout over the dog's howls. "Who the hell are you?"

Jess had envisioned a dozen different scenarios for this meeting. None of them had included yelling out her identity on the front porch of a shack that might collapse around her at any moment.

Yet confronting Whittier like this gave her a fierce satisfaction. No prep. No posturing. Just the blunt announcement.

"I'm Helen Yount's daughter."

"The fuck you say."

His red, flaking rims narrowed to slits. For long moments he squinted at her face; then his bloodshot eyes made a slow, insulting journey from her neck to her knees. All the while, the frenzied dog lunged at the end of its tether.

Jess saw Whittier's lips move, but couldn't hear over the din. When she shrugged and indicated as much, he staggered onto the porch.

"Shut up!"

To enforce the snarled command, he snatched up a rusted hubcap and hurled it, Frisbee-like, at the animal. The vicious metal caught the dog square between the eyes. With a yelp, the Rottweiler went down. Blood spouted from a gash, and its red eyes were filled with hate when it retreated to a shallow depression scraped in the dirt.

The effort of heaving the hubcap started a rattling cough in Whittier's chest. The hacking went on forever, bending him almost double. Finally he groped for the porch support to pull upright, spit a gob over the rail, and took a swill from the bottle still clutched in his hand. Whiskey dribbling down his chin, he turned back to Jess.

"What I said," he got out in a rasping growl, "was you sure don't take after your mama. She had a pair of tits on her could get a man hard just brushing up against 'em." His lips curled back over stained dentures. " 'Course, Helen liked for men to do more 'n just feel her jugs. 'Specially when she was juiced up."

"I didn't come here to discuss my mother."

"No? Then what'd you come for?"

"To look you in the eye," Jess said softly, "and see what kind of man would rape a woman who worked for him."

"Rape, hell. If you're talkin' 'bout that time the sheriff come out to the Blue Crab 'cause one of the customers thought he heard Helen yellin' and carryin' on, it weren't rape. Your mama wanted it. Was beggin' for it."

"Is that why it took five men to hold her down?"

"I told you, she was juiced up." Leering, he cupped his crotch with his free hand. "Truth is, Helen had a craving for this little jigger. God knows, I give it to her often enough."

She'd thought he'd show at least a vestige of remorse or shame. His boasting sickened her.

"I doubt that." Cool contempt dripped from every word. "Even juiced up, as you claim, my mother wouldn't let a scum like you touch her."

Rage mottled his unshaven cheeks. "You stupid bitch. You've caused nothing but trouble since you rolled into town. First McConnell, then Clark. Well, you ain't takin' me down!"

As far as Jess was concerned, Delbert McConnell and Ron Clark deserved whatever place in purgatory they now inhabited.

"Do you think the statute of limitations protects you, Whittier? Guess again. You're going to burn, you bastard."

The hate that twisted his face and propelled him across the porch told her she'd miscalculated both the man and the amount of whiskey he'd consumed.

"You shouldda drowned when you went off the bridge! Why the fuck didn't you drown?"

The Jim Beam bottle swung in a vicious arc. Jess barely had time to throw up a forearm to protect her face and jump back. In the process, her heel snagged on a rotten board.

After that, everything seemed to happen at warp speed.

Tumbling off the steps, she hit the dirt with jarring force. The .38 flew out of her tote on impact.

Snarling another curse, Whittier made a dive for the gun. The weapon was beyond Jess's reach, but a wild scissor-kick sent it skimming through the weeds and trash. Whittier staggered up, lurched for the gun, and fell right on top of it.

Jess was scrambling to her knees when an ominous growl raised the hairs on the back of her neck. With a rattle of chain link, the Rottweiler sprang.

"Whittier! Look out!"

Her attacker jerked his head up. His face frozen in horror, he stared straight into the jaws of death.

Chapter 15

The first officer who arrived at the scene in response to Jess's 911 call threw up his lunch.

He'd barely wiped his mouth clean and pulled out his notebook to take her statement when the wail of sirens heralded the arrival of the EMS ambulance. Advising Jess that he'd be right back, the deputy sheriff went to greet the med-techs.

She sat on an overturned oil drum, spattered from head to toe with blood, her left hand still fisted around the porch slat she'd wrenched free and used to beat off the Rottweiler. Wayne Whittier sprawled in the dirt a few yards away. The mangled flesh and torn cartilage of his throat and face had already attracted swarms of flies. The dog lay in a crumpled heap beside him.

Jess knew it was wrong, knew something inside her had tilted seriously off center, but at the moment the death of the abused animal

numbed her more than that of its owner. Maybe
she'd feel something for Whittier later, when the
shock wore off. Regret, perhaps. Or guilt.

No. Not guilt. Whatever else might come, it
wouldn't be guilt. Uncurling her fingers one by
one, she let the bloody porch slat drop to the
dirt.

The police didn't recover the .38 until the
med-techs got ready to transfer Whittier's body
onto the gurney. By then the media had aug-
mented the small army of medical and law-
enforcement personnel. Panama City reporters
with access to police scanners had converged on
the scene, jockeying with each for the best camera angles and fighting like crows for their share
of the gruesome kill.

The Walton County sheriff arrived hard on
the media's heels. Like Jess, Steve was in jeans
and a knit shirt, but the badge clipped to his
waist formed a solid wall between them. He cut
a path straight to her, but didn't speak more
than a dozen words after confirming she wasn't
hurt, that the blood drenching her clothes
wasn't hers.

She understood. In his mind, she'd stepped
over the line, descended to Whittier's level. Pro-
faned her mother's memory. She also understood the taut lines in his face when he
approached her some time later with the bagged
.38 in his hand.

"Is this your Smith & Wesson?"

"Yes."

"Has it been fired?"

"No."

"Why not?"

She lifted her head. His mirrored sunglasses hid his eyes, but she could feel them drilling into her.

"Why didn't I shoot the dog before he ate Whittier's face, you mean?"

"Answer the question."

The harsh command whipped feeling back into her, small, stinging needles that straightened her spine and brought her head up.

"I told your deputy what happened, Sheriff."

"Tell me."

"Whittier swung at me. I dodged the blow, caught my heel on a loose board, and fell off the porch. The revolver slid out of my tote."

His tight, closed expression gave no clue whether he believed her.

"Whittier went for it, but he was drunk. He stumbled and landed right on top of the gun. It was under him when the dog attacked. I couldn't get to it. I tried to pull the dog off by dragging on its chain, but it was too strong, and its jaws . . ."

A hot, sour swell of nausea rolled through her belly.

"Its jaws were locked," she finished grimly.

Another vehicle pulled into the clearing just

then, a sedan with a blue-and-gold seal on the side. Steve flicked it a narrow glance, then turned back to Jess.

"Are you aware that carrying a concealed weapon without a permit is a felony in this state?"

"I have a permit. I applied for it right after I moved back to Florida."

A muscle ticked in the side of his jaw. Jess could guess what he was thinking.

"Yes, Sheriff. The thirty-eight was in my possession when I arrived in Florida. Do you think I used it to smash in Delbert McConnell's skull? Or held it to Ron Clark's head and forced him to put a hose to his mouth?"

"What I think," he said softly, "is that you'd better talk to an attorney before you volunteer any more information than you already have."

She dipped her head a mere inch, just enough to acknowledge the warning.

With that small nod, the iron band around Steve's chest screwed even tighter. Advising her to lawyer up went against his every professional instinct. Ruthlessly he suppressed his cop's inherent urge to follow the spoor of blood. Just as ruthlessly he resisted the impulse to wrap his hands around Jess's arms, haul her off that rusted oil drum, and throw her into his cruiser before she said something that would widen the crevasse yawning under her feet.

Three of the five men who'd assaulted her mother all those years ago were now dead. Each of the deaths occurred under highly unusual circumstances, to say the least. All had happened since Jess's return to Florida.

The string of coincidences would make a rookie's nose start to twitch, and the detective from the Florida Department of Law Enforcement who was taking a good look at the corpse before the med-techs wheeled it away was no rookie. Jim Hazlett took his time. Like most good cops, he recorded the details of the scene in his own mind before talking to the responding officer.

Unwrapping a stick of Dentyne in a futile attempt to kill his vicious nicotine craving, Steve strolled over to join him. He rarely regretted leaving the sophisticated resources available to the Atlanta PD, but this was one of those times he didn't fully appreciate being sheriff of a sparsely populated county dependent on FDLE assistance in investigating violent crimes.

Not that this was technically a crime scene, he reminded himself grimly. Not yet, anyway.

"Afternoon, Sheriff."

"Hello, Hazlett."

Already drenched with sweat after only ten minutes in the hot sun, Jim Hazlett tipped Steve a nod. As Steve had anticipated, his cop's nose was already twitching.

"Seems like the folks in Walton County are finding more 'n' more ways to get dead these days."

"Seems like."

The detective's glance drifted to Jess. "I understand that's Lieutenant Colonel Blackwell. Is she the same Lieutenant Colonel Blackwell who was heavy on your suicide's mind last month?"

"Yes. And the same Colonel Blackwell who went off the Mid-Bay Bridge ten days ago."

Steve wasn't telling Hazlett anything he didn't already know. Nodding, the investigator confirmed that he'd already discovered the link between Jess's accident and Wayne Whittier in the Florida Crime Information Center's computers.

"I saw the Okaloosa County boys put a rush on their request for the paint analysis of that incident. Also saw where you'd tagged Whittier's 'seventy-six caddy as a potential match." Swiping the back of his hand across his glistening upper lip, Hazlett eyed Steve thoughtfully. "What do you know about the deceased that I don't, Sheriff?"

Steve made a quick sweep of the media before replying. The incident at the Blue Crab and Jess's connection to the three recent deaths would hit the news sooner or later, but there was no need to precipitate the headlines by feeding information into a supersensitive boom mike.

Turning his back on the cluster of reporters, he lowered his voice and spoke directly to Hazlett. "According to Cliff Boudreaux, Whittier was one of five men who sexually assaulted Colonel Blackwell's mother twenty-five years ago."

"No shit."

"The incident occurred at the Blue Crab, a dive Whittier used to own. Helen Yount waitressed there."

"I remember the place. Up on Highway Twenty, wasn't it?"

"Right. Yount left town the same night as the alleged rape. No charges were filed."

With an almost audible whir, the wheels of the investigator's mind spun into overdrive. "Let me guess. Your suicide was one of those five men."

Steve forced a nod. "So was the floater we pulled out of the bay a few weeks ago."

His lips rounding in a soundless whistle, Hazlett looked to Jess once more. When he shifted his attention to the plastic evidence bag in Steve's hand, his eyes gleamed with the joy of the hunt.

"Be interesting to find out whether the colonel always totes a thirty-eight when she goes calling."

Now. Steve had to say it now. If he withheld his personal interest in Jess Blackwell, he'd compromise them both and completely destroy any chance of being able to help her.

"I met Colonel Blackwell for the first time the night of Clark's suicide. I think you should know we've gotten close since then. Very close."

The investigator blinked. "Well, now," he

said, feeling his way cautiously. "Is the fact that you two have, uh, gotten close going to cause complications, Sheriff?"

"No. You do your job. My people will do theirs."

"Fair enough." He made another swipe at the shiny beads on his upper lip. "Guess I'll go see what the colonel has to say about all this."

Just in time, Steve bit back the suggestion that she might prove more cooperative out of the heat and the blood-spattered clothes that were attracting swarms of gnats and flies. At this point, he wasn't sure just how cooperative Jess should be.

By the time Jess was told she could leave, her head throbbed and her skin itched from the combination of sweat and dried blood. One of the EMS techs had given her a package of moist towelettes, but the paper proved ineffective on the gore caked in the creases of her neck and arms and legs.

She should call her boss, Jess thought as she abandoned the oil drum and pushed to her feet. Better Colonel Hamilton heard about this from her than see his supply squadron commander on the ten-o'clock news. Again.

Hitching her tote over her shoulder, she picked her way through the weeds. With each step she tried to summon the calm she'd need to face the reporters waiting for her to leave the sanctity of the taped-off accident area.

That was what this was, she reminded herself fiercely. An accident. Unless and until someone made a public statement to the contrary.

"Colonel Blackwell!"

"Colonel! Over here!"

Bracing herself, she approached the barricade of video-cams and boom mikes. She knew an appeal for consideration would be useless, but tried anyway.

"I'm sorry. This has been a horrible experience. I need to clean up before I—"

She should have known that blood would play better for the cameras than squeaky-clean. Ignoring her plea, the eager reporters peppered her with questions.

"Why were you here?"

"How did you know the deceased?"

"Did you drive out to see Mr. Whittier on air force business?"

Shaking her head, she pushed past them. The newshounds followed, nipping at her heels.

"Where were you when the dog attacked?"

"Did Whittier incite the attack?"

"Is this incident in any way connected with your accident two weeks ago?"

The question came zinging over the heads of the other reporters. Startled, Jess made the mistake of glancing around and almost took a boom mike in the eye.

"I'll answer that."

Steve shouldered his way to her side. Sweat ringed the armpits of his yellow polo shirt, and his face glowed a ruddy red under his tan, but no one mistook him for a civilian bystander. His air of authority guaranteed him as much attention as his badge.

"As some of you are obviously aware, Colonel Blackwell's vehicle was forced off the Mid-Bay Bridge two weeks ago. The incident is being investigated by the Okaloosa County sheriff's office, so you'll have to ask them for an update."

"Come on, Sheriff! Give us something to work with here."

"I can confirm that paint scrapings removed from the colonel's car were sent to the crime lab in Tallahassee for comparison with the National Automotive Paint File. I can also confirm that the scrapings were a bright yellow in color."

The video-cams shifted, zoomed in on the dented, chrome-laden Cadillac parked beside Whittier's shack. The reporters scribbled furiously in their notebooks.

"So you think it wasn't just a drunk driver who plowed into her?"

"Until the paint analysis comes back, it's too soon for me to say what I think. Although"—his glance drifted to the bottles lying amid trash in the yard—"there's certainly the possibility that alcohol was involved in that incident."

Like a school of hungry sharks, they devoured that tidbit.

"What about today?"

"Was alcohol involved in this incident, too?"

"Possibly. We'll furnish you a copy of Colonel

Blackwell's statement, in which she relates that Mr. Whittier appeared unstable when she confronted him. So unstable he stumbled and fell and was unable to protect himself from the dog's attack."

He was covering for her, Jess realized. Implying that she'd driven out to this dump to take on the drunk who'd almost killed her. She supposed she should feel grateful, but they both knew he was just delaying the inevitable. It was only a matter of time until the past hit the headlines.

Terminating the interview a few moments later, Steve escorted her to her vehicle. "Can you drive?"

"Yes. Steve, I—"

"Get in the car. The video-cams are still recording."

Biting her lip, she climbed behind the wheel of the Expedition.

"Go home. Get cleaned up." His jaw worked. "Call a lawyer."

The door thudded shut.

Jess went home, cleaned up, and called her boss. Her respect for the military chain of command went too deep to go outside the system before notifying her supervisor.

Colonel Hamilton wasn't at his quarters, but he responded to the brief message she left on his recorder less than an hour later.

"What's this about an off-base incident, Jess?"

"A man was killed. A civilian. Not one of ours," she added quickly. "I thought I'd better brief you on it before you see it on the seven-o'clock news."

"Okay, shoot."

"It's . . . it's complicated, sir. I'd rather tell you in person."

"No problem. Peg and I are baby-sitting the grandkids. Why don't you swing by my quarters? We'll escape to the deck to talk."

His wife called out in the background, seconding the invitation, but warning Jess she might get pressed into service at the swing set if she wasn't careful.

Eglin's director of logistics and his wife lived on base. From the outside the one-story cinder-block house looked as unpretentious as its neighbors, but the fifties-era bungalow had been renovated a number of times over the years and came with an unobstructed million-dollar view of the bay.

A thick canopy of live oaks shaded the flag-stone patio at the rear of the house. After a friendly greeting, Peggy Hamilton good-naturedly shooed their five lively grandkids back in the house. The colonel waved Jess to one of the high-backed sling chairs around a glass-topped table.

"Would you like a glass of lemonade?"

Jess accepted gratefully. Lip-puckering tart

and icy cold, the drink worked magic on her dry throat.

"All right," the colonel said when he claimed his seat. "Give me the details. Who died and how are we involved?"

"Not we, sir. Me. I was involved."

Hamilton's brows snapped together. "You're not going to tell me you're in some way responsible for this man's death, are you?"

"No, sir," Jess replied carefully. Folding her hands in her lap, she traced her thumb over scarred skin of her right hand. "I'm not going to tell you I'm responsible for his death. But there's a distinct possibility the off-base authorities will."

Chapter 16

On Colonel Hamilton's advice, Jess arranged to meet with the commander of Eglin's security forces after she left his quarters.

The chief of security had already received a heads-up from the Walton County Sheriff's Department. As a courtesy, local law-enforcement agencies notified Eglin's Central Dispatch whenever military personnel were involved in an off-base incident. Jess filled the top cop in on the details of Whittier's gruesome death, including her connection to the man, and drove home.

She didn't sleep at all that night.

Whittier's death headlined the local edition of the *Daily News* the next morning. Jess left the paper unread on her kitchen table and went to take a shower. She'd scrubbed from head to foot for almost an hour last night, but she could still feel the scratch of dried blood on her skin.

When she emerged from the bedroom, her answering machine blinked fast and steady. She hesitated before hitting play. She'd left the repeated calls from radio and TV stations unanswered last night and expected more this morning, but it was Steve's voice that jumped out at her.

"Jess. Call me."

She reached for the phone, let her hand hover over it for long moments.

No. Not yet. Not until she'd talked to the attorney, as he'd advised, and knew exactly what she'd dragged him into.

She managed to force down half a slice of toast before putting on her uniform and driving back to the base that afternoon for a meeting with a JAG from the office of the Area Defense Counsel. The on-call ADC was young—too young, Jess thought at first, but her professional manner soon dispelled the Sunday quiet of the legal office.

"I saw the story in the paper this morning," she said, "but I'd like you to tell me what happened in your own words."

Wrapped in the cloak of attorney-client privilege, Jess started with Wayne Whittier's death and worked her way back in time to the Blue Crab. The JAG's face sobered when Jess related the recent demise of three of the five men who'd allegedly assaulted her mother.

"And all three of these deaths occurred since you arrived at Eglin?"

"Yes."

"Can you substantiate where you were when the first two men died?"

"Do I have an alibi, you mean?" She shook her head. "No."

"For either death?"

"McConnell supposedly went overboard during the tropical storm that hit just a few days after I arrived. I understand they fixed the time of death to within a three- to five-hour time frame, part of which I spent at the base, part at home. Alone."

"I see."

"I was also home the night Clark died."

"Alone?"

"Alone."

The JAG sat back in her chair and peered at Jess over the rim of her glasses. "I'm sure you understand that you'll have to obtain civilian counsel to represent you if you're charged with a criminal offense committed off duty and off base."

"Yes."

"Any such charges, of course, could become a part of your military record." The young attorney paused. "You could also face potentially serious conflict-of-interest charges if you have reason to believe an employee under your supervision once assaulted your mother."

"I'm aware of that."

Thoughtfully, the JAG pushed her glasses up the bridge of her nose with one finger. "Have you spoken to Mr. Petrie at all about the incident?"

"No."

"Does he know you suspect him of being involved in the alleged assault?"

"I don't know."

"Are you his direct supervisor?"

"No. He works for the lieutenant in charge of the fuels branch. My civilian deputy is the reviewing official on his performance evaluations."

"But you can influence those evaluations, along with any recommendations for merit pay increases?"

"Yes."

"Not good, Colonel. Definitely not good. You should think about detailing him to another squadron until this situation is sorted out. Or perhaps transfer him to Hurlburt."

Jess had already thought about moving Petrie to the base just across town. She'd been thinking about it since Steve had dropped the man's name that night on his boat. She was still thinking about it when she drove off base some time later.

Granted, her initial reaction when Steve named Petrie had been one of vicious intent. If she remembered correctly, her exact words were something to the effect that she intended to make the bastard sweat blood. Yet the desire for vengeance that had burned so hot and bright that night on Steve's boat had now chilled to icy dispassion.

She'd have to move Petrie, Jess thought as she drove, get him out of her squadron, send him to the special operations base across town. Although Hurlburt's fuels operation wasn't as large as Eglin's, the branch chief slot was currently vacant. If they civilianized the slot and Jess recommended Petrie . . .

No! She'd work a lateral transfer or a detail, but she was damned if she'd recommend him for a promotion, even to save herself from the storm that had begun to swirl about her. She was damned if she'd do *anything* until he returned from wherever he'd hidden himself and she looked him in the eye.

As she had Whittier.

She got the shakes then, fierce shudders that hunched her shoulders and racked her whole upper torso. The tremors were so intense she had to pull over to the side of the road, so violent she sat gripping the steering wheel with both hands and tried desperately to focus on the McDonald's arches just ahead. On the hot-pink hydrangeas bunched at the curb. On anything but the image of a black-and-tan Rottweiler with ears back and fangs bared, going for Whittier's throat.

The shakes subsided, but the fierce effort required to blank out the horrific images took Jess right past the turnoff for the Mid-Bay Bridge. She kept driving, deciding to take the long way around the bay and give herself time to think.

Gradually, the sprawl of new homes and golf

courses thinned and the road narrowed from four lanes to two. Cypresses formed a dense canopy overhead. As the bay crept within yards of the road, she passed through the towns of her youth. Seminole, Villa Tasso, Choctaw Beach. She didn't slow, didn't look to either side. Nor did she make the conscious decision to stop at Steve's until she turned south on Highway 331.

As the Expedition approached the dirt road that led to his private little bayou, Jess debated whether she should fish her cell phone out of her black leather clutch and call first. He might not be at the boat. More to the point, he might want to maintain the distance he'd deliberately put between them at Whittier's place.

He was a cop, she reminded herself grimly. He wore the same badge as the man who'd escorted Helen Yount out of town all those years ago. If Paxton wanted to continue to wear that badge, he had to separate himself from Helen's daughter. Jess had no idea when he was up for reelection, but she could imagine what it would do to his chances if it got out he'd rolled around between the sheets with a woman he suspected of extracting a deadly vengeance on the men who assaulted her mother.

If that was what he suspected.

Jess had to know. With a desperate need she didn't stop to examine, she flicked on the directional signals.

The sheriff's unmarked cruiser was parked in

the turnaround beside the dock. The hatch of the *Gone Fishin'* was open. Mellow jazz floated from inside the cabin, sending the reedy wail of a sax across the bayou. Smoke curled from a small grill attached to the rear rail.

Steve slouched in a deck chair tipped back at a comfortable angle, one bare foot propped against the rail. A ball cap shaded his eyes from the sun now blazing a gold trail across the water. The smoke from the grill evidently provided adequate protection from mosquitoes, since all he had on in addition to the cap was a pair of wet swimming trunks.

The trunks were green, Jess saw as she slid out of the SUV, a bright, parroty green splashed with pink and orange hibiscus. For reasons totally beyond her comprehension, the baggy shorts blunted the razor's edge of her tension. Leaving her purse in the car, she walked out onto the dock.

"Mind if I come aboard?"

He stayed angled back, one foot on the rail, the other on the deck, his eyes shadowed by the brim of the cap. Jess's nerves did a slow tango until he drawled out a reply.

"Watch your step. The deck's wet."

With the boards rocking gently under her feet, she edged past the cabin and joined him at the rear of the boat. Her glance went to the foil-wrapped package on the grill.

"What are you cooking?"

"Shrimp remoulade." He cocked his head. "Hungry?"

Food seemed to be their neutral ground, their safest ground.

"I haven't been able to eat anything since . . . since yesterday," she admitted, dropping into one of the chairs bolted to the deck.

His face shuttered, Steve leaned forward to haul on a thin nylon tied to the rail. At the other end of the rope were anchored the remains of a six-pack. Extracting a dripping can from the plastic sleeve, he popped the top and passed it to her.

"You sure you want to talk about yesterday, Jess? I'm an officer of the law, remember?"

"I never let myself forget it."

"Good."

While she tipped her head and let the cool beer slide down her throat, his glance roamed her dark blue uniform slacks and light blue shirt.

"Did you just come from the base?"

"Yes. I had a meeting with the Area Defense Counsel."

"And he advised you to talk to me?"

"No, she didn't. But I wanted to ask you . . ."

She framed the question in her mind half a dozen ways before deciding just to lay it out.

"Do you think I deliberately shoved Wayne Whittier at that dog?"

"If I did, you'd be sitting in the county jail right now."

The blunt reply lifted most of the weight pressing in on her chest. His next comment shoveled it back on again.

"I do, however, think it's more than mere co-incidence that the men who reportedly assaulted your mother are suddenly dying off."

"I think so, too," she said softly. "I'm the link. The only link so far."

Steve knew he should end the discussion there. He didn't want to ask the question that had kept him awake most of last night, was almost afraid to hear the answer, but the need drove him just as it had Jess a few moments ago.

"Why did you drive out to Whittier's place yesterday?"

"I wanted to stand toe-to-toe with him and make him understand that the law might not have meted out justice, but his retribution would come. Sooner or later, he'd burn in hell."

"Well, shit. Is that what you told Hazlett?"

"Who?"

"The FDLE investigator."

"Not in so many words, but that's what I intend to tell Billy Jack Petrie if he shows his face at work again."

Steve's fist went so tight the aluminum beer can crinkled inward. "What do you mean, 'if'?"

"Petrie knows what he did. He's also got to know I can't have him in my squadron."

"That's not how you felt the first time his name came up between us."

"Hey, I'm only human. Of course I thought about using my position as his commander to hammer him, but I can't. I won't."

Steve said nothing. There was more coming. He knew her well enough now to be sure of that much, anyway.

"I'm guessing he may be using the time he took off to rethink his career options," she said after a moment. "Hopefully he's planning to apply for a position at another base. If he isn't, I'll arrange to have him transferred. What's between us isn't going to be played out on the job."

Christ, she made him sweat more with every word. Didn't she see how close she skirted to offering a motive for the three deaths, if not the means? Didn't she care?

"How about what's between us, Jess?" he asked curtly. "How do you see that playing out?"

"I think we both saw yesterday that it can't play at all. You put on the skids and backed away, just as I had to. . . ."

Disbelief whittled his anger to a sharp spike. "You thought I was backing away?"

"You had to. I understand."

"The hell you do."

His bare feet hit the deck. He came out of his chair, and got her out of hers in one swift jerk. Her beer jabbed cold against his belly.

"My main concern yesterday was to keep you

from falling into the pit you insist on digging for yourself. As I would have explained if you'd bothered to return my phone call."

"Steve—"

He drew her up then, so tight her arms folded against his chest, so close her mouth hovered mere inches from his.

"I'm so far from stepping back that I'm surprised you don't feel me bumping around inside your skin. You're sure as hell bumping around inside mine."

It would be so easy to stretch forward, mold her body to his, draw him further into the morass. Jess couldn't do it.

"As you reminded me so pointedly just a few minutes ago, you're a cop. Your credibility is on the line here. You've got to distance yourself before it's too late."

"It's already too late. I let Hazlett know he'd have to go through me to get to you."

"Why, for God's sake?"

"I told you. You're inside me. I can't get you out. Correction, I don't want to get you out."

She wasn't prepared for the need that cut into her heart and left it raw and bleeding.

This was the wrong time, the wrong man. Desperately, Jess tried to hold out against the craven desire to sink into his arms, forget the past, and ignore the future. She managed to hang on until Steve summoned a lopsided grin.

"We'll figure out tomorrow when it comes.

Right now, the only decision we have to make is whether we eat now or later."

"You're the cook," she said, surrendering the fight with barely a whimper. "You decide."

Steve had already made his choice, but the knowledge that she'd eaten nothing but a piece of toast all day reprioritized his immediate needs.

"Go below. Get out of your uniform and into something comfortable. I'll dish up the stew."

When she ducked through the hatch, it dawned on Jess that her universe had just shifted, realigning along unfamiliar patterns. She'd been wary of Steve Paxton since the first night he'd knocked on her door, still wasn't sure just what she should and shouldn't say to him. Yet for now, for what was left of the night, they were allies. Friends. Lovers.

Her heart thumping in slow anticipation, she descended the companionway stairs. The galley was as neat as the last time she'd come aboard. Only a roll of tinfoil and the shrimp shells cluttering the stainless-steel sink gave evidence that Steve had prepared his evening meal here before going topside to cook it. As before, his laptop computer sat on the drop-down mahogany table. Her heart gave a painful thump as she passed it.

The stateroom beyond the galley wasn't much larger than the bathroom in Jess's condo, but cleverly fitted compartments kept his belongings neatly stowed. Like the galley, the stateroom was almost spartan in its austere neatness. No keys or loose change cluttered the wood surfaces. No discarded uniform items lay tossed across the bed.

The only personal items were two framed photographs. One obviously depicted his family—father, mother, three siblings, including a teenage Steve. The second showed two police officers, one black, one white, arms hooked over each other's shoulders. Jess's gaze lingered on the photos for some moments before she pulled out a drawer in search of a replacement for her uniform slacks and blouse. She settled for a faded maroon T-shirt with *APD* stenciled in black letters across the front and back. The T-shirt hung to midthigh and wrapped her in the scent of Tide and sun. After liberally spraying her arms and legs with the can of mosquito repellent she found on a shelf, she padded barefoot back through the galley.

They ate with their feet propped on the back rail, scooping spoonfuls of the spicy concoction of shrimp, onions, and rice from wooden bowls, savoring the heat building inside and out. They said little, she and Steve. There was little they could say without stirring dark waters best left untouched.

Slowly the hot, muggy darkness wrapped around them. The jazz CDs that had been playing when Jess arrived finished and the deep-throated bullfrogs took over. Cocking her head, she listened to the chorus of night sounds.

"It's so quiet out here," she murmured, "even with all that noise."

"That's one of the reasons I like living here."

"Is it? What are the others?"

"The mobility. The absence of anything even remotely resembling a yard to mow. The freedom to strip down and dive in whenever I want to."

"You swim here?" She eyed the bayou doubtfully. "Aren't you worried about snakes or alligators crawling around in the weeds beneath the surface?"

"I have the channel dredged every couple years to keep it clear and deep enough for the boat." Reaching for her bowl, he dropped it beside his on the deck. "Want to give the bay another try, Jess?"

"The last time I went in these waters," she reminded him with a grimace, "I almost didn't come out."

"This time I'm going in with you."

That might have offered her some comfort if it hadn't hit too close to home.

Pushing out of his chair, he snagged her hand and gave it a tug. "Ever made love in the water, Jess?"

"Not in salt water, and not—"

"This end of the bay is river-fed fresh water." Ignoring her protest, he pulled her to her feet. "Cool and clean and soft as silk."

His palms planed her hips, raising little goose bumps as he skimmed the T-shirt up and over

her head. Bending, he grazed her bare shoulder.
The scrape of his teeth raised more shivers,
more heat.

"So are you," he murmured against her skin.
"Soft as silk and a movable feast for the mosquitoes. We'd better go in before they eat you
alive."

He cut into the water with barely a splash and
bobbed to the surface some yards away. Ripples
undulated across the water, so seductive, so
deadly.

Jess stood at the rail, her stomach clenching
at the sinuous movement. She remembered all
too vividly how the dark beast below had held
her in its maw until she'd fought free of her
submerged Mustang and clawed to the surface.
Remembered, too, how she'd swum to a bridge
abutment and clung to the cold steel for what
felt like hours until rescue arrived.

The terror of that night tried to sink its teeth
into her once more. The husky promise in
Steve's voice when he urged her to take the
plunge had her setting her jaw. Shimmying out
of her bra and bikini panties, she followed him
over the rail.

He was right. The bayou was cool and clean
and so welcoming Jess soon buried the horror
of her last excursion into these waters under a
thick layer of pleasure.

The silvery wash of moonlight on the dark
surface helped. So did Steve's adroit maneuver-
ing as he kicked out of his trunks and caught

Jess just as she surfaced. They curved together, joined at chest and hip, gliding like dolphins through the night. His hands and mouth worked their magic; his body buoyed hers.

Their splashing echoed in the sudden, startled silence. Their ragged breathing grew almost as loud as the bullfrogs' now-stilled chorus. With the water kissing her breasts and Steve hungry at her mouth and throat, Jess wrapped her legs around his waist and tried to take him into her. He seated himself, thrust hard, and sent them both under.

When they surfaced, Jess spit out the mouthful of bay she'd nearly swallowed. "I thought you said you knew how to do this."

"I did," he admitted, "in my younger, considerably more athletic days."

"I wish you'd shared that particular piece of information with me before you lured me in."

She squirmed, attempting to tread water without sacrificing the smooth, delicious friction of his flesh inside hers. She succeeded only in pushing them both down into the depths. They broke the surface again, gasping.

"I don't think this is going to work!"

"Sure it is."

Keeping her body locked against his, he rolled onto his side and swam toward the boat. Each time he contracted his muscles for another scissor-kick, he withdrew an inch or two. With every smooth lunge forward, he shot in again. By the time he grabbed one of the mooring lines

and anchored them both, Jess had forgotten her
terror of the bay, forgotten her session with the
JAG this afternoon, forgotten everything but the
feel of Steve's body inside hers.

Chapter 17

The following Monday morning, the *Daily News* broke the story linking Whittier and four other unnamed local residents to an alleged assault of a waitress at the Blue Crab twenty-five years ago. The same story identified Jess as Helen Yount's daughter and speculated with chilling detachment on the real reason behind her visit to Whittier the afternoon he died. The reporter also hinted that authorities were reassessing the findings in the recent deaths of two more of the men involved in the supposed incident at the Blue Crab.

Jess had expected the stories, had expected as well the curious glances and rumors that buzzed like dog flies around the supply squadron Monday morning. The civilian attorney she consulted later that afternoon advised her not to acknowledge or address them in any way.

She couldn't avoid addressing one issue, however. Calling in her deputy, she laid out the problem.

"Did you read the paper this morning?"

"Yes." His face grave, Al Monroe fingered his silver Harley-Davidson belt buckle. "Did the reporter have that story about an attack on your mother right?"

"As far as I know."

"Hard to believe something like that could happen 'round here."

"Bill Petrie was one of the five men who attacked her, Al."

"Awww, hell! You sure about that?"

"I got his name along with the others from a police source."

"I've worked with Billy Jack for a lot of years," Monroe said, shaking his head. "He and his wife used to come to dinner before my Luanne took sick."

"I have to move him," Jess said flatly. "I can't have him in the squadron."

"Shouldn't you discuss this with him first? He's back from leave."

She fully intended to talk to him, but not about the transfer.

"Even if we both agreed to let the past die," she told Monroe, "every performance evaluation or merit pay raise Petrie comes up for would raise doubts. I'm going to work a detail to another unit as soon as possible."

It was the wisest course. The only course. To

protect herself, Jess had to get the fuels superintendent out of her squadron. The fact that she was protecting Petrie as well left a bitter taste in her mouth.

After a series of phone calls, Jess discovered that a transfer would take longer than she'd anticipated. Her counterpart at Hurlburt was on temporary duty in the Balkans and not expected back for another two weeks. Since he was the only one with the authority to accept a civilian of Bill Petrie's rank, the move was put on hold until his return.

Nor could Civilian Personnel find a fit for Petrie elsewhere on Eglin itself. His background and experience were all fuels. He was too specialized to place in any other field. The best Jess could do was a two-week detail to a quality-assurance team chartered by Colonel Hamilton to look at ways to improve customer service within the logistics complex.

Jess called Petrie into her office early Tuesday morning to personally deliver the news of his move. With Al Monroe there to act as a witness, she let the man sweat for long, tense moments before breaking the charged silence.

"I assume you saw the story in the paper yesterday?"

The civilian nodded, his face grim. He didn't look as though he'd spent his leave in restful pursuits. Like Jess, he had dark circles shadowing his eyes. The skin stretched tight over his cheekbones appeared almost a pale gray in contrast to his shock of coal-black hair.

"On the advice of my attorney," Jess said evenly, "I'm not going to discuss the details of the story with you except to say I have information indicating that you participated in the reported assault against my mother."

"On the advice of *my* attorney," he got out raggedly, "I have no comment."

Well, now she knew how he'd occupied his time during the past week.

"To avoid the potential for conflict of interest," she told him, "I'm detailing you effective today to Colonel Hamilton's quality-assurance team. I'll work out a permanent arrangement later."

His throat worked. Above the open collar of his shirt, his Adam's apple bobbed convulsively. "We've got a mess on our hands. I'm . . . I'm needed here."

More than she was, he seemed to imply.

"Lieutenant Ourek is placing Sergeant Babcock in charge of recovery operations," Jess informed him with a dart of savage satisfaction. Her decision to give Babcock a last chance had already paid off in spades.

"Ed's a good man," Petrie said gruffly, "but purging those underground pipelines and emptying the storage tank of the polluted fuel is a huge job, something none of us has ever done before."

Under other circumstances, she might have given him some credit for his concern about the mission. The best Jess could do at the moment was bite back the reminder that he'd authorized the deviation to the sedimentation levels in the first place.

"I appreciate the magnitude of the task," she said flatly. "We'll get it done."

He looked to Al Monroe, whether for assistance or sympathy she neither knew nor cared.

"You'll report to the LGX office this afternoon. That's all, Mr. Petrie."

The polite form of address almost choked her, but she managed to keep her expression blank and her hands still until both Petrie and Al Monroe turned to leave.

"Close the door, please," she instructed her deputy.

The moment it snicked shut, Jess curled her hands into claws and gave herself up to the fury she'd kept so rigidly in check.

The bastard! He was there with the other four that night at the Blue Crab. If Jess had harbored the least doubt before, she didn't now. She'd seen the guilt in his eyes, had heard it in his voice.

She wasn't through with Billy Jack Petrie. She knew it. He knew it. She'd made sure he'd seen that in *her* eyes.

Shoving Petrie into a separate compartment in her mind, Jess spent the rest of the day bird-dogging her request to headquarters for additional R-11s and coordinating the emergency contract to haul off the contaminated fuel. The Defense Fuels Center would award the contract, but Ed Babcock, Lieutenant Ourek, and Jess all helped hammer out the requirements.

Her head was pounding by the time she pulled into her driveway just after eight that evening. She lifted a hand, intending to hit the garage opener, when she caught a glimpse of a green-and-tan police cruiser a dozen or so yards away.

Shifting the Expedition into park, she left it idling and walked the dozen yards. The uniformed deputy sheriff at the wheel climbed out at her approach. Tall and ramrod straight, he greeted her politely.

"Evening, Colonel."

"Good evening. Were you waiting for me?"

"No, ma'am. Just doing a drive-by."

His glance was guarded under the brim of his gray straw Smokey the Bear hat. He'd recognized her, obviously, or had connected the name on her fatigues to the newspaper stories.

"Do patrols from the Walton County Sheriff's Department routinely drive through this development?"

"No, ma'am," he said again. "Not routinely."

Letting out a slow breath, Jess nodded. More questions tumbled through her mind as she walked back to her car, but only one man could provide the answers.

Steve arrived at Jess's condo an hour later. She hadn't called him. She hadn't needed to. His deputy had notified him of her arrival . . . and of their brief exchange.

He read the storm warnings the moment she opened the door, but she waited until he'd set the paper bag he carried on the coffee table in the living room and claimed the easy chair before issuing an icy demand for an explanation.

"Am I under surveillance?"

"Not by my department."

"Then how do you categorize these 'drive-bys'?"

"As what they are, periodic drive-bys. They started the night you went off the bridge," he added in answer to her look of patent disbelief. "I wasn't satisfied your vehicle was rammed by a drunk driver, Jess. I'm still not satisfied."

Her eyes widened. While she processed his blunt announcement, Steve kneaded the knotted muscles at back of his neck. Christ, he was tired. He'd had a bitch of a day, and the call from the Okaloosa County Sheriff's Department hadn't improved matters. He still had several hours of paperwork waiting for him at his office, but he'd wanted to deliver both his news and the contents of the brown paper bag in person.

It didn't take Jess long to grasp what he'd come to tell her.

"You hinted to the media that it might have been Whittier who shoved my car off the bridge. Has the lab in Tallahassee matched the paint scrapings from my Mustang to Whittier's Cadillac?"

"No."

That would have been too easy, Steve thought wearily. Too neat.

"The lab matched them to a Buick Regal. As it happens, an elderly Panama City couple reported theirs stolen the same day you went into the bay."

Shagging a hand through her hair, she sorted the implications. "The possibility a stolen vehicle shoved my car through the guardrail doesn't prove the hit-and-run was anything but accidental."

"No, it doesn't, but I'm betting we'll find that yellow Regal under fifty feet of water one of these days, neatly and very deliberately wiped clean of all prints."

" 'One of these days' doesn't exactly do it for me, Sheriff."

"Me, either. That's why I brought you this."

Leaning forward, he unfolded the brown paper bag and slid out a padded leather gun case. The zipper hissed open to reveal a gleaming automatic.

"It's a nine-millimeter Berretta."

"Standard issue for the U.S. military," she murmured.

"That's why I brought it. Are you familiar with it?"

"I carried one for six months in the Balkans."

"Did you fire it?"

"At something other than a paper target? Yes. Once."

"Good."

He extracted a spare clip from the bag, along with a box of bullets. Folding her arms, Jess observed him slide the clip in, chamber a round, and lay the Berretta carefully on the coffee table.

"I wonder what your friend at the Florida Department of Law Enforcement would say if he knew I was armed and dangerous again."

"He knows. He also knows my people are doing periodic drive-bys. Hazlett thinks both are a good idea."

The implication that she didn't top the FDLE detective's top-ten list of criminals sent a spear of relief through Jess.

Steve caught her sigh. Rising, he skirted the coffee table and trailed the back of his hand down her cheek. "We're not out of the woods yet."

"I know."

"Did you talk to a civilian attorney?"

"Yes. He advised me to notify him of any and all contacts by the police."

His mouth curved in a wry grin. "You should think about it next time you open your door to a cop."

"I also talked to Bill Petrie."

His knuckles stilled their lazy path. "When?"

"This afternoon. In my office. With my deputy—"

"Dammit, Jess!"

"With my deputy present to act as a witness," she finished. "I told Petrie I was moving him out of the squadron. He wasn't happy about it."

"Oh, great. Nothing like handing out another reason to shove you off a bridge!"

"I had to move him. You know that. Professionally, the situation was untenable for both of us."

"And personally?"

"He was one of them, Steve." She tipped her chin, her eyes flashing. "He didn't brag about it like Whittier did. On the advice of *his* lawyer, he didn't say anything at all, but he was one of them. I saw it in his face."

"So what?"

She reared back. "Excuse me?"

"So what if he was one of them? I can't change what happened and I can't charge him with a rape that happened twenty-five years ago, even if there were any evidence to prove it actually occurred."

"Then why is he running so scared?" she shot back. "Why did he take off a whole week, and go see a lawyer before he came back to work? Why was he shaking in his boots the day I walked into his office and found him staring at McConnell's picture in the paper? And why the hell did Ron Clark say my name just before he killed himself? What did he think I could do that would drive him to suicide?"

The razor-edged frustration in her voice stabbed into Steve like one of the vicious switchblades he used to take off the punks on Atlanta's streets. More than any impassioned plea of innocence, that angry heat convinced him Jessica Blackwell had no direct hand in the realtor's death.

"I don't know the answers," he said in response to her barrage of angry questions. "I'm missing something. I've been missing it right from the start, but I'm damned if I can figure out how or why. Just keep the Berretta handy. And for God's sake, call nine-one-one if anything—*anything!*—looks, sounds, or smells wrong to you."

"I will."

"Better yet"—he hooked an arm around her waist, wanting to see her reaction, needing to feel the tremor that rippled along her spine—"call me."

The frustration went out of her, edged aside by a different need, every bit as sharp and compelling.

"I can't, Steve. I won't. I've told you before, I don't want to drag you into this mess any deeper than I already have."

"Yeah, well, seems I remember telling you that it's too late. I'm already in over my head, and I'm not looking for a way out."

She made an inarticulate sound, lost when his mouth covered hers, but he didn't have any trouble deciphering the urgent fit of her hips against his.

Their joining was hard and swift, with little

foreplay and no skilled weaving through layers
of sensual pleasure. As if they both sensed the
need to take what they could, while they could.

When Jess dragged on her clothes and walked
with him to the door a half hour later, she felt
as though he'd left the imprint of his body on
every square inch of hers. His scent was on her
skin, his stubborn determination to risk his career on her mind. She caught him at the open
door and drew him back for another, almost
desperate kiss.

"It's okay," he told her softly when she
couldn't say the words that went with the kiss.
"We'll figure this all out, Jess."

He left her standing inside the glass storm
door, wondering just what the heck "this" referred to. While moths beat against the porch
lamp, she leaned against the doorjamb and
watched the night swallow the taillights on his
cruiser. When the red glow had faded into the
distance, her glance drifted to the docks fifty or
so yards from her door.

If they worked "it" out, Steve could moor the
Gone Fishin' at the dock. Or Jess could shoehorn
some of her belongings into a stateroom the size
of a closet and camp out at his private bayou.
The realization of how far she'd come since the
first night she opened the door to Steve had Jess
shaking her head.

She had the door half-shut when she caught
a movement on the dock. She gave the drifting

shadow only a passing glance, would have written it off as the tilt of a mast on a swell if it hadn't taken shape and definition. Strange that someone would be out on the pier so late.

Squinting at the indistinct figure, Jess saw him raise something to his shoulder and caught the glint of moonlight on steel. The glint transfixed her for a fraction of an instant. That was all she needed to decide the gleam might not look, sound, or smell wrong, but it definitely *felt* wrong. She jumped to the side, out of the light spilling from inside the condo, and was about to slam the heavy wood panel when the crack of a rifle shot split the night.

The glass storm door shattered. Deadly splinters cut into the wooden door, flew sideways, sliced into Jess's hand and arm.

Her first reaction was shock. Her second, fury. *No! Not again!* She wasn't letting this unseen bastard have another chance at her.

Whirling, she snatched the Berretta from the coffee table and raced for her bedroom. She was out the back patio door and running for the far end of the building before the echo of the rifle shot had stopped ringing in her ears.

Chapter 18

Bent low, Jess rounded the end of her building and darted through the pool of shadows cast by the live oaks to the bay's edge. The thick tangle of native palmettos lining the shore had been thinned to give the condos' residents an unobstructed view, but enough of the shrubbery remained to provide a dark backdrop as she ran for the dock.

Halting just short of the wooden pier, she crouched beside a spiky palmetto. Her heart jackhammered against her ribs. Her breath came in raw gasps. Biting down hard on her lower lip to silence the painful rasps, she searched for the fatal gleam of light on steel, tried to separate the shadows, filter out the faint tinkle of the boats' rigging hitting the masts, tried to sense movement, any movement.

To her disgust, she heard nothing, saw nothing but porch lights popping on all up and down her row of condos. Cautiously, occupants poked their heads out to investigate the loud crack they'd heard just moments ago.

Jess agonized for a few seconds, reluctant to reveal her position but more afraid the shooter might take aim at her innocent neighbors.

"Stay inside!" she yelled. "Call nine-one-one! Someone fired a shot through my storm door. He may still be out here."

Most of the curious ducked back and slammed their doors. One brave soul shouted to someone inside his place, then made a dash for the utility pole beside the tennis courts. When he tore open a metal box and flipped a bank of switches, powerful, high-intensity floodlights illuminated the courts, the sand volleyball pit, and the dock.

Jess had no idea how long she squatted beside the palmetto, her pulse hammering and her eyes aching as she scanned the dock and the clustered buildings. It felt like hours, but was probably only minutes before the wail of a siren pierced the night. Minutes more before an unmarked cruiser screamed into the parking lot and fishtailed to a stop. Bubble light flashing a furious red, headlights blazing, the vehicle provided a solid bulwark between Jess and the pier.

Her heart in her throat, she saw Steve throw himself out of the cruiser and into a defensive crouch, his head low, his weapon high in a two-fisted grip.

"Steve! The shot came from the dock."

"Get down!"

"I think it was a rifle."

"Put your face in the dirt, dammit!"

He took off at a run, and Jess didn't even consider dropping down to the dirt. Someone had tried to kill her. Twice! The first time had scared the hell out of her. This time it infuriated her.

More to the point, she wasn't letting Steve charge into harm's way without someone to cover his back. Her breath hitching, she raced toward the dock, hunched over, awkward, the slap of her bare feet lost amid the thud of his boots. Every nerve in her body bunched in expectation of another flash of fire, another deadly crack.

Gasping with relief, she almost fell against the tree trunk–size piling at the foot of the dock. "Do you see anything?" she said between pants to the figure shielded behind the opposite piling.

"No," he said in a snarl, "but right now you're in a hell of a lot more danger from me than from your shooter!"

She believed him. He looked so furious she wouldn't have been surprised if he'd turned his gun on her and pumped a bullet into her foot to keep her from following him onto the pier.

"Temper, temper," she murmured, her eyes on the long plank passageway leading to the end of the dock.

Steve whipped his head around, sure that the blood roaring through his arteries had affected his hearing. He couldn't detect the slightest echo of fear in her voice, and her face showed only a fierce determination.

"There must be at least twenty boats moored at the dock," she whispered, seemingly oblivious to the danger she'd put herself in. "He could have taken cover in any one of them. How are we going to do this?"

"We aren't going to *do* anything," he ground out. "We are going stay right here and wait for the backup I called for."

"I'll back you up."

"The hell you will."

The scream of sirens cut off further argument.

The drama ended within a half hour.

A phalanx of deputies peeled into the walled community in response to their boss's call and spilled out of their squad cars. At Steve's shouted direction, they cordoned the area around Jess's building. When a special response team in helmets and thick, bulletproof vestments moved forward, Steve yanked Jess from her crouch and fell back.

They stood behind his cruiser while the response team searched the dock, boat by boat. She sensed long before they finished that they wouldn't find the shooter. He must have made his escape while Jess raced around the end of her building. Digusted, she plopped down on her neighbor's stoop to keep out of the way while Steve and his deputies went door to door.

Only then did she notice the blood streaking down to her wrist. Grimacing, she plucked several long slivers of glass from her forearm before accepting the towel offered by her neighbor.

She was still on the stoop when Jim Hazlett arrived sometime later. The FDLE detective hadn't taken time to change out of his tennis shoes and baggy Bermuda shorts. His bald crown gleaming in the wash of floodlights, he nodded to Steve.

"Evenin', Sheriff."

"Hazlett."

The terse reply made the detective blink and told Jess she wasn't off Steve's shit list yet.

Eyebrows elevated, Hazlett turned to her. "Well, Colonel, you sure do keep things lively."

"That's one way to put it."

"Care to tell me what happened?"

She waved a hand toward the shattered glass next door. "I was standing at the door and saw what looked like a shadow on the dock. The next instant, the glass exploded."

"Why were you standing at the door? Had you heard something?"

"I, er . . ."

She avoided looking at Steve while she fumbled for a way to keep his name from being irrevocably linked with hers. To her dismay, he bulldozed right in.

"Like a fool, she was watching me drive off. In the process, she made herself a perfect target."

"I didn't expect someone to be out on the dock with a rifle to his shoulder."

"You should have! What the hell did we talk about right before I left your place tonight?"

Hazlett's brows soared again. So did those of every deputy and neighbor within earshot.

Enough was enough. Gathering her dignity, Jess rose.

"I need to put some iodine on these cuts. Shall we finish this interview inside?"

Ignoring her firm declaration that she could tend to the cuts herself, Steve followed her into the bathroom. He didn't say a word as he unwrapped the towel and held her arm under the cold tap, but the grim set to his jaw broadcast his feelings with perfect clarity.

While rivulets of pale pink washed down the drain, he ran his fingers lightly over the shallow, daggerlike slashes in her skin to make sure she'd removed all the glass splinters. Jess relaxed under his gentle touch, only to jump and yelp out a protest when he ruthlessly poured a half bottle of hydrogen peroxide over her arm.

"Hey! That stings!"

"Tough."

The rest of the bottle splashed onto her skin.

"Steve, for Pete's sake!"

Yanking, she tried to break his hold. His fingers almost crunched the bones in her wrist as he jerked her forearm back over the sink.

"You know," she said through gritted teeth,

"getting shot at tonight pissed me off royally. You're about to generate precisely the same reaction."

"Is that right?"

He crowded her against the sink, his eyes blazing a clear blue fire.

"You might have been pissed, but when dispatch radioed the location of the ten-thirty-three your neighbor called in, I was scared shitless. And then, when you ran onto the dock—"

His mouth clamped shut. His throat worked. Fascinated, Jess counted the number of times a muscle ticked on one side of his jaw. The count was up to five when he broke the strangled silence.

"When I left here earlier, I was pretty sure that what I felt for you leaned a whole lot closer to love than lust. Now I can't decide whether to kiss you or wring your neck."

"Better go for the kiss. There's an FDLE detective in the other room, remember?"

He didn't go for either. With an indistinguishable sound halfway between a grunt and a groan, he gathered her in his arms and held her. Just held her.

When they joined Hazlett in the great room, their adrenaline had stopped pumping and the cold reality of a crime scene had set in. One uniformed officer snapped shots with a Polaroid. Another stood by, waiting until he finished to gouge into the wooden front door and retrieve the bullet. A third meticulously swept glass shards into plastic evidence bags.

Detouring to the kitchen, Jess put on a pot of coffee before joining Steve and Jim Hazlett in the great room. The two men had covered much the same ground she and Steve had covered earlier. Both cops were now convinced that the incident on the Mid-Bay Bridge was no accident . . . any more than the shooting tonight. Someone wanted Jess dead.

"Why?" Hazlett puzzled, studying her thoughtfully. "What do you know that someone doesn't want you to know?"

"I don't have any idea."

"Think," he urged. "Did your mother ever talk to you about the men who assaulted her?"

"No."

"Did Whittier drop any surprises or unexpected tidbits of information when you confronted him?"

"No."

"What about—"

Steve cut in. "Maybe we're wrong."

"Wrong how?"

"We're assuming these attempts on Jess's life are related to the incident involving her mother," he said slowly. "Could be we're wrong."

"Could be," Hazlett agreed. "It's the most logical connection, but you and I both know logic doesn't always play in the mind of a killer."

Leaning his elbows on his knees, Steve followed his train of thought. "What about your job, Jess? Is there anything going on at the base that could have made you a target?"

What *wasn't* going on? She'd taken over from a commander under criminal indictment for allowing the illegal dump of solvents. She'd butted heads with the EPA over cleanup measures. She'd shut down Eglin's pipeline and put out a polluted-fuel alert that curtailed flying operations at bases all along the coast. One of her first acts as commander was to demote a belligerent tech sergeant—

Abruptly, Jess yanked the reins on her thoughts. She refused to go down that road. Despite their rocky start, she trusted Ed Babcock. She'd put him in charge of a massive fuel recovery operation.

Just to be sure, though, she made a mental note to stop by the credit union and have a chat with Eileen Babcock. It wouldn't hurt to find out if her ex-husband had dropped by her apartment tonight, as he apparently did on a regular basis.

Hating the doubts and danger swirling around her, Jess blew out a long breath.

"There's a lot going on at the base. If you want me to go through it all, we'll need the pot of coffee I just put on. We'll also need to notify Eglin's Office of Special Investigations that you're requesting information regarding military matters."

"You get the coffee," Steve suggested. "I'll notify the OSI through appropriate police channels."

Dawn streaked through the plantation shutters covering the windows when the conclave in Jess's great room finally broke up. Air Force Special Agent O'Daniels left with a pad full of scribbled notes and a promise to brief the officers in his chain ASAP. Jess intended to do the same as soon as she showered, changed into her uniform, and drove to the base. She wasn't looking forward to another session with Colonel Hamilton—or to running the gauntlet of media gathered in the parking lot outside her condo.

She peered through the shutters as Hazlett and O'Daniels waded into the throng. The OSI agent declined all comment. Hazlett, apparently, provided minimal information, just enough to whet their appetites, Jess guessed. Sighing, she snapped the shutters shut and caught Steve's eye.

"You know they're going to glom onto the fact that you were here last night."

"I know," he said with complete indifference. "I'm sure they'll also glom onto the fact that I'll be here tonight."

"Come again?"

"I'll be here every night, until we nail whoever wants you dead. Or"—he swept the condo a considering glance—"you can move in with me. The quarters are tighter, but the *Gone Fish-*

in's remote location and private road give the media less access. Your choice, Jess."

She might have taken umbrage if her thoughts hadn't drifted along very similar lines just before a bullet shattered her front door.

"What if I choose neither A nor B?" she asked curiously.

"Not an option. Your place or mine?"

"Mine," she conceded. "At least I have TV."

His rapier-swift smile promised little tube time. "I'll go out and feed the sharks. One of my deputies will follow you into work. Call me when you're ready to come home."

Considerably sobered, Jess went to shower and change into her uniform.

Whatever Steve fed the sharks seemed to placate them. The headlines that blazed across the front pages of the local papers the next morning detailed the shooting at Jess's condo. But they made no mention of the fact that the sheriff had taken up residence with a woman whose name figured repeatedly and mysteriously in the demise of three local men.

It wasn't until two days later, when Congressman Calhoun was found dead of a broken neck at the Silver Acres Retirement Center, that the media went for the jugular.

This time, the headlines all but accused Jess of pushing the congressman's wheelchair down the short flight of flagstone steps to the patio where he'd been found just before breakfast.

And this time, Steve made no bones about the fact that he'd been in Jess's bed, making love to her, the entire night before.

Editorials in the print media pilloried the Walton County sheriff. TV and radio talk-show hosts pontificated at length about his loss of objectivity and questioned his ability to conclude this or any other investigation. The former deputy who campaigned against Steve in the last election painted an even blacker picture, barely skirting a lawsuit with hints that the sheriff had been seduced by a vengeful daughter who had now eliminated four of the five men who'd wronged her mother.

Although the initial investigation found only Congressman Calhoun's prints on his wheelchair and concluded he'd rolled off the steps accidentally, his funeral attracted network attention. When neither Steve nor Jess would provide a comment, the three-ring circus focused on a solemn-eyed Dub Calhoun. Suitably weepy, Maggie clung to his arm.

Chapter 19

The last days of July gave way to a blistering-hot August. Slowly Jess grew used to Steve's presence in her house and in her bed. She even grew accustomed to his habit of returning every scattered magazine and carelessly tossed uniform item to its rightful place.

She experienced a good deal more difficulty adjusting to her leash, however. That was the only way she could describe the tight surveillance shared by the air force Office of Special Investigations, the Eglin security forces, and the Walton County Sheriff's Department.

"It's been two weeks since the shooting," she pointed out to Steve over a late-evening meal of salad, parmesan-crusted chicken, and spinach fettuccine. "Almost a week since Calhoun died. When will we get the official lab report on the rifle shell and the boot print your people lifted from the dirt by the dock?"

"The official report won't give us any more

information than the unofficial call I got the day after the shooting," he said between rhythmic crunches on the raw carrot slices decorating his salad. "The shell is a Remington EtronX Fifty electric-primed rifle cartridge. They come twenty to a box, ten boxes to a case, and are available at any hunting-supply store in the country for twenty-five dollars a box."

Frowning, Jess nursed her wineglass in both hands while he forked in more carrots. The man ate the most regular meals, she'd discovered. Healthy, nutritious, and disgustingly balanced. Anticipating the minifeasts he insisted on crafting each evening, Jess had resorted to satisfying her fast-food addictions at lunch with quick forays to Anthony's Pizza or the Burger King on base.

"The boot print might have yielded better details," he continued calmly after he downed his carrots, "if a certain gun-toting lieutenant colonel hadn't run through it two or three times."

She didn't dignify that with a reply. "It's still hard to believe that everyone on our list of possible suspects produced airtight alibis."

The number of people with a possible grudge against her had left Jess more than a bit shaken. In addition to Bill Petrie, the list included the grieving widows of Ron Clark and the Reverend McConnell, both of whom had been questioned about their knowledge of their husbands' involvement in an incident at the Blue Crab twenty-five years ago. They had to hate Jess for coming back and opening old wounds, smearing their husbands' memories in the process.

The original list had included Congressman Calhoun. His son. His daughter-in-law. Ed Babcock. Even the captain of the tugboat who'd delivered the polluted fuel and now faced stiff fines for improperly purging his barges. Like all the others, the boat captain produced witnesses to vouch for his whereabouts. He'd been offloading fuel in Texas at the time.

After two weeks of interviews and questions and soul-searching, she and Steve were no closer to an answer than they were before.

"How long do we continue the surveillance?" she asked, swirling the wine in the blue-glazed goblet.

"As long as it takes."

"I run an organization as big as or bigger than yours. I know these extra patrols and escorts are eating into your operating budget."

"I'm not worried about my operating budget."

"Then what about your professional reputation? How many more editorials and talk shows will it take to convince your constituents to initiate a recall?"

Calmly, he knifed into his chicken. "We've had this discussion before. Several times, in fact. Serving as sheriff of Walton County is just a job, Jess. It won't destroy me if I'm voted out of office." His eyes met hers over a forkful of steaming, crusted chicken. "Not like it would if the shooter got to you."

Her heart pinging, she lifted her glass and tipped it to her lips. A sardonic glint came into his eyes.

"You suppose the day will come when you won't put some barrier between us every time I try to tell you how I feel about you?"

She hid behind a flippant grin. "Anything's possible, Paxton."

Blowing out a breath, he let his glance stray to the framed three-by-five photo on the shelf above the sink.

"You said you were like your mother in every way that counts."

"I am."

"Was she afraid to let down the barriers, too?"

"If you listen to the people around here, my mother let down her barriers all too often."

The comment held only a trace of rancor. It was truth from any perspective but hers.

"Tell me about her, Jess."

"Why?"

"I've always heard that a man can see the daughter in the mother. I'd like to know if you measure up to your mom."

That brought a smile. "I try."

"So tell me about her."

Swirling the ruby red merlot in the bottom of the goblet, she gathered her thoughts. How to describe the woman who'd given Jess such unconditional, uncritical, and unceasing love?

"Mom didn't have much luck when it came

to choosing her men. She quit high school to run off with a drummer. If I remember the story right, that affair lasted less than three months. She went through a whole string of bums after that, including the man she thinks was my father."

Jess could almost catch the flash of her mother's irrepressible grin in the garnet depths of the merlot. Helen had always managed to shake off the hurt of being dumped, claiming it didn't matter as long as she had Jess. And it hadn't mattered, until the daughter was old enough to understand the labels others attached to her mother's approach to life and love.

"Money was tight, but I never remember lacking for school clothes or Christmas presents. She worked hard. Picking cucumbers. Sewing tobacco. Wiping down cars at one of those automatic car washes. Waitressing. Mostly waitressing."

Jess used to hang out at the pancake house in Pennsylvania. She'd eaten most of her meals at the Sonic in North Carolina where Helen carhopped for a few months. Gradually the establishments where her mother worked had grown less and less family-oriented.

"I don't remember when she started drinking. I think I was about five or six. The drugs started not long after that."

She lifted her gaze and flashed a warning. She didn't want pity, and refused to accept anyone's vision of the past but her own.

"I never went to school hungry. I never had to wash my own clothes or put my hair in ponytails. Whatever she did at night, my mother always, *always* dragged herself out of bed in the morning and got me off to school."

"Sounds like you were her anchor."

"She was mine, too. All we had was each other until she met Frank."

"Your stepfather?"

"My father. He adopted me right after he and Mom married."

The memories came faster now, spinning through a collage of Arizona's desert heat, afternoons spent in the garage where Frank wrestled with rusted radiators, her mother's painful weaning from alcohol and drugs. The joy of Jess's commissioning and early years in the air force. The agony of watching Helen die.

Absently, she massaged her right hand. "Frank never finished high school either, but he's the kindest, most generous man I know. You'd like him, Steve."

"Sounds as if I would."

Unlike the fiancé she'd brought home for such a short, disastrous visit. Steve would see past the dirt under the nails and the ill-fitting dentures, just as the down-to-earth mechanic would look beyond the lazy smile, the weathered skin, the Arnold Schwarzenegger shoulders and pecs.

And the badge. The badge wouldn't freeze Frank as it had Jess for so long.

"Maybe you should call him," Steve suggested. "Let him know what you've been going through."

"I started to last week, just to hear his voice. I don't want him to know about this . . . this mess, though. There's no point in upsetting him."

"You might want to reconsider, Jess. Your mother could have told him something she didn't tell you."

Her fork stilled. Blankly, she stared at Steve. It had never occurred to her to ask Frank about the Blue Crab. The roadside dive was part of Helen's past, Jess's past. What happened in that smoky back room took place years before they'd drifted into Arizona.

"So you've abandoned the theory that the attempts on my life have no relation to the assault on my mother?"

"I haven't abandoned anything," Steve said calmly. "Finish your dinner; then we'll give your father a call."

Jess caught Frank Blackwell in the middle of his favorite TV game show. She could hear the audience whooping and cheering in the background as the contestants shouted out their bids for various products.

"I'm glad you called," Frank said, muting the TV. "I was gonna give you a ring this weekend if I didn't hear from you. How's your new job going?"

New? So much had happened in the past

three months that Jess felt as though she'd commanded the 96th Supply Squadron all her life.

"It's going." She hesitated a moment before taking the plunge. "If you do call here, don't be surprised if a man answers."

"A man, huh? Sure hope he's got more bottom to him than the last one you hooked up with."

"I'll put him on and let you decide. His name's Steve, by the way."

Wedging into a corner of the sofa, she curled her feet under her and listened with unabashed curiosity to the one-sided conversation. Patiently, Steve replied to Frank's grilling, which included queries about his present employment—cop. His hobbies—fishing, hunting, and the occasional round of golf. His intentions where Jess was concerned.

"We're still negotiating," he said, hooking a brow in Jess's direction.

After another couple of exchanges, he handed the receiver back. She couldn't think of a way to ease into the past, so she took a deep breath and plunged right in.

"Did Mom ever talk to you about the time we lived here in Florida, Dad?"

"Once or twice."

The guarded note that crept into his voice straightened her legs and brought her upright on the sofa. She flashed Steve a quick look, nodding when he gestured to the red button on the phone.

"I'd like Steve to hear this. Mind if I put you on the speaker?"

"Guess not."

Hitting the button, she settled the receiver in the cradle. The scratchy echo in the speaker assured her she hadn't lost Frank.

"Did Mom mention working at a place called the Blue Crab?"

"Can't say as I remember the name of the place."

"What do you remember?"

"Just that Helen had some rough times while she worked there. Got in over her head, went from poppin' pills to the bad stuff. The son of a bitch she worked for kept her supplied."

Steve cocked his head, his brows slicing down. "Wayne Whittier peddled drugs?"

"Why am I not surprised?" Jess muttered.

"If this Whittier character is the bastard Helen worked for," Frank put in, "he's bad news, Jess. Real bad news."

"Not anymore. He's dead, Dad."

"Good riddance."

"Yeah," she said softly. "Good riddance. Did Mom tell you anything else about Whittier, or talk about the customers at the Blue Crab?"

"Not that I recall."

Frank had little more to add. Helen's past had always been her business as far as he was concerned. Jess hung up a few moments later and curled back in her corner.

"What do you think?"

"I think I'll take tomorrow morning off and get in a little fishing," he answered slowly.

"Well, whatever works for you."

The dubious reply drew him back from wherever his thoughts had taken him.

"Walton County isn't Miami or Atlanta, Jess. We don't depend on snitches or pay informants. Word gets around here. If Whittier was dealing drugs at the Blue Crab, Sheriff Boudreaux knew about it."

"So?"

"So I'm curious why he didn't mention that bit of information the last time we talked."

"Maybe he didn't think it was pertinent."

"Maybe."

Steve also thought it curious that he'd found no mention of drugs in Whittier's long and otherwise colorful file in his department's computer. He'd stop by the office on his way up to Boudreaux's tomorrow, he decided. Have his folks run another, expanded query. Could be they'd missed something besides the drugs.

"What about you?" he asked when he trailed Jess into the bedroom some time later. "What have you got on the schedule tomorrow?"

"Just the usual," she said wryly. "Stand-up. Staff meetings. Dumping about four million gallons of polluted fuel."

Steve might have evinced a greater degree of interest in her planned activities if she hadn't reached for the hem of her T-shirt and dragged it over her head at that precise moment.

Chapter 20

The sun made a valiant attempt to penetrate a thin layer of clouds when Jess drove across the Mid-Bay Bridge the morning after her phone call to her father. Steve tailed her as far as the turn-off to Highway 20. A patrol car picked her up from there.

She waggled her fingers to Steve in farewell, then rolled her shoulders and slumped against the leather seat. Aches from the previous night's lovemaking tugged at her muscles.

If Steve experienced similar aches this morning, he hadn't let on. He'd been preoccupied the whole time he downed his disgustingly healthy breakfast of bran flakes, sliced bananas, and fresh-squeezed juice. So preoccupied he forgot to rinse his dishes and stow them neatly in the dishwasher.

Jess felt her mouth curve in the beginnings of a smirk. Away from his boat, the man might just develop a few human habits after all.

*   *   *

Any inclination to grin disappeared the moment she drove through Eglin's back gate. The sun speared through the gray clouds long enough to paint the tank farm just off to her left in a shimmering haze. Despite the heavy overcast, weather forecasters had predicted temperatures in the triple digits today. Not exactly ideal conditions for pumping millions of gallons of contaminated JP-8 out of a storage tank and into a long string of barges.

The first tug was supposed to nose its way into Weekly Bayou at seven-thirty. Jess had called her command center to verify the ETA before she left her condo. She'd also left word for Al Monroe to cover stand-up and Colonel Hamilton's staff meeting this morning. She wanted to observe this phase of the recovery operation firsthand.

Ed Babcock had already arrived at the fuel dock when she pulled up. So had Lieutenant Ourek and the NCO in charge of dock operations. The muggy heat stained the lieutenant's cheeks brick red. Damp rings circled Sergeant Weathers's armpits, and he appeared only too happy to defer to Sergeant Babcock's far greater experience and expertise for answers to Jess's questions.

"It should be a pretty straightforward operation," Ed reported, his boots thudding as he led the way down the metal gangplank to the floating dock. "We'll reverse the pumps to bring the fuel down from the storage tank. The tug captain and his crew will tend the connectors and monitor the fill levels in the barge compartments."

"Why do I think you're making this sound too easy?"

"It is easy, as long as the crew stays on their toes. Although . . ."

"Yes?"

A frown creased his brow as he darted a quick look at the sky.

"With this heat and the low cloud cover, the fumes are going to be intense."

He kept his tone casual, but Jess noted that his wrestler's shoulders were tight under his freshly laundered fatigue shirt.

"The captain has to make sure his men don't overdo it and breathe in toxic levels. All it takes is for one of those guys to get dizzy and trip over a crowbar or bucket. A single spark could ignite the fumes."

Or a single cigarette, Jess thought, repressing a shudder. She hadn't forgotten Babcock's story about tossing a crewmember about to light up into the bayou.

Lieutenant Ourek leaned forward, squinting toward the bay. "Here comes the first tug. Right on schedule."

"Good," Ed muttered. "Let's hope that means the captain knows what he's doing."

Shedding their fatigue shirts, he and Sergeant Weathers climbed into the launch moored to the dock and prepared to deploy the containment boom. Rivulets of sweat trickled between Jess's breasts as she bent her elbows on the rail and followed their progress.

"We need a new boom," Lieutenant Ourek worried, watching the two men hook the end of the buoyant line. "That one's older than I am."

Jess bit back the comment that just about everything within sight was older than the fresh-faced butter-bar.

"Did you include a new boom in your budget submission for next fiscal year?"

"I've included it for the past three years," he replied glumly. "It keeps getting redlined."

"How much are we talking about?"

His eyes brightened behind his rimless glasses. "Less than twenty thousand for the Super Swamp Boom manufactured by American Marine. It's a calm-water containment system, with twenty-two-ounce PVC fabrics and hot-dipped galvanized steel ballast chains."

Whatever those were.

"I'll see what I can do," Jess promised.

Eglin ought to be able to wiggle twenty thousand out of headquarters, seeing it was Ed Babcock who'd identified the SF445 problem. The engine run-ups Colonel Hamilton had ordered were still in progress, but preliminary results indicated potentially severe damage to the nozzles over an extended period of time. If Headquarters balked at coughing up the additional funds, Jess could twist some arms at the Defense Fuel

Center. Maybe link a new boom to this recovery operation.

Pushing back the brim of her 96th Supply Squadron ball cap with its silver oak leaf on the crown, she wiped her forearm across her forehead. Her fatigue shirt lay plastered to her back, and her toes were already swimming inside her leather boots. This looked to be a long, long day.

"What's the latest estimate to empty the entire storage tank?"

"Well, it usually takes fourteen to twenty hours to off-load a typical barge load of a million gallons and pump it up through the filters to the tank. By removing the filters and reversing the pumps, we estimate the fuel will flow down into the barges almost a third faster."

She performed the quick mental calculation. Four million gallons of polluted fuel. Four barges to fill. Ten to fifteen hours per barge.

"Sixty hours to completely purge the storage tank."

"Right," the lieutenant confirmed. "We'll need an additional forty-eight hours to cleanse it and the pipeline."

That was four days minimum, assuming her people worked around the clock, which wasn't going to happen. Exhaustion too often led to carelessness, and carelessness when handling highly combustible fuels could mean disaster.

"You made it absolutely clear to the Defense Fuels Center that I want the barges to arrive on a staggered schedule, with sufficient time for our people to take a break between loads?"

"Yes, ma'am."

"Hold the tug captains to the ETAs. I don't want one of them slipping in early, thinking to shave a few hours off his trip."

Promising to monitor the schedule personally, he stood beside Jess as the first tug pushed its two petroleum barges past the waiting launch. The moment the tug cleared, Sergeant Weathers sent the launch across the narrow throat of the bayou, dragging the boom behind. Once secured to the anchor chains, the floating barrier completely segregated the tug from the bay behind it and would—hopefully!—contain any oil that might spill over its sides.

With the boom deployed, Weathers brought the launch back to the dock. The two NCOs climbed out, joining Jess to watch the lead barge inch into position. The crew seemed to know what it was doing, she thought as they prepared for docking, but she didn't draw a full breath until the barge had gently bounced against the bumpers and been secured.

Once it was docked, the crew stripped down and muscled the hose connecting the underwater pipeline into place. That done, they set about filling the first of nine separate compartments of the barge.

Even with the pumps reversed and the filters open, emptying the massive storage tank of the

contaminated fuel was slow, dirty work. Oil
gushed into the barge's compartment, splashing
onto the crewmembers and coating them with a
bright sheen. Fumes trapped by the gray clouds
clogged the air, so thick Jess was sure she could
reach out and grab a fistful of the shimmering,
noxious curtain.

At the tug captain's invitation, she boarded
the barge and squatted beside the compartment
hatch to watch the oil flow. Every rattle and
bump of the hose or hull made her nerves skit-
ter. As Ed Babcock had pointed out, it would
take only one spark. . . .

Later, much later, she would learn the explosion came after a whole shower of sparks.

The only consolation, if there was any to be
had in a disaster of that magnitude, was that it
didn't result from human error or carelessness,
but from one of those capricious acts of nature
that no one—*no one*—could have predicted or
prepared for.

Their first and only warning came too late to
prevent the holocaust.

When her cell phone rang, Jess had returned
to her observation point beside Lieutenant
Ourek and had just glanced at her watch. The
first compartment had been filled in under an
hour and a half. The crew had already started
on the second.

Unbelievably, it was only ten past nine. Lord,
it seemed later than that. A lifetime later. Her

head pounded from the fumes and there were still seven more compartments to fill after this one. Just on the first barge.

The past hour and a half had given Jess an even greater respect for her fuels management people, who labored under these abominable conditions every day. Thinking of ways to let them know she appreciated their work, she dug her pinging cell phone out of her shirt pocket and flipped up the lid.

"Colonel Blackwell."

"This is Al." Her deputy's voice conveyed a note of raw urgency. "I wanted to make sure our people got the call from the command post."

"What call?"

"The coast guard station at Destin just reported a freak cloud formation out over the bay. Two water spouts have been sighted, one of which was only a mile offshore and heading our way."

Her heart in her throat, Jess skimmed the horizon. She'd become so absorbed in the barge operation, she hadn't even noticed that the low-hanging clouds had darkened from gray flannel to flint.

"The command post's issued a tornado alert," Al reported grimly. "The sirens should go off any moment."

"Right." Snapping the phone shut, Jess whirled on the lieutenant. "We've got a tornado alert."

"What!"

"Come on."

They started for the barge, intending to alert the others, at the same moment Sergeant Weathers came racing up the metal gangplank, his face ashen and his handheld radio squawking.

"The command post's put out a tornado alert."

"We just heard."

"I've instructed the crew at the pumping station to halt the fuel flow. I need to tell Ed to secure the barge compartment."

"Do it," Jess ordered. Swinging back to the lieutenant, she pulled together her whirling thoughts. "Alert your on-call operators to stand by in case we have to initiate spill-containment procedures."

"Yes, ma'am."

"Do you have a copy of the spill response checklist with you?"

"It's in my vehicle. I'll—"

He broke off, his eyes widening. Every trace of color drained from his cheeks.

"Dear God!"

Jess spun around, knowing what she'd see. Still, she wasn't prepared for how close the waterspout was. Or how fast it moved.

The thin, pewter funnel towered above the bayou, spiraling from surface to sky. Mesmerizing in its soft, soughing hiss. Graceful in its lethal power.

As the trees on either side of the bayou began

to whip from side to side, Jess screamed a warning to the NCO grimly supervising shutdown operations.

"Ed! Behind you!"

He twisted, took one look over his shoulder, and leaped for the hose from the underwater pipeline. The flow had slowed, but hadn't yet cut off. Shouldering aside the stunned, gaping crewmembers, Ed wrestled with the nozzle.

"Clear the barge!" the tug captain shouted in English, then again in Spanish. "Clear the barge!"

"The damned thing's coming right down the bayou," Lieutenant Ourek got out, shouting now to be heard over the rattle of wind and trees. "You'd better get off the dock, Colonel."

"I will, as soon as our people are clear."

She shot a glance at the deadly waterspout, then whipped her gaze back to the men racing along the length of barge. A solitary figure still fought the hose.

"Ed! Let it go! Take cover! Now!"

Even as Jess screamed the order, she knew it was too late. Weekly Bayou seemed to rise, as if begging to be drawn up into the air. The resulting wave lifted the tug, then sent it careening into the rear barge. It, in turn, shoved the forward barge into the dock.

The pylons gave. The floating platform tilted under Jess's boots. The long metal gangplank buckled, shot upward. Folding almost in half, the structure began a slow, agonizing descent.

With sickening certainty, she knew it would crash onto the barge's open compartment. She saw Ed take a dive to one side, go down, throw up his arms to protect his head from the twisted steel.

She leaped for the deck, hit it running. The awful shriek of metal grinding against metal assaulted her ears, almost drowning the tornado's deadly hiss. Wind and water whipped into her face, her eyes, her mouth as she grabbed Ed's arm and dragged him free of the mangled gangplank.

"It's going to blow!" he yelled, staggering to his feet. "The whole damned thing's going to blow!"

Jess never saw the spark that ignited the fuel. With a desperate lunge, Ed shoved her over the side. She tumbled into the bayou at the same instant the world seemed to explode.

Chapter 21

Steve walked out the rear door of the low, single-story building housing the Walton County Sheriff's Department in DeFuniak Springs a little past nine a.m. and headed for his cruiser.

Long habit narrowed his eyes to check the prisoners from the adjoining county jail detailed to work grounds maintenance. The same habit had him scrutinizing the appearance and attitude of the guards who supervised the prisoners.

This morning he gave the grounds detail only a cursory once-over, however. One nagging question occupied his mind. One question only.

Why was there no record that Wayne Whittier bought or sold drugs?

Steve had found no reference linking him to drugs in the computer, in old police logs, or in reports of local busts dating back to the days of the Blue Crab. He might have shrugged off Frank Blackwell's claim that Helen's boss at the

Blue Crab had supplied her with cocaine if not for a vivid memory.

He could feel the rowboat rocking under him. See the turtle sunning on a branch. Hear Cliff Boudreaux's deep voice as he related how Helen was flying high the night she was assaulted.

On rum and coke.

The kind you snorted.

Cliff knew drugs were going down at the Blue Crab. So why the hell hadn't he marked the roadside dive and its owner as—

"Sheriff!"

The shout snapped Steve's head around. His shift lieutenant hurried out, the hazy sunlight glinting on the accoutrements of his dress-down uniform.

"Marine Ops just called in a weather warning. The coast guard station at Destin reported a squall spinning up out on the bay."

Steve squinted at the low-hanging clouds to the south. They didn't look threatening, but a good twenty-five miles separated DeFuniak Springs from Destin.

"Any reports of injury or damage to ships?"

"Not so far."

"All right. Keep me advised."

"Will do."

The call from Dispatch requesting immediate activation of the Emergency Operations Center came when Steve was a mile from the turnoff to Cliff Boudreaux's place. Grabbing his mike, he keyed the transmit button.

"In response to what emergency?"

"Eglin reports an explosion and major fire. They're requesting all available assistance from local fire and police departments."

His first thought was that one of Eglin's aircraft must have gone down. His second, that the liquid nitrogen used to drop the temperature in the gigantic climatic laboratory on base to minus seventy degrees had somehow exploded.

Only as he rekeyed his mike did Steve remember Jess's four million gallons of polluted fuel.

"Activate the Ops Center. I'm returning to base immediately. Advise me as soon as you know what's on fire."

"It's their tank farm," the dispatcher replied. "The whole damned thing's gone up. The guys at our substation say you can see the black cloud of smoke all the way across the bay."

Chapter 22

Jess had read histories of the Japanese attack on Pearl Harbor. She'd watched CIA and military intelligence videos of the oil fields the Iraqis had set afire when they retreated from Kuwait. She'd participated in disaster-response exercises where old aircraft and even whole buildings were blown up.

But never, *ever*, had she imagined anything like the hell that surrounded her when she thrashed to the surface of Weekly Bayou.

A black, impenetrable cloud shot with flames surrounded her. Scorching heat seared her skin and threatened to blister her eyeballs. Smoke burned into her mouth, her lungs. The deafening roar blocked all other sound.

Squeezing her eyes shut, she gulped in the black, oily smoke and jackknifed back under the water. She had no way to judge her direction as she scissored wildly with legs and arms. The frantic movement propelled her forward.

Toward the dock? The shore? The burning barge?

Her chest screamed with agony before she surfaced again. A sob of relief tore at her throat. *Thank God!* She'd cleared the burning ring of fire! She rolled to her side, intending to strike for the grassy shore. Caught sight of the body floating facedown a few yards away.

The burned, burly torso and shredded fatigue pants could only belong to Ed Babcock. Another sob ripped from her throat. She wouldn't let it go, refused to cry out to the immobile figure. Swimming to his side, she flipped him over and hooked an arm under his chin.

Smoke billowed across the bayou, thick and blinding, as she kicked toward shore. She heard a splash, felt hands grab at her shirt, at her arm, at the body she towed behind her.

"I've got him."

Lieutenant Ourek's blackened face thrust through the smoke. His glasses were gone. So were his eyebrows.

"I've got him, Colonel. Let go."

With the aid of the oil-blackened Sergeant Weathers, who came running up at that moment, Ourek struggled to lift Ed Babcock's heavy body out of the water. Jess crawled up the bank on hands and knees, weak with relief that at least two of her people had survived the explosion.

Too exhausted to do more than sink back on her heels, she could only pray as Ourek pumped

Babcock's chest and Weathers breathed air into his lungs. They were still working on him when she gathered enough strength to push to her feet.

Damage assessment. She needed to conduct a damage assessment. Direct the crews of rescue vehicles she heard wailing in the distance. Take control of the fire before it won control of her.

To her dismay, the situation was worse, far worse, than she'd imagined. The forward barge had exploded. Burning fuel coated the wreckage, the empty barge behind it, the crumpled dock. Flames danced like Saint Elmo's fire along the mangled metal gangplank, making their inexorable way toward the dock operations building.

"Stay with Ed until help arrives," she croaked at the two men. "Then come find me. I'll need your expertise."

Shoving her wet hair out of her eyes, she stumbled into a jog, covered a few yards, then broke into a run. She was racing around the end of the bayou when the underwater pipeline erupted. Shooting straight up out of the water, spewing a fine spray of oil, it, too, caught fire. Horrified, she watched flames burst to life inside the pipe itself.

If the pump crew hadn't stopped the flow of oil . . .

If the fire followed the pipeline to the pumping station . . .

If it jumped the station and reached the massive storage tanks beyond . . .

Praying as she'd never prayed before, Jess ran for the greenish yellow fire truck tearing down Eighth Street.

The first firefighters to arrive on the scene wore full protective gear, with hoods and respirators to allow them to operate in the thick, black smoke. While the others grappled with the hose, one of them half dragged, half carried her behind the shield formed by the massive pumper.

"This way, ma'am," the firefighter shouted through the speaker in his hood. "We'll get you on oxygen and—"

"I'm okay," Jess yelled back, almost weeping in relief at the protection from the blistering heat. "Where's the chief?"

"He's just pulling in."

Jerking free of his hold, Jess stumbled toward the emergency vehicle that squealed to a halt amid a growing army of pumpers and tankers. Eglin's civilian fire chief jumped out to conduct the initial on-scene assessment, direct the response, and set up his mobile command post. Jess reached him seconds later.

"I'm Lieutenant Colonel Blackwell, Ninety-sixth Supply Squadron commander."

Although she'd trained with the Eglin Disaster Response Force only a few times since her arrival at the base two months ago, Jess's years of experience stood her in good stead. Swiftly she recapped the horrifying chain of events and gave the fire chief her best estimate of the num-

ber of military and civilian personnel present at
the time of the explosion, many of whom were
still trapped within the towering fortress of
smoke.

"We need to contact the crew at the pumping
station!" Jess gasped. "Make sure they've completely shut off the flow of fuel."

The chief was on the radio before she finished.

When Steve fought his way past the traffic
backed up for miles outside Eglin's gate, day
had seemingly turned to night. Soot drifted
down onto the logjammed vehicles like ebony
snow. Smoke blackened the sky and completely
blocked the sun that had followed the freak
storm.

He'd already received an initial report from
the scene, advising him of the scope of the disaster, but the brief report in no way prepared him
for the fortress of smoke and flames that greeted
him inside the gates. The nightmarish scene
would have hit him even harder if he hadn't
also received a personal call from Eglin's chief of
security, assuring him that Lieutenant Colonel
Blackwell was on-scene and actively engaged in
disaster-control efforts.

Despite those assurances, his heart almost
dropped into his boots when he finally arrived
at the access control checkpoint and spotted the
lone female in hard hat and protective gear huddled with a group of grim-faced officials.

Hair blackened by soot and oil straggled

down her back. White circles ringed red-rimmed eyes. He could read exhaustion in every line of her body, but when he flashed his badge and fast-talked his way through the checkpoint, he knew better than to suggest she take a break.

She looked up, startled, when he appeared at her side. "Steve!"

"You okay?"

"Yes. I asked the Security Forces to relay a message to your Central Dispatch. Didn't you get it?"

"I got it," he said gruffly. "I had to see for myself . . . and check on our troops. Walton County's got a hazmat team and five pumpers on-scene, and half my deputies working traffic control off base."

She shot him a grateful look. "The response from the communities around Eglin has been nothing short of incredible."

"Any casualties?"

"One so far. A crewmember from the petroleum barge. Two of my men were burned pretty badly."

His gaze skimmed the dozens of pumpers positioned around Weekly Bayou. High-pressure streams of water pierced the flames rising from the charred barge hulks, dousing them with little discernible effect.

"What's the estimate to put out the fire?"

"Another couple hours. We shut down the pipelines in time to keep the fire from backing up to the tank farm, but we'd pumped almost forty thousand gallons into the barge before it went up."

Wearily, she shifted her handheld radio and scrubbed the heel of her hand across her forehead.

"The explosion destroyed our containment boom, and the tide carried the burning fuel into the bay. We've called in two C-130s outfitted with RADS—a Retardant Aerial Delivery System. They should arrive within the next half hour."

The fire-fighting C-130 tankers had dumped millions of gallons of retardant on the forest fires that had charred a good portion of the Florida panhandle a few years back. Steve could only hope they proved as effective on the bay.

"I'll get out of your hair," he said. "You can reach me through Dispatch if you need me."

She gave him a distracted nod and headed back to the command center. She'd taken only a step or two when her radio crackled. She put it to her ear, answering as she walked.

Suddenly she froze. Steve saw her chin come up. Her entire body went rigid. She shook her head once, as if in fierce denial, then whirled.

"Where's your car?"

He jerked a thumb at the cruiser parked at the edge of the logjam of emergency vehicles.

"Let's go!"

"Go where?" Steve demanded, breaking into a lope to keep up with her as she ran for his car.

"Up the hill. To the tank farm. Hurry!"

He didn't like the sound of that. Shoving the key into the ignition, he jerked the cruiser into gear and brought it around.

"Care to tell me what the problem is?"

"That call was from my squadron's command operations center. They wanted to advise me Billy Jack Petrie is at the pumping station."

A chill flowed into Steve's veins. "Yeah?"

"They say he wants to talk to me."

"Now?"

"Now," she answered through tight-clenched teeth. "Or the whole base might blow."

Chapter 23

Bill Petrie was waiting at the gate to the compound that housed the pumping station and tank farm. The tan-painted building enclosing the pumps sat at one end of the compound. Thick pipes rose from the earth, bent at a ninety-degree angle to snake through the building, then dropped back into the dirt on the far side. Behind the station loomed the five massive storage tanks.

Steve's cruiser squealed to a halt beside the chain-link fence topped with razor wire. Jess leaped out before the car rolled to a stop.

"You wanted to talk?" she shouted. "Talk!"

"There's another line. One put in years ago, before the present dock was built."

She reeled back a step or two. Her frantic mind had conjured up a dozen different reasons for Petrie's abrupt demand to see her. That wasn't one of them.

"Our grid maps don't show a secondary line."

"The contractor who put in the new line capped it, but it's still there." He leaned forward, his dark eyes desperate. "I'd just started work in fuels when they built the present dock. I watched it go in, watched the contractor lay the new pipeline. I'm telling you, the old line's still there."

"Why doesn't it show on the grid?"

"It *did!* I swear it did!" He thrust a shaking hand through his hair. "The engineers must have thought it had been removed when they updated the base maps. Hell, I didn't even remember it until I heard the explosion and found out what happened. I called Al Monroe. He said to get my ass down here immediately and show Lieutenant Ourek where the old line is."

"Ourek's in the hospital."

"I just found out. That's why I had the command center contact you." His eyes blazed into hers. "You've got to trust me on this, Colonel."

Jess didn't think twice. The past played no part in the raging inferno of the present. Grimly, she shoved the handheld radio that linked her to the on-scene command center into the pocket of her scorched fatigue pants.

"Show me."

Almost sagging in relief, Petrie snatched up a crowbar and started across the compound. Jess followed, but the thud of footsteps brought her whirling around.

"I'm sorry," she said to Steve firmly, regretfully. "This is a restricted area."

He nodded, clearly unhappy at being left behind but respecting her authority. "I'll wait for you here."

Her boots raising puffs of dirt, Jess followed Petrie past the pumping station to what looked like a small toolshed tucked up against the far side of the fence. Its metal sides had rusted with age. Dust and cobwebs obscured the solitary window. A padlock secured the rusted hasp on the door.

"No one could remember where the key is," Petrie said, grunting as he wedged the crowbar inside the hasp. He wrenched the bar downward twice before the lock gave and he put his shoulder to the door.

The fumes that erupted when the door gave should have warned him. They certainly warned Jess. She shouted an instant warning.

"Petrie! Don't go in there!"

He swung around. The crowbar in his hand banged against the metal building. For the second time that day, an explosion knocked Jess off her feet.

The blast was a small one, thank God, fed by the fumes that had collected in the shed and not spewing fuel. Swearing a blue streak, she picked herself out of the dirt and stumbled toward the shack. Petrie was buried under a pile of burning rubble.

The fumes were already dissipating, but Jess had no way of knowing whether oil might explode through the abandoned pipeline at any moment and spark another, massive explosion. Gritting her teeth, she reached for the crowbar.

Steve was charging headlong across the compound when he saw her lift a metal bar and swing at what looked like a prone body. For the space of a single heartbeat, shock jolted through his body. Even as his boots pounded the dirt, his mind screamed a silent protest.

No, Jess!

No!

When he reached her seconds later, she'd pried up a twisted sheet of metal.

"Drag . . . him . . . out!" she said, panting, levering all her weight against the crowbar. "Hurry!"

Between them, Jess and Steve dragged Petrie clear of the shack and rolled him in the dirt to smother the flames that licked at his clothing. Satisfied that they'd beaten out the deadly tongues of fire, they rolled him onto his back.

While Jess leaned her hands on her knees and sucked in deep, rasping gasps of air, Steve frowned down at the man's waxen face and blue lips.

"Hell!" Laying a hand along the side of Petrie's throat, he searched for a pulse. "I think he's having a heart attack. Get on your radio and call for help. I'll start CPR."

Steve tilted Petrie's head back and cleared his airway before straddling his hips to finger down to the pressure point on his sternum. As he locked his hands and began the rhythmic count, Jess put out the call for an EMT crew. She followed that with a request for a fire-suppression team to lay a heavy coat of retardant over the shed and make sure the pipeline stayed capped. That done, she dropped the radio and crawled to Petrie's side. Dragging in a breath, she put her mouth to his.

Chapter 24

Twenty-six hours later, the last of the flames had sputtered out, the barge crew had been fully accounted for, and Jess ached in every muscle and joint in her body. Yet she insisted that Steve drive her by the hospital before they went home to eat, shower, and collapse.

They met Eileen Babcock in the burn unit. Her auburn hair tumbled haphazardly from its clips and she'd cried away every trace of makeup, but her delicate face lit with joy when Jess rapped softly on the door.

"Colonel! Come in!"

Jumping out of the chair she'd pulled up beside her ex-husband's bed, she rushed across the squeaky-clean tile floor. Her hand came out, as if to shake Jess's; then she abandoned all pretense at formality, threw out her arms, and gave the colonel a fierce hug.

"I could have lost him," she said when they

separated. Her throat working, she fought the tears that rushed into her eyes. "I came so close to losing him."

Jess wasn't sure whether the petite redhead referred to her divorce or Babcock's close brush with death, but from the woman's fierce expression, it was clear Eileen didn't intend to let Ed slip away from her again.

The heavy load on Jess's heart eased a fraction. She still faced a hell of a mess and long-term cleanup efforts. The investigation into the explosion would probably take months. She'd have to weasel funding for a new dock and pipeline out of Headquarters. Yet out of disaster had come the small, piercing joy of watching Eileen Babcock return to her husband's side and gently take his unbandaged hand.

"Colonel Blackwell's here, Eddie."

The NCO was swathed in gauze bandages. An IV dripped into his arm, and the head he slowly turned on the pillow was missing big patches of hair. His lips pulled back in what Jess sincerely hoped was a grin and not a grimace.

"Thanks for . . . pulling me . . . out from under . . . the gang . . . plank," he rasped in a hoarse croak.

She smiled down at him. "Thanks for shoving me into the bayou. The docs say you're going to be okay. Do you need anything?"

His glance drifted to the woman holding his hand. "I have every . . . thing I . . . need."

*   *   *

Jess had another stop to make at the hospital, but she put it off until she'd checked on Lieutenant Ourek and those of the barge crew who'd required medical attention. Impatient to get back to his fuels operation, the lieutenant was already badgering the docs to release him.

That left only Bill Petrie.

He'd received treatment in the ER and spent the night in the Cardiac Care Unit. According to the charge nurse, he was due to be transferred to a civilian facility for follow-up care later that day.

With Steve beside her, Jess made her way past the CCU's glassed-in cubicles. The click of life-support equipment and the familiar, piney scent of antiseptic brought back haunting memories of her mother's last days. As a consequence, she couldn't force even a semblance of a smile when she reached the cubicle where Bill Petrie lay.

Like Eileen Babcock, his wife hovered at his side. She was a thin, nervous woman whose eyes went wide with fear when Jess introduced herself.

"You're the one," she whispered.

Shrinking against the bed, she clutched her husband's hand. Her glance darted to Steve, took in the badge clipped to his belt. A little whimper escaped her lips.

"It'll be all right." In a ragged whisper, Petrie tried to reassure her. "I'll make it right."

"Don't talk to them, Billy Jack! Don't tell them anything!"

"I have to, sweetheart. I can't . . ." His eyes closed, then opened slowly. "I *won't* carry this burden anymore."

With a calm that suggested he'd anticipated just such an eventuality, Steve stepped around Jess. "Before you say anything, I need to advise you of your Miranda rights."

Shock rippled through Jess as she listened to him remind Petrie of his right to an attorney . . . and that anything he said could be used against him later in a court of law.

Petrie's face whitened during the brief recital, but he ignored his wife's plea that he talk to his lawyer and forced himself to meet Jess's eyes.

"I'm sorry about what we . . ." He stopped, swallowed, started again. "I sorry about what we did to your momma. I was drinking that night. We all were. I know that's no excuse."

"You're right," Jess agreed with ice in her heart. "That's no excuse."

"Whittier said she just got what she wanted," he continued after a painful moment. "Old man Calhoun agreed. But we couldn't put it out of our mind."

"We being?" Steve asked, the cop in him determined to nail down every detail.

"Me, Ron, Delbert."

Petrie looked beyond them to the window. Sunlight streamed through the miniblinds, as if in grotesque mockery of the dark memories that had invaded the cubicle.

"That's when Delbert found the Lord. He

spent the rest of his life trying to do good and praying for forgiveness. Ron and me . . . We just lived from day to day."

He dragged his gaze from the window to Jess.

"Until you came back. We none of us ever thought Helen's daughter would come back."

"But I did."

"You did. Ron near 'bout shit a brick when he ran a credit check on the colonel who wanted to lease a condo from him and saw her mother's name. That's when we—"

"Billy Jack!" his wife begged. "Don't say anything more!"

"That's when we got together. All six of us. Out on Delbert's boat."

"Six?" Jess said in surprise. "But I thought—"

Steve silenced her with a quick chop of his hand.

"The storm whipped up so quick that day," Petrie whispered, his tortured gaze going back to the window. "Just like it did yesterday."

Jess's breath caught. The Rev. Delbert McConnell went overboard and drowned the day Tropical Storm Carl hit. Her glance went to Steve, but all his attention was focused on the man in the pale blue hospital gown.

"We weren't far offshore," Petrie recounted in his papery whisper. "We hadn't planned to go out on the bay. All we needed was a private place to talk, where no one could see us. Or hear us. Delbert wanted to tell the truth. He was always wanting to tell the truth. We shouted at each other over the wind, argued until the swells got too heavy. Delbert insisted we had to come in and went to start the engine."

Steve stepped into the heavy silence that descended. "And that's when his leather-soled shoes slipped on the wet deck?"

"Billy Jack," his wife cried in anguish. "Please!"

"That's when Sheriff Boudreaux shoved Delbert overboard," Petrie said quietly. "He hit his head on the gunwale going in. We stood there, all of us, and let him drown."

Jess didn't speak another word until she and Steve walked out of the hospital into the blinding sunlight. Her mind numb, she paid no attention to the startled stares her scorched uniform and oil-drenched hair snagged from passersby.

Only after Steve escorted her to the cruiser and tucked her into the passenger seat did she break her stunned silence.

"I can't believe it. Sheriff Boudreaux was blackmailing them for all these years. All five of them."

Steve didn't want to believe it, either, but he couldn't deny the truth that had been staring him in the face for the past two days. His mentor, his friend, the man who'd personally selected him as his successor, had skimmed a share of the profits from Whittier's drug trade.

Now Steve knew that Boudreaux had also traded his silence about Helen Yount's rape for

Congressman Calhoun's political support through four elections. He'd strong-armed Ron Clark into cutting him a deal for his farm, a deal so sweet that any jury in the world would consider it extortion. He'd bled Bill Petrie and his wife dry of their savings. He'd even harangued Delbert McConnell into campaigning for him from his pulpit. Then he'd shoved the reverend into the bay to silence forever his guilty conscience.

Just as he'd shoved Jess's Mustang through the guardrail of the Mid-Bay Bridge.

A coldness settled in Steve's gut.

"I'll take you home," he told Jess, keying the ignition.

"Me? What about you?"

"I'm going fishing."

"No, Steve! You can't go after Boudreaux. Not alone, anyway. I won't let you. There's been too much hurt, too many deaths already."

"You've done your job the past few days, Jess. Now I have to do mine."

Chapter 25

Jess adamantly refused to let Steve drop her off at her condo. The best he could do was extract a promise from her to stay in the cruiser when he led a small convoy of patrol cars through the patchwork quilt of farms north of DeFuniak Springs.

He'd taken a few moments at his office to splash cold water on his face and change his uniform. His eagles glinted at the collar of his gray shirt. His green trousers with their gray stripe down the legs showed knife-edged creases. He carried an extra clip for his .45 on his belt, and two boxes of shells for the rifle mounted on the rack behind him. Cinnamon spurted with every pop of his gum as he drove past mile after mile of peanut fields.

The sun was directly overhead when they reached the turnoff to Boudreaux's place. Steve had timed their arrival deliberately to eliminate the shadows that might obscure his line of sight.

The dirt road that stretched straight as a scar through the ripe fields would announce them, just as it had the last time Steve came up here to fish. He didn't worry about the dust pluming out behind the vehicles. His instincts told him Boudreaux was expecting him.

His instincts proved right. Cliff Boudreaux lounged against one of the pillars that supported the wraparound porch. His ball cap rode low on his forehead, shading his eyes. His belly strained the buttons of his shirt. He carried a double-barreled shotgun tucked in the crook of one arm.

Steve halted the cruiser well outside the shotgun's range. Patrol cars pulled up on either side. Reaching behind him for the rifle, Steve speared Jess with a hard look.

"Stay in the car."

She wasn't about to risk his life by pulling his attention from Boudreaux.

"I will."

Shouldering open the car door, Steve climbed out. The brim of his peaked hat shaded his eyes, but Jess couldn't miss the grim set to his jaw as he instructed his troopers to position themselves behind patrol cars.

"Keep him covered," he ordered softly, "but do not—I repeat—do not fire unless or until I give the order."

Steve made the walk to the porch slowly, his eyes on Boudreaux. His predecessor greeted him with his standard drawl.

"Hey, Sheriff."

"Hey, yourself, Sheriff," Steve replied.

"I've been expecting you."

Sighing, Boudreaux hefted the shotgun a little higher in his arm. Steve heard the thud of rifles hitting the patrol car roofs behind him. Slicing his hand in a vicious arc, he signaled to his men to hold their fire.

"Took you long enough to figure things out," Boudreaux commented. His glance flicked to the cruiser. Something close to regret drifted into his eyes. "I didn't like going after your woman, but you know how it is. Once you get into these things, there's no easy way out."

"No, Cliff. I don't know."

"No, I guess you don't. You've always been squeaky-clean, haven't you, boy? You couldn't even pump a bullet through the bastard who murdered those babies at the YMCA."

He cocked his head. A small smile played at his lips. "Think you can pump a bullet into me, boy?"

"I don't think. I know."

"That's what I'm counting on."

Steve whipped up his rifle at the same instant Boudreaux swung the shotgun. Before either could pull the trigger, one of the deputies fired. The crack of his rifle spooked a second deputy.

Cursing, Steve dropped to the dirt as a fusillade zinged in from both sides and spun the figure on the porch around.

Chapter 26

Jess propped her bare feet on the rail of the *Gone Fishin'*, angled back her deck chair, and tipped her face to the moon. Water dripped from her hair to the deck. The deep-throated croak of bullfrogs crooned a soporific lullaby.

It was late. Past eleven, she thought. But the night that had witnessed so many sleepless hours now rocked her in a cradle of sheer exhaustion.

She should go below. Curl up next to Steve. Let him work more healing magic with his hands and mouth and hard, driving body.

Smiling at the needles of anticipation that pierced even her thick blanket of fatigue, she closed her eyes. She'd just sit here for a few minutes more and listen to the frogs while the bay dried on her skin.

Steve found her sound asleep, one leg hooked over the rail and her body slumped awkwardly

in the deck chair. Shaking his head, he scooped
her up against his naked chest.

"What?" She lifted her head, blinking. "Is it
time for work?"

"No, Jess. It's just a little after midnight.
We've got all night yet."

"No, we don't," she grumbled in protest.
"The night's halfover."

He hesitated, remembering how she'd shied
away from any talk of a future before, yet
couldn't hold back the soft promise.

"We'll have more. A whole lifetime of
nights."

"And days," she muttered sleepily into his
neck. "I want days."

Grinning, he carried her across the deck. "You
got 'em," he promised softly. "As many as you
can handle."

Merline Lovelace

"[An] incredible talent for creating spine-tingling suspense and fiery romance." —*Rendezvous*

DARK SIDE OF DAWN

When chopper pilot Joanna West pulls the handsome grandson of a former president from a fiery car wreck, she's swept into a dangerous passion that she can't resist...

0-451-20355-0

To Order Call: 1-800-788-6262